Praise for
New York Times and USA Today Bestselling Author

Diane Capri

"Full of thrills and tension, but smart and human, too."
Lee Child, #1 New York Times Bestselling Author of Jack Reacher Thrillers

"[A] welcome surprise….[W]orks from the first page to 'The End'."
Larry King

"Swift pacing and ongoing suspense are always present…[L]ikable protagonist who uses her political connections for a good cause…Readers should eagerly anticipate the next [book]."
Top Pick, Romantic Times

"…offers tense legal drama with courtroom overtones, twisty plot, and loads of Florida atmosphere. Recommended."
Library Journal

"[A] fast-paced legal thriller…energetic prose…an appealing heroine…clever and capable supporting cast…[that will] keep readers waiting for the next [book]."
Publishers Weekly

"Expertise shines on every page."
Margaret Maron, Edgar, Anthony, Agatha and Macavity Award Winning MWA Past President

FATAL

FALL

by DIANE CAPRI

ALSO BY DIANE CAPRI

The Hunt for Jack Reacher Series
(in publication order with Lee Child source books in parentheses)

Don't Know Jack (The Killing Floor)

Jack in a Box (*novella*)

Jack and Kill (*novella*)

Get Back Jack (Bad Luck & Trouble)

Jack in the Green (*novella*)

Jack and Joe (The Enemy)

Deep Cover Jack (Persuader)

Jack the Reaper (The Hard Way)

Black Jack (Running Blind/The Visitor)

Ten Two Jack (The Midnight Line)

The Jess Kimball Thrillers Series

Fatal Enemy (*novella*)

Fatal Distraction

Fatal Demand

Fatal Error

Fatal Fall

Fatal Edge

Fatal Game

Fatal Bond

Fatal Past (*novella*)

Fatal Dawn

The Hunt for Justice Series

Due Justice

Twisted Justice

Secret Justice

Wasted Justice

Raw Justice

Mistaken Justice (*novella*)

Cold Justice (*novella*)

False Justice (*novella*)

Fair Justice (*novella*)

True Justice (*novella*)

The Heir Hunter Series

Blood Trails

Trace Evidence

CAST OF PRIMARY CHARACTERS

Jessica Kimball
Brentwood Stephenson
Joshua Nelson
Elisha Harvey
Charlene Mackie
Alistaire Meisner
Margot Meisner
Henry Morris
Karl Blackstake
Crystal Mackie
John Whiting
Barbara Whiting

FATAL FALL

*"Where there is mystery,
it is generally suspected there must also be evil."*

— Lord Byron

CHAPTER ONE

Randolph, Washington
Monday, September 26
5:00 a.m. Pacific Time

IT WASN'T EASY.

Moving a body never was.

The new grave was a mile from the old one, deep in a thick wooded area. A better location. Well hidden. He'd chosen the first location under pressure, but it had served well for more than a decade. This second grave should last forever.

He touched the sores on his hands where blisters had formed and burst. Fall's rain and humidity had weighted the soil and compacted the ground. The digging had taken much longer than expected, but it was finished. The hole was ready.

Now he needed the body.

Carrying his shovel, Karl Blackstake set off for the old grave. The undergrowth in the woods was heavy. He changed directions often, looking for an easier route. Branches clawed at him as he pushed through. He held the shovel in front of his face to fend off the worst of the thorns.

He trudged through deep darkness. He shined a weak light on the ground ahead of his footfalls. Red. The least observable color, in case someone was watching. He grunted. Red light was the least illuminating, too. He backtracked several times, eventually exiting the woods a half mile farther than he'd intended.

Out in the open, he had to sacrifice the weak red light, but from here, he knew his route.

Thirty minutes later he reached the old grave. He'd dug it fourteen years ago at the base of a substantial nine-foot gray steel fence post. The border fence had been under construction back then. It ran for more than a mile, intended to keep trespassers off the property. Beyond the fence in the opposite direction was a ribbon of trees maybe a hundred feet thick, and beyond the trees lay a minor road.

The fence was a massive structure with thick steel cables running horizontally between the steel posts. Three rows of barbed wire ran along the top. It was an intimidating sight, and it was intended to be so.

It had been constructed years earlier when vandals had knocked down a low fieldstone wall that had been intended to serve the same purpose. The wall had failed to keep trespassers away. The new fence would not.

A giant tractor had dug holes for the steel fence posts. The holes were deep into the soil. He'd put the tractor's efforts to his own use back then. The tractor had dug the old grave and done a decent job of the task. The body could have stayed there until it decomposed. It was a perfect plan at the time.

But some do-gooder lawyer up in Seattle had won a court

order allowing local complainers to move the fence and build a new pathway. Something about an old covenant that he had no time for. All he knew was that the body couldn't be here when the workmen arrived to move the perfectly good fence at the end of the week.

At the gravesite, he drove his shovel into the ground. He removed the grassy layer from the top of the grave and set the grass to one side. He'd use the sod to cover the hole after he filled it in with dirt.

The wet soil clumped around the shovel's blade. His boots slipped in the mud. Sweat ran down into his eyes. He cussed at the stinging rivulets and wiped them with the back of his filthy hand. He probably looked like a coal miner or something. A long, hot shower was going to feel great when he finished the job.

The ground was tight at the base of the fence post, and trees were close on the other side. He had trouble getting good leverage on the shovel. He had to dig from an awkward position to avoid damaging the structure. It meant he had to use his weaker, left arm, making the digging slower and harder. The sores on his hands developed new blisters that bled when they burst. Blood mixed with sweat and rain made the shovel handle slippery. He grunted as he pushed the shovel into the ground, again and again.

Two feet down, Blackstake leaned his shovel against the fence and straightened his back. He could feel the individual vertebrae popping back into their proper location. *Click, click click.* He rotated his hips, stretching out his cramped muscles.

He'd been a lot younger when he had buried the girl. His grave digging days should have been over long before now. He could have hired younger men with stronger muscles to do the job. Trustworthy men who could be counted on to keep their mouths shut. But his boss didn't trust anyone else to handle the biggest secrets. Blackstake felt a wry grin steal across his mouth. This was very definitely a skeleton in the senator's closet.

Blackstake looked up the hill in front of him. Sunrise was maybe an hour away. The moon was a thin sliver, low on the horizon, its light cold and weak, but sufficient for his purposes. At the top of the rise was the mansion, three stories and sprawling. His employer, Senator Meisner, his wife, and a small cadre of kitchen staff, housekeepers, and day-to-day security lived on the premises. Soon, the staff would be rising. Time was short.

He cracked his knuckles. Blackstake knew the mansion's routines. He was a member of the security team. He'd been lucky. He came out of the navy right as Meisner started his run for senator. They were a perfect fit—Meisner needed someone with his special blend of skill and resourcefulness, and he needed a job.

The mansion's white walls were pale in the weak moonlight. By day the place was visible for miles. Visible to the media, too. Though the senator hadn't announced his intention to mount a bid for the presidential race in two years' time, he was driving hard to raise funds and a few of the more savvy media outlets had prematurely connected the dots. He lived under a spotlight now that required more discretion than usual. Neither he nor Meisner was happy about the increased scrutiny.

Around the mansion was the gravel driveway, though to call it a driveway was a misnomer. It was fifty feet across and known to the security team as the killing zone because running on its rough surface was impossible.

In a couple of weeks, covered pathways would run from the house to the lawns. The start of the preparations for Meisner's first serious fundraiser. Marquees would be positioned at the end of those pathways, giant tent structures that would cocoon the occupants in luxury, insulating them from the Northwest's rainy weather while providing the vaguest impression of being outdoors. A fancy catering company from Seattle would stock the marquees with food, flowers, and all the other baubles that impressed the rich.

Guests would land their helicopters on the pad at the rear of the property, and be whisked to the reception. He grinned. The whisking would be done by beautiful and expensively dressed women, handpicked by the senator for their conviviality.

The senator would then ply the one trade he was superb at. Talking. He would direct his focus to each person in turn, deftly praising their accomplishments, complimenting their spouses, and hinting at how he really wanted to support their pet project. The rich were far more petty than ordinary people. They had no idea as to what they wanted to change in their lives, so they just picked something. It didn't appear to matter what that was, as long as they had something. Meisner had said that to him, and he believed it because once the conversation reached a conclusion, they would stare each other in the eye, give a firm handshake, and Meisner's political coffers would be a hundred thousand richer.

There had been lean times, but Meisner had solved his cash flow problems in the same way aristocracy had solved such problems for centuries. He had married into money.

Blackstake picked up his shovel. The brief respite had eased his aches. He attacked the ground with renewed vigor. As he progressed deeper into the earth, the soil ran back into the hole.

He broadened the hole, extending it into a short trench, aligned with where he remembered he had hidden the body.

Lights came on up at the mansion. Blackstake sweated. He was running late. The sun wasn't up, but its light was reflecting off the sky. The world around him was gaining that milky black and white effect of the earliest moments of dawn. If he could just get the body out of the ground and hidden in a wheelbarrow before it really got light, he'd look like any ordinary workman.

Another minute's digging and a shiny surface became visible. The plastic bag in which he had wrapped the girl. He worked his way around the edges, clearing the mud until he could lever the shovel under the body. He had torn the bag and punctured it with his knife, to allow nature to reclaim what was hers.

He brought a plastic wheelbarrow alongside the hole. He slid a plastic sheet under the body and lifted it out. His muscles strained at the weight, his back protested, but in a few moments the body was secure in the barrow and covered by another plastic sheet. Out of sight.

Moving the soil back into the hole was easier than digging it out. He tamped down the layers and set the turf last. Sweat poured down his face, but he wasn't finished. He had a mile to cover before sunrise.

The sun was on the verge of breaking over the horizon. He secured his shovel to the wheelbarrow.

A buzz sounded. Not loud, but close.

He ducked down. The sound came from the woods. He moved his head left and right. The noise was diffuse, bouncing off the trees and hiding its source. He pulled out his gun. He'd already fitted the silencer, though the sound of gunfire in the stillness would carry a long way.

He shed his jacket and folded it double. He pulled himself up the wires that held the fence in place. The tension made them almost rigid. At the top, he laid his jacket on the rows of barbed wire. Thick layers of fabric rendered the knife-sharp barbs ineffective. He rolled over the top, and slid down the other side, outside the fence.

He stood still. The buzz continued, but there was no chatter or laughter. No shuffling of feet or whispered conversation. Probably one person, then. One, he could deal with. A team presented bigger problems.

The sound was faint. The buzzing waxed and waned, partly from the distance and partly from the shielding effect of the trees. He moved toward the road. It was one of the most open areas of the thin ribbon of woods. Even so, the tree canopy filtered out almost all light.

The buzz stuttered. He froze, rotating his head, fruitlessly searching for direction. The faint buzz grew louder. The pitch rose and fell. He strained to see in the blackness but saw nothing.

He heard movement, footsteps on leaves, but couldn't judge the exact location. If someone was in the woods he had to find them. He pushed onto the edge of the forest, where the trees met the minor road that ran along that side of the estate.

He kept his fingers tight around the gun's grip, his finger against the trigger with the barest pressure. He searched the road in either direction. There was no car and no sign of life. He moved to another tree, kneeling down and resting his weight against its trunk for protection.

The wet tarmac glistened in the dim light. He had a good position, elevated with a clear view of almost a quarter of a mile in either direction. All he needed was a target.

The buzz's tone rose to a squeal and stopped. He turned. It

was behind him. He stared into the mottled darkness between the trees. There were only two choices. Keep his position and take out anyone who emerged, or head back into the woods and risk missing the target. He rolled his shoulders. He could miss the target even if he waited there.

He turned back to the woods. The sound had stopped. He had come straight through the trees to the road, so whoever was making the noise had to be to the left or right. He chose right, and moved fast, gun first.

The wet leaves slapped at his clothes. Faint light penetrated the foliage.

The trees thinned out. He saw a faint outline of the fence. He'd have to double back, covering a different angle and more ground. He swore to himself.

A branch broke to his right. The crack rang out through the damp air. He dropped to his knees, amid the undergrowth. He searched to his right, training his gun across the ground. Nothing moved. He saw only trees and the thick ground layer of weeds.

He moved forward, tree to tree. Swift movements from one camouflaged position to another. Ahead lay an opening, maybe twenty feet across. It was clear.

He exhaled. The sound of the breaking branch had been too loud suggesting a branch too big to have been broken by a woodland animal. He swung a full three-sixty, his gun trained, his eyes straining into the gloom.

Another branch cracked. Loud. Close. He jolted back, dropping to his knees behind the protection of a tree trunk. The sound had come from above. Far above. He pressed close to the tree, searching upwards. He saw branches moving, perhaps forty feet above him.

He stared. Someone was climbing? Had they seen him and

now thought they were going to hide? He frowned. How stupid were they? As high as they had climbed, they were well within range. He hefted his gun and stopped. Even with the silencer, a gunshot would be too loud.

He watched leaves shake high above him. Perhaps they weren't as stupid as they first seemed. They were forcing his hand. They might survive a few shots. Tree limbs had plenty of stopping power, and the noise would bring the estate's guards running.

He cursed. He was running out of time. He had to act. He holstered his gun and pulled out a hunting knife. Its blade glinted in the pre-dawn light. He prepared to climb after them. A knife was his best weapon.

The sight of a knife was usually enough to make ordinary people freeze. Their throats closed up. Their mouths hung open. Often, they would simply hold their breath. Exactly the wrong actions if they hoped to survive.

He steeled his muscles for the task ahead. He really had only one choice. The risk of discovery was unacceptable. He would have to deal with the intruder.

Above him, wood splintered. The climber screamed. High pitched, perhaps female. A large chunk of the tree peeled off, crashing and tumbling as it fell, striking branches and limbs on the way down. Blackstake ran for the edge of the clearing. Somewhere in the blur, the screaming continued.

The tree limb hit the ground in a flurry of leaves and twigs. A sharp smack. The screaming stopped abruptly. The climber had fallen all the way down along with the limb.

On the ground was a mess of branches and leaves. The sound of falling debris stopped. Silence returned to the darkness.

Blackstake leaped forward through the undergrowth. He ran

flat-out. Bounding across the opening. Closing the gap on the unsuspecting intruder. He raised his knife, his momentum carrying him forward, his arm tensed for the pounding blow that would drive the knife into the intruder's chest.

He reached the fallen limb and froze.

The intruder lay prone on the ground. A boy. Young. The crest of some middle school on his jacket. His hair was a jumbled mat. Even in the dim light, Blackstake could see he had suffered a head injury that covered one side of his head with blood. His mouth was open, but he made no noise.

Blackstake hesitated, hunting knife held high. The boy had been standing not fifty feet from the girl's grave. He might have seen nothing or everything. Leaving him alive was too big a risk. Unnecessary.

He adjusted his grip on his knife. He'd seen a lot of head trauma before, and the boy's was extensive. Blood on the boy's body glistened in the growing light.

He lowered his knife. The boy wasn't going to make it. He'd fallen at least forty feet. He'd been climbing a tree, doing something stupid. He'd be found dead, and people would come to the same conclusion.

If he added further injuries to the boy, an autopsy would likely show them.

He slid his knife into the sheath. He would leave the brat to die. It was the least risky option.

Under the boy's collar rested a set of cheap headphones. Tinny. He leaned closer. They were silent, probably broken in the fall. He looked up the tree. The boy couldn't have seen anything at the gravesite, really. If he had, he would have run away. Fast. He wouldn't have wasted time listening to music and climbing a tree.

Blackstake walked away. He climbed back over the fence and pulled his jacket after him. He picked up the wheelbarrow and set off across the field. He had almost a mile to walk.

He kept close to the fence, dragging the wheelbarrow behind him. Morning dew soaked his boots and jeans. He leaned forward, his legs pushing hard, following the same path he had taken earlier.

Light was growing all around him. He kept his head up, and his grip tight on the barrow's handles.

Thirty minutes later he arrived at the edge of the thick woods, just as dawn broke over the horizon. He gave a great sigh. He was going to make it. He'd finish soon. No one had seen him. Or at least, no one who could possibly talk about what they'd seen.

An hour later, the girl's body was back in the ground, and the vegetation around her new grave was carefully arranged to cover the disturbance.

On his return to the manor, he saw that the fence post had collapsed and pulled another post along with it. Despite his care, his digging had undermined its footings. He shrugged. The fence was slated to be moved anyway.

He kicked off his muddy boots and ignored the housekeeper's stares as he walked through the mansion's basement in his filthy clothes. He entered his private apartment and dumped his clothes in the trash. Later he would incinerate them.

He showered, and fell, exhausted, onto his bed.

His day's work was done.

CHAPTER TWO

Denver, Colorado
Monday, September 26
10:00 a.m. Mountain Time

JESS KIMBALL PUSHED HER curtains back as far as they would go, letting the Denver sunshine sweep away the deserted apartment feeling. The air was stale. Dust motes swayed in the sun's rays.

She spent very little time here. No wonder the place never felt like a home. She'd create a real home someday. After she found her son. Until then, this almost abandoned apartment was as good as anywhere else for stashing what few belongings she possessed between the trips required by her *Taboo Magazine* assignments.

She rinsed out her coffee machine and washed a mug. She hadn't been here for weeks. Everything had acquired a thin layer of dust that made her sneeze. The machine gurgled and hissed, and filled the single mug. Coffee for one. She wondered if Peter drank coffee now. His fourteenth birthday was three months ago.

Maybe he was still too young, but Jess had been drinking coffee at age eleven.

Her fridge was barren, and she'd eaten her last protein bar last night. She sat in the room's only armchair and looked out of the window. Small white clouds dotted the deep blue sky. She could see the mountains in the distance.

She blew off the steam and sipped her coffee, savoring the burning sensation in her throat. She felt a bit uneasy. The apartment seemed too quiet. Her life now was chasing exciting stories for *Taboo*, not enjoying morning solitude. She was still too young for peace and quiet. Maybe she'd become addicted to adrenaline along with the caffeine.

She blew out a long breath and shook her head. No. Not adrenaline. It wasn't a quest for excitement that drove her.

It was justice for the victims that pushed her beyond her limits. She couldn't right all wrongs, and sometimes families were beyond anything justice could offer. But crime victims deserved justice. Justice shouldn't always serve the rights of criminals at the expense of victims. Victims needed an advocate like Jess. Especially when the system failed. Which, in Jess's view, happened all too often.

Like her son, Peter. The system had failed him. Failed her. She and Peter deserved justice, too. And they'd have it. One day. Until then, she'd do what she could for other victims.

She looked around the empty apartment. She rarely socialized. Work came first. But did she really need to put her own life on hold forever? As her assistant, Mandy, warned her all the time, Jess wasn't getting any younger. She grinned. Maybe Mandy was right. Maybe she should think about finding the right guy one of these days.

Her phone buzzed. Not the normal ring, but short, sharp

buzzes. She put down her mug and hurried across the room.

She didn't need to look at the name on the display before stabbing the talk button. "This is Jess Kimball."

"Good morning, ma'am." Brentwood Stephenson's warm drawl was unmistakable. Her chief investigator. The man she'd hired to lead the effort to find her son, missing twelve years now. Definitely not her prince charming, but that wasn't why she needed him.

Stephenson sounded like the sort of person for whom the words "southern gentleman" were invented, but she'd hired him because of his years in the Dallas PD. It was his record, not his manners that made him her number one choice for the job. His gallantry and unflappable calm were simply a welcome bonus.

Jess perched on the arm of the cheap sofa. Her heartbeat quickened. Stephenson wasn't due to call today. "I'm here. What's up?"

"Still alive? Haven't heard from you in a few days. You know I always worry about my clients." He laughed, teasing her as he often did. "Mainly because the dead ones don't pay up."

She put a smile into her voice because she felt emotional all of a sudden. She was tired. Exhausted, really. That must be it. She'd cried all of her tears for Peter long ago. "Well, I'm still alive, and I believe you're still getting your monthly retainer straight from my bank account?"

"I do believe I am. Every month. On the dot. Which is why I'm calling." He paused and his voice dropped an octave. "I heard from a contact. Washington State Police."

Jess leaned forward, crushing the phone to her ear.

"They have a boy in the hospital." Stephenson's teasing had stopped. His tone was deadly serious.

She swallowed. "And?"

"I don't want you getting your hopes up."

She brushed his concern aside. "Tell me everything."

"Jess, I barely know anything. In fact, I wasn't even going to call you. But the boy might not make it. I thought you had a right to know and make up your own mind."

"I'm okay." Her voice squeaked. She took a deep breath and sighed deliberately into the mouthpiece. "Just tell me what you do know, and we'll take it from there."

"A boy, seems about the right age. Admitted to a hospital in a small town southeast of Seattle this morning. Randolph, Washington." He paused and she could hear him inhale. "Head trauma. Bad. They've got him in a medically induced coma."

"Isn't that dangerous for a head injury? To sedate him?" She'd meant to wait for his full report before asking questions, but her worry had popped out of her mouth of its own accord.

"Sometimes. It can be. These docs seem to know what they're doing. It's a good hospital. State-of-the-art, I'm told."

She hoped he was right. "What else?"

"No ID on the boy yet. Police are doing everything to find out who he is. They'll be on TV, Internet, everywhere." He took another deep breath and held it a moment before he spoke again. "When they admitted him, the only thing they got out of him was a name."

She gritted her teeth. She knew what was coming. She'd been down similar roads before.

"It's why I called you." Stephenson paused as if to soften the blow. "He said his name was Peter."

Tears welled up in her eyes. Her jaw trembled, tapping her teeth against each other. She clamped her mouth shut and breathed deeply for control. Was this her Peter? After all these years? Could it be true? She grabbed a tissue from a box and dabbed the moisture from her eyes.

"Jess? Are you still there?" Stephenson's voice came from the speaker, tiny and distant.

Her heart beat in pounding thumps, and she snatched short breaths, avoiding tears, but barely. She'd been through this so many times. But this time felt different, and she wasn't sure why.

"Jess, you're worrying me. Do I need to send Denver PD over there?"

She knew he'd make good on the promise, so she brought the phone back to her ear and cleared her throat. "I'm here. Just a little under the weather today. Sorry."

Stephenson kept talking, giving her time to collect herself. He was an intuitive man, which was one of the things that made him a good investigator. "It could be him. It's possible. Not likely, but possible."

"Right." She choked the word out between snatched breaths.

"Look, Jess." His tone was gently stern as if he was talking her off a ledge or something. "Keep calm. There are millions of Peters in the world. This isn't the first one we've run across who is the right age and lacking ID, right?"

"But you think this one could be him." She wiped her nose. "That's why you called, isn't it?"

"Possibly. He was found in a small town, but his picture wasn't recognized at the schools there, which is strange. No one seems to know who he is or where he came from." Stephenson paused a beat. "His parents haven't been located. He might have run away or been dropped off. We just don't know yet."

"Where?" Jess breathed hard, sucking air deep into her lungs, pushing back the emotions rolling over her composure.

Stephenson wouldn't call without good reason. She cleared her throat again. "What hospital is he in?"

"Only one in that town, but it's a pretty good one. Randolph Memorial Hospital. ICU."

"Do you have a picture of him?"

"Not yet."

She felt the decision make itself. "I'm going."

"That's not a good idea, Jess. Not yet. This kid's suffered a head trauma. It's bad." His warnings fell into the silence and disappeared.

"If it's not him, maybe I can help." She paused to steady her breathing. "If it is him, I need to be there when he wakes up."

"Docs are not upbeat about his chances," Stephenson said warily.

She squeezed her eyes shut. "Then I need to go now."

"They might find the parents any minute." He wasn't the type to give up easily on his best judgment.

"Look, Brent. I appreciate you looking out for me. I do. But if he's my Peter, no matter what happens, I have to be there." Her voice broke, and she coughed to conceal her uncharacteristic emotion. Maybe she was losing her mind. Other mothers she'd met over the years had slipped over the edge into madness, eventually. She'd never thought the same might happen to her.

"It's only been a couple of hours since they found him," Stephenson said. "We'll have more info later. Why not wait until we know more?"

"Send me any information you get as soon as you have it. Thanks, Brent. I'll keep in touch." Jess hung up and booked the next flight out of Denver to Seattle. She'd send a note to her assistant and deal with a car rental and everything else from the airport.

She felt better, stronger, for making the decision. It was the right move.

If the boy wasn't her son, she'd catch a flight back in the morning.

CHAPTER THREE

THE PHONE IN BLACKSTAKE'S basement kitchen buzzed. The mansion had its own internal telephone system. Extravagant when it was installed. Unnecessary in the age of cell phones. But the system had advantages. No records were created. No log of calls or recorded conversations. When his phone rang, he answered immediately.

The boss spoke before Blackstake had a chance. "Security tells me three local police officers are milling around the area where you were busy last night."

Blackstake's blood ran cold. He punched buttons on a TV monitor to bring up the closed-circuit cameras pointed toward where he had been working. The distance and the thick forest challenged the camera range. He could make out three figures moving in the woods, but little else.

"I'll deal with them."

"Why are they here?"

"I'll find out."

"I was told an ambulance arrived and departed."

Blackstake took a deep breath. The ambulance must have been for the dead boy. He should have reported the boy's death earlier, but he'd assumed the body would lie there for a long time. Days, perhaps.

He sighed. "There was a boy down by the fence. An idiot. Climbed a tree and fell out of it."

"Did he see you?"

"Definitely not. Any boy with an ounce of sense who sees me digging up a body is going to run a mile. He isn't going to play Tarzan up a tree."

Another long silence. "Then why are the police here?"

Blackstake pursed his lips. "Like I said, I'll find out."

"You do that. Report back immediately."

The phone went dead.

Blackstake donned hiking boots and a thick jacket and left the mansion.

A police presence after someone had found the dead boy wasn't surprising, but it raised his adrenaline.

He remembered every single tool and weapon he had carried with him the night before. He counted them off. He ran through the list twice. He'd brought everything back with him. No question.

His clothes had been ripped and torn. He'd probably left fragments. Disturbed soil at both gravesites might be discovered. Forensic trace evidence was likely, if a crime scene team scoured the area. But why would they?

He ground his teeth. Speculation was useless. He needed facts to assess his risk and evaluate options.

He took a golf cart with oversized tires down the hill and angled to the left of the police to a gate in the fence. He recognized the police captain, Nelson, his lackey Gardner, and their trailer-trash dispatcher Charlene Mackie. They were on their knees, sifting through the undergrowth. What the hell were they looking for?

He used a master key to unlock the gate. Nelson stood as he approached.

"Problem?" Blackstake said, with a concerned frown.

Nelson nodded. "Could say that. You on the senator's staff?"

"Karl Blackstake. Security." He shook hands. "So, what happened here?"

Nelson pointed. "A boy fell from that tree. The cottonwood."

Blackstake looked up. The tree was huge. The trunk disappeared into the canopy of leaves, but he guessed it was a good hundred feet tall. "Folks walk through here all the time, as you know. We try to keep them out, but you know how unsuccessful that's been." He glanced at Gardner and Mackie and shrugged. "Kids climb the trees, even though we'd prefer they didn't."

"He fell forty feet," Nelson said.

Blackstake whistled. "Will he be okay?"

Nelson shook his head. "He's hanging on in the ICU. Stable for the moment. But not good."

"Broken bones?"

"Several." Nelson nodded. "And significant head trauma."

"What was he doing all the way up there?" Blackstake pursed his lips and tried to look concerned. The kid should be dead already, but head traumas could go either way. Tricky thing, the brain.

Nelson shrugged. "He's still unconscious. The doctors are probably going to keep him that way for a while."

Blackstake grimaced. "Parents with him?"

Nelson shook his head. "He didn't have any ID. The only thing he's said so far is his first name. Peter. No last name."

"But you'll find the parents, surely?"

"We hope. We've guessed his age. We're checking the schools and we've asked the media to help."

"You didn't find a backpack or anything with his name and address in it?" Blackstake cocked his head. "Seems like every kid I see is carrying a backpack these days."

Nelson shook his head. "We've gone over the ground twice. There's nothing else here."

"How do you know he fell from this tree?"

Nelson pointed to a yellow gash high up the trunk. "Looks like the tree limb couldn't hold his weight."

Blackstake looked up. The gash hadn't been visible in the early dawn light.

Blackstake walked to the fence. He followed the immediate portion of the path he had taken at dawn, dragging his boots across the ground, disturbing everything he could reach.

Nelson followed.

Blackstake shook the fallen fence post. The steel cables that ran to the neighboring posts flapped.

"These steel posts are strong. This one couldn't have been knocked down by that boy without some kind of help."

"No."

"Petty vandalism then. Unrelated to the boy."

"Seems like," Nelson said.

Blackstake raised his eyebrows. "You think there was someone else here with him?"

Nelson snorted and shook his head. He gestured to where the boy had landed. "Believe me, no civilized human being would have left him there alone. It's a miracle he's alive."

"Poor kid." Blackstake nodded. "He's lucky you found him."

"Pure luck," Nelson said. "A couple of high school kids decided to take a shortcut. They found him earlier this morning. We interviewed them, but they don't know anything."

Blackstake nodded again. He handed over a card with the senator's security office phone number on it. "Will you keep us updated on his progress?"

Nelson took the card. "It won't be a liability issue if that's what you're worried about."

Blackstake shook his head. "I'm sure the senator would like to express his sympathies to the parents. If you let us know when they're found, we'll arrange something."

Nelson nodded.

"I've got to get back. And I'll call for repairs to the fence."

Nelson nodded again.

Blackstake turned and stepped over the fallen fence post, stomping a few extra times on the surrounding dirt for good measure, and returned to his golf cart.

The encounter had gone better that he expected. Nelson and his team had found no evidence that Blackstake had been there earlier.

The boy had survived. That was a surprising disappointment. But one that should remedy itself soon enough. If he lived, he'd more than likely have amnesia of the events surrounding his injury. Head trauma often produced memory loss of the actual event.

If none of that worked out, there were other options. He'd deal with that problem when and if the boy woke up.

Nelson seemed convinced the boy's fall had been an accident. None of the three cops had taken any interest in the first gravesite.

All in all, it was as good a result as he could hope for considering the boy hadn't died as expected.

He took the golf cart back up the hill, much happier now than when he had descended. The boss would be pleased.

CHAPTER FOUR

Randolph, Washington
Monday, September 26
3:00 p.m. Pacific Time

SIX HOURS AFTER STEPHENSON'S phone call, Jess pulled into the Randolph Memorial Hospital parking lot. She'd been delayed following the TSA protocol to check her Glock through to Seattle, and collecting it at her destination. It was a hassle. But she never traveled without it.

The gun was secured in its case in the trunk now. She wasn't licensed for concealed carry in Washington, so she'd have to leave it there. But knowing her Glock was with her made her feel safer. The Glock and her *Taboo Magazine* credentials were the only protection she'd ever needed.

She walked swiftly along the sidewalk and entered the hospital through the main entrance. The building and grounds were impressive. The lobby's atrium was larger than she'd expected. It rose four floors and seemed to run the full length of the building. She walked around a few oversized potted plants to the reception desk.

There was a line of visitors waiting to ask questions. The woman behind the desk looked harassed. She gave out forms and hand-waved directions.

Jess used the time to check local news sites on her phone. As Stephenson had said, local authorities were circulating a picture of the boy. It was a hand-drawn sketch, probably because a photo of the damaged child would be too disturbing. The news reports requested the parents come forward and posted tip lines for people to call in with information. The latest reports said the boy's parents hadn't done so.

It was three in the afternoon. The boy had been admitted around eight in the morning, not long after he'd been discovered by two local teens. Jess bit her lip. The media ads had been going out since midday. The parents should have been located by now.

She swallowed. She needed to keep her hopes in check.

The parents might not know about their son's situation. It was Monday, a school day. The image of the boy wasn't a photograph, and some people would need a more accurate portrait to recognize him.

She stopped speculating. Guesses would get her nowhere. She needed more and better information. If she couldn't get it here, she'd find out what she needed to know somewhere else. She was a reporter. She could uncover anything, given enough time.

Jess was next in line when she spotted a sign for the ICU. She walked around the reception area and headed for the doorway. The fewer people she had to explain her presence to, the better.

She walked through to another reception area in ICU.

Beyond the desk, Jess saw more wires, tubes, beds, monitors and other equipment found in every intensive care unit. Stephenson was right. This was a state-of-the-art facility. She breathed a little easier.

Around the ICU central nurse's station were several cubicles, each with a privacy screen. At the far end of the room were two doors labeled "isolation."

A nurse parked a gurney against a wall in the corridor and walked behind the reception desk. A sign on the desk said her name was Elisha Harvey, R.N. She smiled. "Can I help you?"

Jess put some conviction into her tone and straightened her spine. "Nurse Harvey, I'm looking for Peter, the boy who was brought in this morning."

Nurse Harvey inched closer. "Are you his mother?"

"I don't know. Maybe." Jess bit her lip. "It's complicated."

Nurse Harvey nodded. She'd probably heard all kinds of stories from patients and families. "Are you a relative?"

Jess took a deep breath. "My son, Peter. He…he would be fourteen years old now."

"I'm sure you understand." Nurse Harvey sat down, put her hands on her knees, and wheeled the chair up to the desk. "I'm afraid we can't let visitors approach our patients without authorization."

Jess rummaged in her bag and produced her Colorado driver's license. Her *Taboo Magazine* credentials usually caused unnecessary panic in hospitals.

Nurse Harvey read the license and nodded again before she handed it back. "I'm sorry. I can't let you in unless we can confirm you are related. Or, if you had a court order or permission from his family?"

Jess shook her head and swallowed, closing her eyes as she

did so. It had been an impulsive idea. Turning up out of the blue on the off chance this young boy might be Peter. Her Peter. And Nurse Harvey was only doing her job. "Can you tell me his age?"

Nurse Harvey shook her head. "I'm afraid I can't give you any information at all, Miss Kimball."

"Blue eyes? Green? Brown?"

Nurse Harvey kept shaking her head.

"I mean if I could just see him. For a moment. I think…If he's mine, I think I could recognize him."

"Do you have any photos of your son?"

"I do. Just a moment." Jess kept Peter's age-progressed pictures with her at all times, for just such an occasion. Not that she needed them to remember what he looked like. She'd used them to persuade people like Nurse Harvey to talk to her before.

But the photos were only computer-generated images, updated monthly. Guesses, really. Made by a machine. From the few photos she'd taken of Peter as a baby. Still, they were the best she had.

She pulled out her phone and flipped to the photo marked *Peter, age 14*. She handed the phone to Nurse Harvey, who accepted it, looked carefully, and then handed the phone back.

"I'm sorry." Her tone and her expression conveyed sympathy, but the result was the same. She wouldn't allow a total stranger to approach a very sick child. Jess should have known better.

"Can I help you?" said a deep voice behind her.

Jess turned. A uniformed police officer. The name tag on the left chest pocket said J. Nelson. She had to look up more than a foot to make eye contact.

"Can I help you?" he repeated, not unkindly. "Captain Nelson. Randolph PD."

"I want to see Peter."

"You're a relative?"

"Maybe." Jess gestured to Nurse Harvey. "We were just discussing that."

"I'm sure you understand we have to put the boy's interests first." He raised both eyebrows as if the statement might have been a question. "If you are not a blood relative or legal guardian, I'm afraid I'll have to ask you to leave."

"I was just telling Nurse Harvey—"

"You lost your boy, and his name is Peter." He nodded. "I presume you reported him missing?"

"Yes. And we've been looking for him for more than twelve long years," Jess replied.

"I sympathize, but the investigation should be pursued through the appropriate channels," Nelson said as if he knew how hopeless such investigations were after more than a decade of looking. "If this boy is your son, you'll be notified as soon as we get the situation sorted out."

Jess opened her mouth to speak.

Nelson cut her off. "I'm sorry for your loss, ma'am. But I will have to ask you to leave now."

Jess sighed. She realized he wasn't going to back down and there was nothing more she could say to persuade either of them. Not yet. Not without more than a computer-generated picture.

He gestured down the corridor. "I'll walk you out."

She nodded.

He walked her through the reception, past the stairs, and into the parking lot. He pointed his chin toward his cruiser. "Let's step over here for a moment."

They walked up to the front of the vehicle. A heavyset woman stepped out. She looked Jess up and down.

"Take her name and address, Charlene. In case we need to contact her. Just for our records." Nelson turned to Jess. "You're not being charged with anything."

"Glad to hear it." She heard the anger in her voice, but she couldn't help it. She'd come so far, waited so long. To be turned away without seeing Peter was more than she would accept casually.

Nelson sat in the cruiser, closed the door, and worked on a laptop attached to the dashboard.

According to her name plate, Charlene's last name was Mackie. She opened a notepad and held out her hand. "May I see your ID, please?"

Jess handed over her Colorado driver's license without comment. Officer Mackie swiped the license and made notes. Then she studied the license. She held up the picture in front of Jess's face. "Jessica Kimball?"

"That's right."

Charlene frowned. "From *Taboo Magazine*?"

Jess nodded.

Charlene bit her lip and bobbed her head, slow and steady. "I wrote to you once."

Jess smiled automatically, as she always did when someone recognized her. "Well…thank you."

"You didn't reply."

Jess shifted her weight. "I'm sorry. I get a lot of mail, and it's hard to remember every name."

Charlene grunted. "I wouldn't expect you to remember me. It was years ago."

Jess pursed her lips and nodded. "What was it about?"

Charlene shook her head. "Not important now."

"But it was back then, wasn't it?"

"Yeah." Officer Mackie nodded slowly. "It was. Back then."

"I hope whatever it was worked out okay." Jess expected things hadn't worked out well, though. The cases she worked on rarely had happy endings.

Charlene Mackie grunted. "What are you here for?"

Jess turned and pointed at the hospital. "I heard about the boy. Peter. He's fourteen and his parents haven't been found."

"And that makes him worthy of a *Taboo Magazine* story?"

"No. If you've read my stories, you probably know my boy was taken from me. He'd be fourteen."

Charlene stared, her mouth open a fraction.

"I guess I'll have to wait and see if this is my boy," Jess said.

Charlene nodded. "I'm very sorry."

Jess shrugged.

Charlene lowered her gaze. "It's rough." She held out Jess's license. "But don't give up."

Jess took her license. "I won't."

CHAPTER FIVE

JESS SAT IN HER rented sedan and went through the notes Stephenson had sent her again. The boy had been found in a local forest. The thick woods were spread over public property and continued onto Senator Alistaire Meisner's private estate. The police report wasn't clear on whether he'd been found on the public or private side.

Which could explain some of the reaction she'd experienced from the locals, Nelson and Mackie, and even Nurse Harvey. The senator was probably a magnet for reporters of one kind or another. When he was here at home in Randolph, he probably shunned attention.

Charlene walked into the hospital. Nelson was still in his cruiser, staring at his computer. He likely knew as much as anyone about the boy.

She walked over to his cruiser and startled him by knocking on the windshield.

He wound down his window. "Help you?"

"I didn't mean to be so abrupt."

"No problem." He pointed to his computer. "I looked you up. Seems you check out okay."

"I told you, my son was taken from me. This boy might be mine."

"People tell me all sorts of things. Doesn't make them true."

Jess gave a weak smile. He was right.

"It's my job to protect the citizens of Randolph," he said. "And that boy still needs protection even if he turns out to be yours."

"I understand." She nodded. "Buy you a coffee?"

He checked his watch. "You know Biscuits in town?"

"I'll find it."

The diner was a standalone building with a parking lot that surrounded all four sides. The window glass was painted white up to the seated customers' shoulder level, leaving only their heads in view, bobbing and turning as they ate and talked.

The "Biscuits" sign was large but lit by only two incandescent bulbs that did little to attract attention to the place. A fact underscored by the three cars and one pickup truck parked in the front of the oversized but otherwise empty parking lot.

Jess circled the building once and parked away from the road, close to a side door. Nelson wasn't here yet.

A waitress met her as soon as she set foot into the hot, humid atmosphere.

"Table or booth?"

Jess looked the room over. It spanned along two sides of an open kitchen and grill. "Booth."

"Before you ask, we're not serving breakfast." She dropped a menu on the table. "Be back in a minute to take your order."

Nelson had arrived before she ordered. She watched him

back his car into a parking spot and squeeze into the side of the booth facing the door. He had all the basics covered for a quick getaway, which meant he'd had good training somewhere and took his job seriously.

She ordered black coffee. He requested yogurt, toast, and coffee.

Jess grinned. "No doughnuts?"

"Not since I left Philly." He patted his flat stomach. "I'm an outdoorsman these days."

"You moved here for your health?"

He shrugged. "Wife's from the Seattle area. But I have to admit, life's better here."

"You don't miss it? The excitement of the big city?"

He shook his head. "The work here's mostly figuring out why someone did something stupid, not looking at the human wreckage of violent crime."

Jess nodded. "Police work isn't always the excitement they show on television."

"And after we catch them, half the time they get off through some legal fine point. Or witness intimidation." He paused for a level stare. "I saw plenty of that."

The coffee arrived. Steaming, hot, fresh. Jess inhaled the aroma.

He spooned three sugars into his cup. "I gave up doughnuts. Can't give up everything."

She poured a spoonful of sugar into her own cup.

"How did you hear about this boy?" Nelson asked.

"I got a call. My son's name is Peter. He's the same age. This boy didn't seem to have any parents. No one knew who he was." She shrugged as if those facts were enough to justify her headlong dash to Randolph.

He wasn't fooled. "And you live in Denver, work for *Taboo Magazine*, and show up in a matter of hours?"

"I have some people looking out for my son. We check out every lead."

"Oh?"

She gave him a flat smile. "I'm not some obsessive nutcase that's going to manipulate the situation just because he has the same first name as my missing son."

He raised his cup. "Glad to hear it. I mean, places like this, people get obsessed over the smallest things."

"I thought you said nothing much happened around here."

"You back to being a reporter now?"

"Seems like I don't have anything else to do." Her coffee had cooled. The sugar was a bad idea. "I don't even know your name."

He patted the tag on his chest. J. Nelson.

"Your first name," she said.

"Not many people want to know a cop's first name."

"I'm a reporter," she teased with a grin.

He grunted, but he smiled, too. "Joshua."

"Joshua Nelson," she said. "Has a nice ring to it."

"I prefer Nelson."

She nodded. "Right. If I can find something worth reporting on in this town, you'll be identified as Officer J. Nelson. How's that?"

"Captain J. Nelson."

She grimaced. "Sorry, I should have known that."

He waved it away. "Nothing worth reporting on in this town anyway. Local paper struggles to find enough to fill a dozen pages. Including the used car ads and the grocery store sales."

"I guess the boy's accident will make it onto the front page."

"Well…"

"What?" she said.

He shrugged.

She leaned forward. "Oh, come on. You know denial just revs up my interest."

The waitress returned with Nelson's food and topped off his coffee. Jess had barely touched hers.

When they were alone again, Jess stared at him. "What's the secret?"

He took a mouthful of yogurt. "There's no secret. Nothing special really. You said local. But he's not from around here."

Jess frowned.

"We found a bus ticket in his pocket. He's from Bamford."

"Which is?"

"Thirty miles south of here." Nelson dug into his yogurt again.

Jess leaned back. "He came thirty miles to climb a tree?"

"Kids have done stranger things," he said.

"It must have been really early in the morning when he left home."

"He was found at eight. The docs think he fell an hour or so earlier." Nelson finished the yogurt and licked the spoon. "We're talking to the bus drivers trying to figure that out now."

"So if he fell around seven, and the bus takes, say, forty-five minutes, he left home around six. Isn't that pretty early?"

Nelson worked his way through a slice of toast. "Middle school starts at seven-fifty. He could be in the band or athletics. They practice early."

"But he skipped school and came here instead." She swallowed a sip of the now cold and sickly sweet coffee.

Her Peter had been taken long before they had developed a

school routine. She'd never dressed him for classes or packed his lunch or waited outside for the school bus.

"You okay?" Nelson said, between mouthfuls.

She took a deep breath. "Sure. Fine."

He stopped eating. "Kids skip school to do a lot of weird things."

"But thirty miles to climb a tree?" She bit her lip. "Is there something special about that tree?"

Nelson spread jelly on his last piece of toast. "Just a tree."

"Doesn't make sense, does it?"

"Why are you trying to make this something more than it is? Kids fall out of trees all the time." He leaned forward. "I know you're worried that he might be your son, but frankly it's far more likely that his parents are at work and won't know he's hurt until tonight."

She pursed her lips.

"I searched the area where he fell with two of my officers. He was off to the side of a path and down a ways through some woods. There were broken branches around the area where we found him. He climbed a tree, and the branch, limb, or whatever he was on, broke. Not mysterious. Nothing complicated. An unfortunate accident. That's all."

"Can I see the place?"

He finished his toast and used his radio to call the station. Charlene told him nothing was happening and he had no appointments. He signed off with a thank you.

He sighed. "Looks like I'm free."

CHAPTER SIX

JESS TOOK HER OWN car, and followed Nelson's cruiser to
the shoulder on the side of a narrow road, not far outside of
town. The air was crisp, and the ground soft with a thick layer of
branches and rotting leaves. She followed him toward the scene
of the accident.

She'd donned ballet flats before she left home, but as
they worked their way up an embankment, she began to
wish she'd worn boots. She'd also grabbed her bag out of
habit, and it was already starting to feel like lugging a
suitcase.

"He climbed up this hill?" Her voice was slightly breathless.

Nelson shook his head and pointed back along the road.
"This path starts closer to town. It winds around some. We took
a short cut because there's an opening in the trees here we can
walk through."

"Did he? Take the short cut?" She struggled to keep up with
him.

Nelson shrugged. "No way of knowing. Unless he wakes up, so we can ask him."

Jess felt the cold air wrap around her. "He's still unconscious?"

"Medically-induced coma. They say it's better for him that way."

The air tightened its grip on Jess's throat. Whether he was her son or not, she wanted him to recover soon.

They'd reached a pathway that ran parallel to a substantial steel fence topped with three rows of barbed wire. Both extended ahead as far as she could see. "That's quite a fence."

"Meisner's," Nelson said as if that explained everything.

He pointed to the right. "That way back to town." He turned to the left. "The boy was found over here."

As they walked, the trees thinned out. Beyond the fence was a gradual incline that continued to a flat peak about half a mile away. In the center of the flat area was a large white mansion. Surrounding it was a broad gravel driveway of the type that once signified wealth and power because of the cost of maintaining it.

The mansion had three stories and dozens of windows. It was Georgian in style, a very formal geometry, complete with white Doric columns across the front. There appeared to be some sort of glass structure on the roof, but the mansion's height concealed all but the very top.

Two figures on horseback rode up the far side of the hill. They rounded the house and disappeared from view.

"Nice house," she said.

Nelson looked up the hill without breaking his pace. "Meisner's place."

"Meisner's fence, Meisner's place. Does he own everything around here?"

Nelson looked left and right. "Pretty much."

Further on, the woods grew thicker, and the trail turned inward. Jess could see nothing but trees. They had to crouch and crawl through some places. Nelson held back branches, handing them off to Jess before they flicked in her face.

They passed a fallen fence post, the wires still attached, but the post leaned drunkenly toward the land it was supposed to protect, its barbed wire close to the ground.

The trail widened again a few feet farther on, and Nelson stopped in a clearing.

From here, Jess could see the mansion, but the blanket of gray sky was concealed by a mesh of branches. The dim light in the opening took on a green tinge.

"That's where he fell." Nelson pointed to a thick old tree and patch of ground where the undergrowth had been trampled down.

Pathways were worn through the weeds, lines where medics had brought in a stretcher, where police had examined the scene. A thick tree limb had been cast aside, the milky-yellow grain of its cross section evidenced a recent break. Several pieces of white debris lay in a pile. Medical wound dressing wrappers hastily discarded by the paramedics.

Nelson picked up the trash and stuffed it into his pocket. "He was in a bad way."

Jess looked up. The tree was tall. A long way up, the same milky-yellow grain was visible on the thick old tree. A circular patch and long gash down the trunk lit starkly in the dim light of the woods. The break had torn the bark downward along a three-foot section of the tree.

"Forty feet up," Nelson said, pointing toward the circular patch where the branch should have been.

Jess whistled as she looked up the tree. It was older and taller than the others in the immediate vicinity. Maybe a tempting challenge for a young boy. A badge of honor. One that had come with a price.

"Four stories is a long way to fall. What were his injuries?"

"Broken bones in his shoulder, right arm, and right leg. Those should all heal." Nelson looked up the tree again. "The head injury is the critical one. The docs are worried about it more than the others."

Jess pursed her lips. She inhaled deeply. "That's a lot of injuries. Even for a fall from that distance."

"But…" Nelson stepped to the edge of the path and pushed the vegetation back with his boot to expose a rock with a dark stain on it. "He was pretty unlucky."

"His head hit that rock?"

Nelson nodded. "I'm pretty certain it was that one." He lifted his boot away and the weeds sprang back into place.

She gestured to the undergrowth. "Can I touch things?"

Nelson shrugged. "This was an unfortunate accident. Not a crime scene."

Jess kneeled and inspected the rock. It had lain on the ground for maybe eight hours since the boy's fall, but the vegetation shielded it from the weather. The stain was large and spread out in inky rivulets. She used her phone to snap a few pictures of the rock and its immediate surroundings.

She eased the rock from the mud and held it up. It was irregularly shaped and maybe three or four pounds. With more daylight, the stains revealed themselves. Peter's blood.

She held the underside of the rock. "You mind if I take this?"

Nelson hummed. "Presumably you're thinking DNA?"

She nodded. "Seems obvious."

He took a deep breath. "Like I said, it's not a crime scene, so I guess that's okay. But Meisner won't like it if he finds out."

"Why? It's just a rock. Is he that possessive of everything on his land?" She pulled a big sheet of paper out of her bag and wrapped the rock in it and placed it carefully inside. "If he squawks, tell him I'll pay for the rock."

Nelson shrugged.

Jess looked up at the scarred tree and back at the depressed soil where she'd removed the rock. "Seems like more than a little unlucky, doesn't it?"

"Under the circumstances, he was lucky his injuries weren't worse." Nelson shook his head. "These rocks are all over this area." He pointed to the flattened undergrowth. "There are several bigger, sharper rocks in that area. If he'd hit his head on one of those, he'd be gone for sure."

Jess stepped off the path. She bent down, eyeing the flattened weeds. They radiated in strange directions, twisting and turning. The result of the medical team's rescue efforts, most likely. She lifted sections of the greenery until she found a rock. It was deep brown. Long buried in the earth. She found another, equally brown, equally buried. She held back the grass. "Why are all of these rocks here? This area isn't particularly rocky anywhere else."

"Fieldstone. They were trucked in." Nelson waved his arm up and down the trail. "Used to be a rock wall along here."

Jess stood and looked along the path. She looked back the way they had come. "How long ago? I mean, there's no sign of a wall or anything."

"Fourteen years ago," said a voice behind her.

Jess turned to see a stout middle-aged man approaching with

a noticeably younger woman close behind him. She was stylishly dressed, and he looked faintly ridiculous in the same garb. Riding hat, tweed jacket, and tight riding breeches that clung to her shapely legs and his thick ones. He waved a riding whip back and forth along the trail. "Used to run along here until a bunch of criminals decided to invade my property and knock it down."

Jess nodded. She didn't recognize him, but she knew who he must be. "This is your land?"

"Knocked it down," he repeated, glaring at Nelson. "Bunch of them labored all night to destroy my expensive fieldstone wall. Criminals. Never caught."

Nelson took a deep breath. "This is Mr. and Mrs. Meisner."

The man flashed a grim smile. "*Senator* and Mrs. Meisner."

Nelson nodded. "Yes, Senator and Mrs. Meisner."

Meisner stepped past Jess and looked at the flattened weeds. "Is this where it happened?"

Nelson nodded again. "Where the boy fell? Yes."

Meisner grunted. "A shame."

"To say the least," Jess said.

Meisner looked at Nelson. "They say he's in a bad way."

Nelson nodded. "Very."

Meisner looked back at the trampled undergrowth.

"Do you know what he was doing here?" Jess asked.

Meisner scowled in her general direction. "How would I know what he was doing here?"

Before Jess could respond, his wife touched his arm.

Mrs. Meisner shook her head. "Terribly sad for the child and his family, of course." Her voice was husky. Sexy.

His expression changed immediately. "Sorry. Didn't mean to be uncaring. I'm concerned for the boy's welfare, naturally. What human being wouldn't be?"

Jess clamped her jaw shut.

"Are you the mother?" Mrs. Meisner asked.

Jess shook her head. No reason to complicate this conversation right now.

"Related?" The senator asked.

Jess shook her head again.

"I have no idea what the boy was doing climbing trees on my property." Meisner shrugged. His phony concern disappeared as quickly as it arrived. "What did you say your name was?"

"I didn't." She held out her hand. "Jessica Kimball."

He gripped her hand. His palm was soft and his fingers fleshy. His gaze crossed her face. She felt his gaze linger on her curls and her mouth. She relaxed her fingers, finishing the handshake. He held on a fraction too long. Easing his grip from her knuckles, sliding his fingers over hers as he released her hand. She resisted the temptation to wipe her palm on her jeans.

Mrs. Meisner was wearing gloves, and she didn't remove them or offer her own handshake.

Jess gestured to the woods. "This is your land?"

He pointed to the left. "All the way to the road."

Nelson took a step closer. "But the trail is a public right of way, Senator."

"Yes, we mustn't forget that, must we?" Meisner sniffed. "It is, however, as the lady said, my land." He kicked at a rock buried in the vegetation. "As was the fieldstone wall I paid for."

"That was long before my time," Nelson said.

"And now, thanks to some bunch of do-good lawyers, I'm going to have to move the fence I paid for to replace the fieldstone. Does that seem right to you?"

"It was all settled in court," Nelson said.

Meisner grunted.

The horses on the other side of the fence whinnied. Mrs. Meisner touched her husband's arm again. "Alistaire?"

Meisner stared at Jess and Nelson another moment.

"Yes, Margot, we must go. There's no problem here that we need to deal with." He looked at Nelson. "I am correct, aren't I? There is no problem?"

"That's right." Nelson lowered his head a fraction. "No problem."

Meisner made a circular motion with his hand. "No more trampling over my property?"

Nelson shook his head. "Just paperwork at this point."

Meisner looked sideways at Jess. "Good. Glad to hear it." He nodded. "If you'll excuse us, the horses are waiting. Keep me informed, Joshua."

He gestured toward his wife who walked off ahead of him. A moment later, Meisner disappeared beyond the trees.

"He's a charmer, isn't he?" Jess said, curling her upper lip.

Nelson nodded. "And rumor has it that he's making a run for the White House next election."

An involuntary shudder ran from her damp feet all the way through to her scalp. "Heaven help us."

CHAPTER SEVEN

NELSON LED THE WAY back through the trees toward their parked vehicles. She opened her trunk, found a large Ziploc bag in her luggage, and sealed the rock inside.

Nelson stood watching her. "You know it will be difficult to prove the integrity of the DNA sample in court."

She placed the plastic bag in the middle of her luggage. "If it gets that far, I'm sure the test can be repeated. This is just personal. If his DNA matches mine, then I'll take the next steps."

She closed the trunk. "So, this is all his land? Even the woods?"

"As Meisner pointed out." Nelson gestured to the fence. "He built that barbed wire fence about fourteen years ago. Cut off the public right of way, which used to run straight across the field the other side of the fieldstone wall."

"The right of way ran directly across the lawn in front of his house?"

"Bingo."

"I've never heard of a public right of way over private land."
She stopped and studied the setup. "I'm not sure I'd like that,
either, if I owned that mansion. People traipsing past my
windows day and night."

"I'm told it was some kind of covenant thing. Dates from the
early 1900s. And it wasn't past his windows. It was only halfway
from the forest to his house. Quarter mile at the closest. But,"
Nelson shrugged, "the new fence blocked the entrance and exit
to the right of way. Now people have to walk all the way around
from the bus stop to get home instead of taking the short cut
across the right of way. Stirred up a lot of bad feeling between
the pro- and anti-camps."

Jess cocked her head. "The what?"

"Pro and anti. For and against." He took a deep breath.
"Look, he's a senator. Brings a lot of money into the area. Which
is good if you're feeding off that money. Those people just want
to keep the old man happy. But if you're not benefiting from that
money, and you live in the low-income housing way on the other
side of the forest, and you just want to get home after a long day,
it's not so great."

"Because?"

Nelson pointed to the right, along the fence. "How would
you like to walk through these woods at night?"

Jess shook her head. "Couldn't he just move the fence
farther away from the trees, so people could walk by more
easily?"

Nelson laughed. "That is exactly what the judge said. He
called it a compromise. Meisner has to pay for a new path and
lighting. It's still a long way from where the path used to run, but
people will be able to walk along a ten-foot easement that will be
out of the woods, at least."

"It took ten years to reach that agreement?" Jess said.

"No. It took eight years until the anti-crowd could convince a fancy Seattle company of lawyers to take the case pro bono. Then it took two years to schedule a session in court. Then it took ten minutes." He offered the same flat smile she'd seen several times now. "Don't you love our legal system?"

Jess looked back the way they had come. "Why was there a gap in the fence? Back there?"

He shrugged. "Fence posts fall over all the time."

"Isn't that a suspicious coincidence? The fence is down, and the boy is injured on the same day?"

He shook his head. "We don't know when it fell over. We just happened to see it because we came here to rescue the boy."

She shrugged. "I guess."

They reached a point where the woods thinned out and Jess could see the big house again. Outside the front, two figures sat on their horses on the gravel drive. She guessed it was both Meisners. She assumed the pair was watching them. "What's she like?"

"Margot Meisner?" Nelson sniffed. "Rich daddy. Very rich. Expects everything her way. Not one to be messed with. They say misery loves company. I think money loves misery, too."

Jess stared up the hill. They had turned their horses and were pointing straight down the hill. Straight toward Jess. It was like a challenge. As if they were smug in their superiority and taunting her.

She knew it was a stupid feeling. They just happened to be on horses on a hill, and she just happened to be on foot, far below. It was an image that had been played out over centuries. It stirred atavistic feelings that probably went back to when that difference really meant something. The difference between warmth and cold. The difference between plenty and starvation, and, she exhaled, the difference between life and death.

She stopped. "Wait."

Nelson stopped a few paces on.

"I want to go back," Jess said.

He looked at his watch. "Why?"

"I'm going to climb that tree."

"Why?"

"Peter climbed it for a reason."

Nelson sighed. "Boys climb trees. An accident happened. There's nothing more to say."

"He must have had a reason." She smiled. "Please. Just a few more minutes."

He sighed. "Lead on."

They returned to the tree. It was old. The thick trunk split in half about ten feet from the ground. Gnarled knots peppered the lower twenty feet of the trunk. Heavier limbs intertwined higher up.

Nelson put his hand on the tree. "You sure you want to do this?"

Jess looked up. "There has to be a reason he was up there."

He shrugged. "Something to tell his pals."

"Maybe he wanted to see something?"

"Like what?"

She put her foot on the lowest of the knots. "That's what I want to find out."

"I can go up instead of you," he said half-heartedly.

She shook her head and began the climb. "I'm smaller. Easier to get through the gaps."

He very carefully placed his hands on the lower part of her thighs and helped her up the first eight feet.

She moved one limb at a time. Like the rock wall climbing she did at the gym. She didn't rush, reaching up one hand, grasping as far as she could, hanging her weight on her straight arm and bringing her feet up, bending her knees, coiling, before pushing upward, arm out straight, to repeat the process.

The tree was ideal for climbing. The arrangement of lumps and limbs was perfectly spaced for her size. It must have been the same for Peter. He was probably smaller than Jess, but with some twisting and turning, progress was fairly easy.

At twenty feet, the foliage to her right thinned. She could see up the hill. One horse was still near the house facing the woods. She guessed it was Meisner.

Jess climbed a few more feet. The view to her right opened up. The house and its land were clearly visible. As was Meisner. Jess's higher elevation allowed her to see around the curve of the hill.

Green fields rolled into a broad expanse of trees in the distance. A lot of trees. A larger forest than the thin ribbon of woods below. Old white painted barns dotted the landscape. To the left of the house, and down the hill was a stable. She saw a man clearing the yard outside.

On the right, halfway between the house and the woods, was a modern looking building. Unlighted windows ran in a continuous line around the walls. Cars were parked on either side. Meisner had some sort of offices on his property.

Jess sat on a limb, her arm around the tree's trunk. She was maybe twenty feet below the milky-yellow gash that marked the place from which the boy had fallen. She looked a long way down. Two full stories of an ordinary building from this point. Four stories to the ground from the broken branch. The extent of his injuries became easier to understand. It was a wonder he hadn't died.

Above her, the tree thinned out. She could reach the height he had reached, but as she looked across Meisner's land, she concluded that she wouldn't see much more from another twenty feet up.

She took one last look at the house on the hill and Meisner, who was still watching her, then worked her way back down, using her arms for balance and her legs to carry her weight. Nelson lifted her the last five feet to the ground.

"What did you find?" he said.

She nodded in the direction of the house. "You can see the Meisner place. Stables. A couple of old barns. Forest in the distance."

"That's all his, too."

She whistled. "Lot of land. And he has an office building."

"He has a small staff. Mostly interns. They need a place to work. Anything else?"

She shook her head.

"Nothing significant? Nothing you can't see from the ground?"

"No."

He frowned. "So he climbed a tree. Like boys have done for years."

"Maybe."

Nelson laughed. "You think he was interested in spying on a senator?"

She gnawed the inside of her lower lip. "Don't know. I won't know until I talk to his parents. Try to figure out what he was doing here."

He frowned. "I know I have no control over what you do, but please leave the parents alone for a while. After we identify them, they'll have enough to worry about, and they don't need to feel any more guilty about not supervising the boy. Unless that DNA comes back the way you hope it will, you've got no cause to talk to them."

Jess took a deep breath. She hated to admit that he was right, but he was. She'd interviewed plenty of grieving parents wracked with guilt and regret over the years, and she knew the feeling intimately, herself. Unless this boy was her son, it would serve no purpose to interview the parents right away. "Okay. You've got my word. You tell me who they are as soon as you find out, and I won't try to talk to them unless something changes."

"And then, you'll let me know before you approach them?"

Why not? It was courtesy she could easily extend. "Of course."

He nodded and walked back toward his car. She kept apace. They passed the section where the trees thinned and the house became visible. The Meisners and their horses were gone.

Nelson held out a hand to help Jess down the slope back to the cars they'd left parked on the side of the road.

"He seems to know you," she said.

"Meisner?"

"Yeah."

"It's a small town, everyone knows me."

"He used your first name. I thought you didn't like that."

Nelson shrugged. "He's a senator. He's not used to being told no."

CHAPTER EIGHT

THE ANTIQUE PEDESTAL TABLE acted like a drum as it amplified the phone's loud ringtone. Blackstake had set up the shrill buzzer to distinguish this particular caller from someone using the mansion's internal telephone system. He grabbed the phone.

"Yes?"

"There's a woman. Jessica Kimball." Meisner paused for breath. A horse whinnied. Given the hour, Meisner was out on his daily ride. "She only gave me her name, but I know who she is. A reporter from *Taboo Magazine*."

"Uh-huh." He stayed noncommittal. When any new topic arose, he let the senator lead. No point in trying to second guess. But in this case, he had the feeling he knew what he might be called upon to do. The magazine's name was familiar. The reporter, too. She'd made headlines in the past as a one-woman crusade for justice. Crusaders were never good news for him or for Meisner. "Where is she?" he said.

"Right now, she's just climbed the tree that boy fell from."

"The cottonwood." Blackstake exhaled. Carefully. Slowly. Releasing the impact that he might not have been as stealthy as he thought without letting the senator hear his concern. "Do you have any connection to this magazine?"

"Not at the moment, but they have featured me a couple of times, and will hopefully do it again when I need them. When it matters."

Blackstake mentally added the words, "When I announce my run for President."

Meisner grunted his contempt. "I want to know what she's doing and why."

"Surveillance then?"

"By you and only you."

A sliver of a smile of professional pride flashed over Blackstake's face. He was loosely associated with Meisner's security detail, but Blackstake was no gate goon. He took no part in the daily business of securing the house and grounds. He handled special assignments. Surveillance. Situations of a delicate, clandestine nature. The only records were kept in his head where they would never be discovered. No physical evidence, no witnesses, and no paper trail.

"Is she here because of the boy?" Blackstake said.

"Maybe. She was with the police captain. Might be a human interest thing. A coincidence, perhaps. If that's all she's interested in, then we're good." Meisner paused. "But it's unlikely. Human interest stories are not the kind of thing she does."

If she was a good reporter, Blackstake knew, there was only one direction her meddling could go. "And if I find her motives are contrary to your position?"

Meisner was silent for a long time. "I cannot afford any kind of prying going on right now."

Blackstake listened to Meisner's measured tone. He heard a new level of caution. Meisner needed significantly more and bigger backers for a Presidential run than he'd acquired for the Senate races. Wider audiences. Larger stakes. No margin for error or suspicion.

Blackstake said, "I understand."

"Good. Keep me informed."

Meisner hung up. The man was abrupt. Some people saw it as disrespect, but Blackstake appreciated it. He had no time for idle chatter.

He tapped his knuckles on the tabletop. What had started as a simple, clandestine operation was gaining too much traffic. The police and now a reporter. Even if they weren't there specifically to investigate the grave, they presented too much risk.

There was a natural explanation for the police presence, but a reporter? Especially one with a reputation for championing justice? She could be looking for filler for a slow news day, but it wasn't likely.

Kimball's presence meant Meisner's concern was valid, and Blackstake's approach was perfect. Investigate, then operate. Locate loose ends, then tie them up. Tight. Fast. Before anyone noticed.

Blackstake cracked his knuckles. Kimball was a risk he knew how to deal with.

CHAPTER NINE

Randolph, Washington
Tuesday, September 27
6:30 a.m. Pacific Time

JESS WOKE WITH THE dawn. She was curled in a ball, her left arm trapped under her stomach. She rolled on her back, and massaged her arm as it awakened from numbness, to pins and needles, and finally to life.

The light had been fading fast when Jess left the woods yesterday. Nelson had suggested the Montpelier Hotel for the night. It was impossible to miss. Perfectly manicured hedgerows lined the edge of a property that looked like an English country estate. A bowling green lawn ran from the roadway all the way to a black and white mock Tudor building. The driveway had the same gravel surface that she'd seen around Meisner's mansion.

Inside was a combination of oak, brass, and years of polish. A large man with an equally large white beard had somewhat condescendingly given her an old-fashioned key on a wooden key ring to the Cavanaugh room, which turned out to be spacious and well lit. Its blocky wood furniture was pleasantly arranged into a bedroom and a sitting area, complete with a writing desk and comfortable chair.

The granite and brass bathroom had been recently modernized, a fact she was grateful for this morning.

She peeled off her clothes and stood in the shower. Steam curled around the bathroom, fogging the mirrors, and settling on the surfaces. She breathed in the vapor, letting the moisture soothe her inside and out.

The hotel towel was thick. She dried off before wrapping a brilliant white terry robe around her. A room service menu stood on the dressing table. She phoned down for coffee, fruit, and toast.

A moment later, her cell phone rang. She frowned. FBI Special Agent Henry Morris. She hadn't spoken to him since she'd returned from that case in Italy a few weeks ago. No reason to. Odd that he'd be calling now.

She picked up the call. "This is Jess Kimball."

"Henry Morris here."

She remembered his voice. Mid-range. Strong. All business all the time. "What's up, Agent Morris?"

"You could call me Henry, for starters."

She heard the grin in his tone and cocked her head. What was going on? "Okay. What's up, *Henry*?"

"Not much. I've been transferred to the Denver Field Office and I've got a break in my schedule. Can I buy you dinner tonight?"

Dinner? She remembered everything about Henry Morris well enough. He was not too handsome, but not too bad. Dark hair, dark eyes, and a scar that slashed his lip on the left side. That, and a nose that had been broken more than once, made his face more interesting than it might otherwise have been.

"I'm out of town right now, but I'll be back in a couple of days, so sure." But she remembered the plain gold band on his left ring finger, too. "Will your wife be joining us? I'd love to meet her."

He paused. "I'm afraid you can't meet her, and I'd rather explain why in person." She could hear his measured breathing. "I've got to run. Let me know when you're back. We'll set something up, okay?"

"Yeah, sure. Sounds good. I'll call you." Jess stood holding the phone after he'd disconnected the call. *What was* that *all about?*

She was dressed when breakfast arrived fifteen minutes later. The simple order had been translated into a work of art with toast done in four types of bread, fruit arranged in geometric patterns, and coffee in what appeared to be a genuine silver pot. The bone china was Royal Albert, no less. The waiter placed the tray on a small table by the window.

Breakfast came with a local newspaper. She unfolded the inky pages and found a thin column headed *Boy Falls*. There was a quick rundown of the location, and his first name. The article ended saying *Authorities are still searching for the boy's parents.*

That wasn't a good thing. Not for Peter, or for her, but it left open a possibility. She checked her watch. It was probably too early to approach the hospital again. But the longer Peter's parents remained absent, the more likely he could be her boy. Things could still go either way, but she needed to know, and she wasn't leaving town until she was sure.

She put the paper aside and started on breakfast.

The coffee was strong. A French roast that livened her

senses more than hot water and beans had a right to do. The fruit was freshly cut. She buttered the toast. The orange marmalade was in a small white serving bowl with a tiny silver spoon. She ladled it on and spread it thickly with her knife. It was sweet and tangy.

She finished her toast and gazed over the manicured lawns. A pair of peacocks strutted past.

She checked her watch, again. She had waited long enough. The hospital staff would be up and running. She had waited more than a decade for the chance to find Peter, she wouldn't wait any longer.

CHAPTER TEN

ON THE WAY TO the hospital, Jess found a store and couriered the bloody rock to Stephenson. She bought extra packaging to double seal the sample and added instructions to perform a full sequence DNA test.

The hospital parking was almost full. Jess toured the lot twice before finding an available space. She reversed in, turned off the engine, and left the car. She bypassed the front desk and took the corridor toward the ICU, avoiding eye contact.

The halls were busy. Patients were being wheeled away for X-rays, EKGs, and ultrasounds. The click and whirr of pumps feeding clear liquids into the arms of patients were the ubiquitous sound of modern medicine. Mornings were the same in hospitals everywhere.

"Miss Kimball?" said a nurse.

Jess turned toward the voice. "Nurse Harvey. Hello. I—"

"Are you wondering about Peter?"

Jess nodded. "I came to see. I don't think his parents…" Jess's sentence trailed off as she saw the look on the nurse's face.

Jess sighed. "They've been found?"

Nurse Harvey nodded. "John and Barbara Whiting. Last night. I thought you might have heard."

"I read the paper this morning. It didn't say anything."

Jess's stomach felt hollow, like she'd been punched in the gut. How quickly the matter was closed. Another dead end. The last in a long line of false leads. Parents found. Simple as that. She'd jumped to an unwarranted conclusion, and crossed half the country based on nothing but unfounded eagerness. Perhaps Nelson had been right to keep her away.

She took a deep breath. "That's good, of course. For him, and the parents. They must have been going mad with worry, and," Jess bit her lip, "I guess they're still worried."

Harvey nodded.

There was a long silence. Jess shifted her weight. "You're sure, I presume. That they're his parents?"

"He's still unconscious, but they know about him, where he goes to school and all that. They have pictures. Him and them. Growing up."

"Right, right. Sorry. I had to ask."

"Sure." Harvey checked her watch. "I have to go. End of my shift."

Jess smiled. "You work long hours."

Harvey nodded. "We're down a couple of nurses. Flu. We're all filling in with extra hours."

"Have you had breakfast?"

She shook her head. "I'm off the clock in a few more minutes."

Questions swirled in Jess's head, but a corridor in a hospital wasn't the best place to get the best responses in an interview. "How about I buy? There's a place in town. Biscuits."

Harvey laughed. "Sure."

CHAPTER ELEVEN

JESS WAS ALREADY SEATED with a coffee in front of her when Elisha Harvey arrived at the diner. The nurse crossed the room, waving her order to a man at the kitchen door. She sat on the vinyl bench seat across from Jess with a thump.

"I'm getting to be a regular here," Jess said.

Harvey flashed a tired smile. "You'll have to be in town a while longer to qualify as a regular."

"I came here with Captain Nelson."

She frowned. "You in trouble?"

Jess shook her head. "We had coffee. He's a nice man."

Harvey nodded. "He is."

"Can I call you Elisha?"

"Most people do, seeing as it's my name." Elisha grinned.

"How's Peter today?"

"I can't talk about my patients, but he's stable."

"Just tell me what was in the news, then. That's public

information." Jess cocked her head. "Did the news report say he was conscious?"

"He has several broken bones, and," she touched her forehead. "Skull damage. Doctors aren't sure if he'll lose his right eye."

Jess winced.

"Docs are keeping him unconscious. Helps with recovery."

"How are the parents taking it?"

"As well as can be expected." The waitress put a plate of eggs and bacon in front of Elisha. The nurse dug in.

Jess sipped her coffee. "What are they like? The Whitings?"

"Normal. She's blond, blue-eyed. Tall. Very pretty." Elisha looked up from her food. "He's nice. Same blond and blue eyes. A little shorter than her. A touch of gray in his hair."

"You never told me what color his eyes were."

Elisha hummed. "Guess it doesn't harm. Brown eyes, brown hair. Similar to you."

"But not blue."

Elisha shook her head. "It is possible. A brown-eyed child from blue-eyed parents."

"Rarely." The issue had come up before in some of the stories she'd investigated. She'd studied the science in several journals.

"Very rare, yes. But it happens."

Jess knew the odds were slim. She didn't argue further. "Nelson said they live in Bamford. Are they originally from this area?"

Elisha shook her head. "Wrong accent. They're probably from the south somewhere, if I had to guess."

"Why did it take them so long to get to the hospital?" Jess wasn't sure how much Elisha would reveal, but she'd keep asking questions until Elisha balked.

"She works in a call center. One of those jobs where you can't have a cell phone because you're supposed to be talking to customers every minute of the day."

Jess nodded. "And him?"

"Warehouse manager. He was still wearing his company shirt when he got there. Some paint company."

"Must be tough, coming home to find their son's in the ICU."

"They're in shock, of course. Stayed at his bedside all night. Slept on bunks in his room. It's perfectly understandable, but it's always difficult to sleep with all the hospital noises, and he's going to need them at their best."

Jess shoved the thought of The Montpelier's luxurious bed to the back of her mind, along with a vaguely guilty feeling.

"Like this morning. They had to have a whole conversation to work out how old he was."

Jess frowned.

"He said fourteen and she said thirteen."

"So, how old is he?"

"Thirteen. That's what they decided."

"Seems odd, not knowing."

"Lack of sleep does funny things to me, too."

"Do they have any idea why he was here?"

Elisha shook her head. "They think he skipped school for fun."

"Did he do that often?"

"No idea." Elisha shrugged. "But they aren't staying with him around the clock like I would be."

"They're not?"

"Not there now, in fact."

Jess nodded slowly, wondering what would cause a mother

and father to leave an injured child alone in the hospital. "I went out to the place where he fell."

Elisha grinned. "Rumor has it you climbed the tree."

"A lot of things about his accident don't make any sense."

"So you did climb it?"

"The first twenty feet or so. Not as high as he went. It was kind of scary. He must have had a good reason for climbing as high as he did."

Elisha shrugged. "I have two boys. They don't need a reason to do anything. Logic doesn't figure into the stupid things they do."

Jess shook her head. "There must have been a reason."

"What could you see from up in the tree?"

"You know Senator Meisner's mansion?"

Elisha screwed up her face and groaned. "Mauling Meisner."

Jess leaned forward. "What do you mean?"

"It's nothing. Rumor. He's just slimy."

"Tell me about it. We shook hands."

Elisha curled her lip. "Likes to think he's a big deal around here. Always telling everyone how good he is to us."

Jess nodded. "A politician."

"Through and through. Was there anything else you could see from up in the tree?"

Jess shook her head.

Elisha finished her food and laid her knife and fork on her plate. "Then I guess he just climbed because he was being a boy.".

CHAPTER TWELVE

ELISHA LEFT JESS AT the diner. Her story about Peter's parents was disturbing. How often had Jess forgotten her own age, or her son's? She must have, surely, but she struggled to recall a specific instance.

Finally, she grinned. There was one time. Years ago. She'd said she was twenty-four, twice, until a friend had pointed out her mistake. Specifically, her friend had pointed the error out to the man Jess had been trying to date. Her grin faded. Not the only reason that relationship hadn't gone anywhere.

But that was the only instance she could recall. And she didn't remember ever forgetting her son's age or his birthday or his precious face or anything else about him. Not one thing. Ever.

And why had it taken them until the end of the day to find their son?

There could be innocent answers. Simple explanations. The

Whitings could surely provide them, but she wouldn't trust the answers without verification.

She left the booth and returned to her car and sent a message to Mandy Donovan, her assistant at *Taboo Magazine*.

A few minutes later, she received an address for John and Barbara Whiting in Bamford, Washington.

A second message followed, from her editor. *New project? Want to tell me about it?*

She smiled. Carter Pierce might be the best boss on the planet, and Mandy sat right outside his office, but she needed time. She texted back, *No and not yet. Thanks.*

A moment later, Mandy followed up with *LOL. Guess you told him!*

There was no point in getting people excited, only to find there's an innocent explanation for everything that seemed at first more than strange. Besides, the motivations of tree-climbing boys were not the kind of story her readers were interested in. They wanted stories about victims of injustice. The kind of injustice that angered normal people and made their blood boil. Peter's case would have to get a lot more serious before Carter Pierce would consider it a *Taboo Magazine*-worthy story.

There were certainly some things that didn't stack up, though. Jess dashed off another message to Mandy, requesting the public record of the birth of Peter Whiting in the hospital nearest to Bamford within the past fifteen years, broadening the time frame to be certain.

The map on her phone showed the Whitings lived in a ranch house on a dead-end road, precisely thirty-three miles, and forty-four minutes from Biscuits.

She turned on her windshield wipers and headed out of Biscuits' parking lot.

CHAPTER THIRTEEN

KARL BLACKSTAKE SAT AT the corner table in the back of Biscuits. He watched the nurse leave, followed a few minutes later by the reporter. He pulled his earphones out of his ears and quit the app on his phone. The sensitive, directional microphone embedded in the phone's thick case had picked up everything the women had said and piped it directly into his ears.

There had been a moment when the reporter had dropped her knife. The microphone's amplification had distorted the noise into a jet-engine loud cacophony that made him flinch. He hadn't dared look up. He didn't want to make eye contact, but she hadn't paid him any attention.

He brought up a second app on his phone and examined a map with a red and blue dot. The blue dot was stationary, centered on the diner. Him, in the booth with a mug of so-so coffee. The red dot was the magnetic tracker he had placed in the wheel arch of Kimball's car. It was moving. Thirty miles an hour. Headed south, out of town, toward Bamford.

As he left the diner, the red dot stopped. He quickened his pace. To form a complete picture of what the reporter was doing, he needed eyes on the subject at all times.

CHAPTER FOURTEEN

BY THE TIME JESS was leaving Randolph, large drops of rain had splattered her windshield. The light jacket she'd packed looked unlikely to keep her dry. She made a last minute turn into the unpaved parking lot of a resale shop at the very end of Main Street.

The store seemed to have everything, from pots and pans to furniture. There was a for-sale board with pine furniture, dogs needing a new home, and someone willing to donate a kidney, under which some wag had scrawled "only one left!"

Next to a table filled with toys, she found a stack of waterproof boots with a wide tread. She tried on three pairs before finding the right size.

At the other end of the store was a rack of dark green workman's jackets. They were PVC with welded seams and creaked as she moved, but the hood and white cuffs would keep her dry for sure.

The girl at the checkout cut off the tags.

Jess climbed back into her car wearing her new gear and headed to Bamford.

She drove a series of minor back roads. They twisted and turned through wooded areas and undulated over hillocks. Lumpy clouds obscured the sun, stealing shadows and leaving the scenery dull in the flat light.

Four miles before the town's outskirts, she passed a police cruiser on the opposite side of the road, pointing toward her. The driver's window was down, and wisps of steam trailed from the exhaust. She watched in her rearview mirror as he J-turned and followed after her. She checked her speed and eased off the gas.

Bamford was signposted left at the next intersection. She took the turn. The police cruiser followed.

The town nestled in a broad dip. She crested a rise and felt as if she were descending from an airplane. The road sloped down for at least a mile. Bamford's main street was a broad slash of signs and lights through an expanse of industrial and suburban buildings that could best be described as generic brown.

She passed a "Welcome to Bamford" sign and slowed down to the posted limit. The cruiser gained on her. Not threatening, but closer than expected on a quiet road in a quiet town.

She passed a light industrial building with a single car parked outside. The roll-up doors were closed, and there were none of the piles of boxes, rusting equipment, or barrels of who-knows-what that accompanied human endeavors.

She took a right, toward downtown. The cruiser did, too. The officer might be heading into town for a late lunch. Or back to the station to write up another shift log. Or, she glanced at her car, maybe he simply didn't trust drivers in rented sporty red cars to obey the speed limit.

Main Street was small stores nestled between bigger stores.

Neon "Open" signs glared from sandwich shops and pizzerias. One or two small chain stores. No Wal-Mart or Target. The town wasn't big enough.

Angled parking spaces lined the sides of Main Street. Pedestrians walked on a concrete sidewalk, dotted with tired looking trees bowing from large wood planters.

Jess chose a parking bay with cars on either side. She slid into the spot, putting on the handbrake, turning off the engine, unbuckling her seatbelt. Looking busy. Doing what normal people do. What people who aren't perplexed by a cop following them for four miles do.

The cruiser rolled past. Slow. On momentum. The driver not pressing the vehicle's accelerator. The windows were tinted, even in the front. She couldn't see the driver, but she felt his gaze. What had she done to warrant the scrutiny?

She'd driven the speed limit, taking in the scenery. She'd done nothing that should have attracted attention. A leisurely drive from one small town to another. Nothing more. She craned her neck to watch but lost sight of the cruiser between the parked cars and leaning trees.

She blew out a long breath. If he'd wanted to stop her for something, he would have done so on the outskirts of town, where it was quiet, and a traffic stop wouldn't have upset anyone but her.

She consulted the map on her phone. The Whiting place was a half-mile east. She memorized the route and backed out of her space. Soon, she drove onto the right street.

The ranch houses she'd seen on the map looked smaller in real life. Middle class homes with a mixed bag of maintenance habits. Some houses were immaculate, and some displayed peeling paint and weeds run amok. The Whiting house was in the former category. A white picket fence, a mown and trimmed lawn, and a selection of potted plants around a frosted glass front door.

A driveway ran down the right-hand side of the house, curving around to a double garage set behind it. There was a join line across the driveway. The Whitings had likely removed a single attached garage and replaced it with a double in the back yard. Not a bad idea with Washington's weather.

There was no gate on the drive. The curtains were open, but she saw no lights inside. She eased her rental onto the driveway, stopping before she reached the house.

Now that she'd arrived, the trip suddenly seemed foolish. She'd told Nelson she wouldn't interview the Whitings, but she could talk to them. She wanted to see these people. See where they lived. Get a sense of them. She had a good grasp of human nature and something about the situation, and these people didn't feel genuine.

She would start by offering her sympathies and best wishes for the boy's recovery. She'd see what kind of people they were. Maybe offer her help, if they needed any. Although she had no idea what kind of help they might need from her.

Mainly, she wanted to confirm that the Whitings were good people and their son was well loved and cared for and, well, actually theirs.

She took a deep breath, stepped out of the car, walked up to the front door, and pressed a large white doorbell button. Inside the house, a gong chimed with deep and extended resonance. She dropped her purse. The strap had come unbuckled. She bent to retrieve it, adjusted the strap, and hoisted it back onto her shoulder.

A white car drove by and parked further down the street while she waited.

Jess peered in through the frosted glass. She saw no one inside. Elisha had said the Whitings weren't at the hospital. Now, it appeared they weren't home, either.

She rang the bell again and listened to its deep boom. Another minute went by. She was patient, used to waiting for people who were struggling to make the decision to either talk or not. But there was no one inside, she was sure of it at this point.

At least that meant she wouldn't break her promise to Nelson. She shrugged. She'd find a way to talk with the Whitings another time.

She followed the driveway around to the back. The garage took up half of the real estate behind the house. The driveway had been integrated into a path and patio, a broad expanse of concrete across the width of the house. Near to her was a back door, and on the other end, double patio doors. On the concrete, four chairs were neatly arranged around a table. An umbrella poked up through its center. It was tied closed. As if no one had used it in a good long while.

She looked through the kitchen window. The surfaces were clean. There were no dishes in the sink. A small breakfast table sat in the corner, its disturbed chairs the only evidence anyone had ever used the room. Barbara Whiting was certainly a neat freak.

"Can I help you?" An old man, a gardening fork in his hand, leaned over the fence.

Jess smiled. "I'm looking for the Whitings."

"They're not in." He wasn't hostile, merely informative.

Jess waved toward the window. "I know. I just…" She cleared her throat. "I just wanted to offer my sympathies."

The old man frowned.

"For their son. Peter."

The man's eyebrows inched down and wrinkled his face in a deep frown. "Peter?"

"That's right." Jess nodded. "He fell from a tree."

The wrinkles on the man's forehead softened. "But he's okay, right?"

Jess bit her lip. "Okay…but not great."

The old man inched backward. "I didn't know."

"It happened yesterday. Early morning."

The man shook his head and tutted.

"Have you seen them since yesterday afternoon?"

The man continued to shake his head. "Last night, I think. Late. And gone again early this morning, like always."

Jess shifted her weight. "Do you know…Peter?"

The man waved his hand. "Course. Known him since he was a baby."

"Do you know why he might have gone over to Randolph yesterday morning?"

The man screwed up his nose. "Randolph?"

"He was in Randolph when he fell."

The man shook his head. "Might have gone with his dad to fly his model plane, I guess."

"He was alone, though."

"He wouldn't do that. He's fearless, that kid." The man shook his head. "But…too young to go that far alone."

Jess nodded. "Has he lived here all his life?"

"Most of it." The man closed his eyes briefly, as if he was trying to remember when the Whitings moved in next door. "Had his first birthday here."

Could that be true? If it was, then Peter couldn't be her son. Her Peter had celebrated his first birthday with her. "How long ago was that?"

The man closed his eyes again, thinking. "I can't remember." He tapped the top of his head. "Not as good as it used to be."

"But he was happy?"

"Course. Bright kid. Good as gold. Never a moment's trouble." He grinned. "He'll be an astronaut or a CEO or something, you just watch."

Jess looked back at the house. "Where did they live before here?"

"Other side of Seattle. One of the islands." He screwed up his face with concentration. "Can't remember now."

Jess waited. The old man shook his head. "Nope. Can't remember."

"Well, thanks anyway." Jess turned to go.

"Wait. What's your name?"

"Kimball. Jess Kimball."

"I see Barbara or John, I'll tell them you stopped by," he said.

"Thanks." Jess smiled at him and turned to go. The buckle on her bag had come undone again, and it fell onto the small strip of flower beds close to the house. This time, the bag's flap opened and dumped half of its contents on the ground. She knelt and collected her possessions. When she stood to leave, the old man was gone.

CHAPTER FIFTEEN

JESS STARTED THE CAR and sat trying to solve the problem with her bag's buckle. Maybe the rock with Peter's DNA on it had been too much weight for the bag and the weight had damaged the buckle or something. She pushed the prong into a smaller hole and snugged the frame tight. She slipped the end of the strap into its retaining loop. The buckle stayed closed after several hard tugs. It should be fine until she could find a better solution.

A sharp rap on the driver's side window startled her. She glanced up. The old man stood outside her door. She lowered the window.

"It was Vashon. I remember now. Where John and Barbara used to live. Vashon Island." He tapped his temple. "Not as bad as I thought it was."

She thanked him and smiled for good measure.

He shuffled from foot to foot. "You said Peter wasn't doing great." He took a deep breath. "Is he…I mean…gonna be okay?"

Jess's skin tingled. She took a deep breath, but gently, not wanting to overplay her concern. "He's in the ICU." She smiled reassurance. "He has good people looking after him."

The old man's eyes glazed over. "Damn." He leaned on the window frame and exhaled. "Good kid."

Jess nodded. "We're all hoping for the best."

He offered a strained smile and waited a moment longer before he straightened up with a groan.

"By the way, where does Mr. Whiting work?" she asked.

The old man's expression was totally blank while he tried to dredge up the answer. And he grinned again when he finally grasped it. "Wilson's Paint. Highway 47. Bit of a commute. Council made them move the company outside of town after one of their places had an explosion. Big one. Down in Arkansas or somewhere like that."

Jess nodded.

He turned, and wandered toward his house, and turned back. "Forty-seven. Can't miss it. Thirty minutes." He waved.

Jess raised her window and brought Wilson Chemical and Paint Company up on her phone. The map indicated it was a thirty-minute drive, just as the old man had said. She rested her phone on the dashboard and pressed the button for route guidance. As a mechanical voice told her to turn right out of the driveway, a white car passed, heading out of the dead-end street. She followed it to the junction. The white car turned left. She turned right.

She followed I-47 as it jinked around hills and mountains. The freeway lay alongside a river that twisted and turned with even more regularity than the freeway. She crossed and re-crossed the water before encountering a flat area with a group of large buildings far off the highway. A road-grime covered sign announced the entrance to Wilson Chemical and Paint. She waited for an eighteen-wheeler to pull out before heading down the well-worn road to the buildings.

Jess cruised the length of the large and almost full parking lot. The view from the road was misleading. What had appeared to be a group of buildings was actually one building that had been subject to endless additions. One side of the building was lined with eighteen-wheelers backed up to open loading docks. Forklift trucks rumbled in and out. Burly men lugged barrels between giant metal racks. A sound like the grinding of rocks shook the windows of her rental. Jess didn't know what work John Whiting performed at the plant, but she was pretty sure it was hard and honest work from the look of the place.

Her phone bleeped, and the mechanical voice announced that navigation was lost. She looked at the display. The signal strength bars were gone. She dialed her office. The phone made a long beep and ended the call with a message that no networks were available.

It wasn't just the work that had cut John Whiting off from the news about his son, then. He was far enough away from civilization to have left the cell phone era. It was easy to see how he hadn't noticed the news in such a remote place.

The machine that sounded like it was grinding rocks changed its pitch, and the vibration moved from the rental's windows to her teeth. She backed out of the parking lot, trying to put more distance between her and the source of the noise. Another eighteen-wheeler passed her, charging hard down the well-worn path to the freeway. She followed in its dust.

The Whitings were, by all visible signs, good people. They seemed to have worked hard for what they had. They surely loved their son. They'd been dealt a blow they didn't deserve, and she'd overreacted. It might be time to call this one another false lead and move on. Maybe.

CHAPTER SIXTEEN

THE AIR COOLED FAST. Blackstake swore. The temperature and humidity of fall in the northwest combined to suck the heat out of the car. He couldn't keep the engine running, and he couldn't get out. So he sat still, his shoulders down, his head lined up with the headrest. His gaze flitting between the side and rearview mirrors.

His phone buzzed. He knew the number. He pressed *on* and waited for the caller to speak.

"Status?"

"Bamford. Whiting's house," he said.

"Are they there?"

"No."

"Then she's looking for something."

"Probably."

"She won't find anything, will she?"

"Absolutely not."

The call ended. There was no thank you or goodbye. He was

used to the abruptness. It wasn't a slight, it was respect. Mutual understanding. No chitchat was necessary or desired.

He placed his phone back in his pocket.

At last, he saw activity in the mirrors. The reporter in her green jacket.

He had a little longer to wait. Then he would make good on his promise. Perhaps he would get lucky, and deal with two problems at once.

CHAPTER SEVENTEEN

JESS RETURNED THE WAY she'd come. She traveled through Bamford and saw no hint of a surveilling police cruiser. She turned at a small sign marked for through traffic, skirted the main street, and stopped at a gas station. The sun wasn't bright, but the glare from the wet roads was tiring, so she bought a pair of cheap sunglasses.

Her phone rang as she walked back to her car, her assistant's number on the display.

"Mandy?"

"Hey. No luck with Peter Whiting. A few born around the country in the right time frame, but not in Bamford."

Jess screwed her face into a grimace. "Arrgh."

"Jess?"

"I should have told you. He wasn't born in Bamford. The Whitings moved there after Vashon."

"Vashon?"

"An island, off the coast of Seattle."

"Wait a minute," Mandy mumbled to herself. "No, no Peter Whitings born in Vashon. The nearest I have to Bamford is Kids Own Medical Center. Fourteen years and three months ago."

"Peter Whiting?"

"Check. Born to John and Barbara."

"Fourteen years ago?"

"And three months. Why?"

"You're sure?"

"That's what it says."

"Can you send me what you have?"

Jess heard typing and the swoosh noise of Mandy's computer sending an email. "Presto, it's all yours."

"You sure you have the right Peter Whiting?"

"Peter David Whiting. He's the only one I can find anywhere near Bamford born in the last fifteen years to a John and Barbara Whiting."

A hard lump had formed in Jess's throat when she heard the middle name for the first time. Her son was Peter David, too. She had trouble getting her question out. "Where's the Kids Own Medical Center?"

"Portland."

Jess swallowed. "As in Oregon?"

"Yeah."

"Wow."

"What's up?"

"That's a long way to go to have a baby for someone who lives in Vashon, Washington."

Mandy blew out a long breath. "Visiting someone, maybe?"

"Maybe. Can you do something else? Find out where the Whitings have lived over the last fifteen years. They live in Bamford now, but before that."

"I thought you said they lived in Vashon."

"I did, but that was before I knew they had a baby in Portland. And look for family, too."

"Okay. Call you back in a bit." Mandy hung up.

Jess checked Mandy's email. It was all text. Computer generated. It listed John and Barbara Whiting as the parents of Peter Whiting. The text listed the birth date, June 15, fourteen years and three months ago, and the location, Portland.

Did the Whitings live in Portland and move to Vashon for a short while before settling in Bamford? And if their boy had celebrated his birthday three months ago, why did they have trouble remembering his age? And why had they decided he was thirteen, not fourteen?

Her son's birthday was not something Jess would ever forget, and she couldn't imagine any parent who would. Peter David Whiting's birthday, according to this, was the same month her Peter was taken.

The possibilities made her stomach churn. For whatever complex or convoluted reason, this boy could be her Peter. Could be. A long way from certain. But was this boy Peter David Whiting? Or was he Peter David Kimball?

She put her hands on the steering wheel. Was she over-thinking all of this? There had to be an answer linking the disparate facts. All she had to do was find it. She could ask the Whitings, and she would. After she had a firm handle on the truth.

She started her car and typed Vashon Island into her navigation system. There were no bridges to the island. She searched her phone's GPS for ferries. She found two routes, one from a place called Fauntleroy, somewhere north of the airport, and the other closer, from Tacoma via the Point Defiance-Tahlequah Ferry. She chose the closest.

A yellow line snaked across the screen, and a woman's mechanical voice prompted her to turn left. Jess pulled out onto the road and followed the voice to I-5 and north toward Tacoma.

CHAPTER EIGHTEEN

THE FERRY WAS SIGNPOSTED several miles before the terminal. She ignored her navigation systems, which routed her around a nearby state park, and followed signs to a double lane road that ran onto a pier. She stopped short of the pier, behind several cars, lined up as if they were about to race across the water. The clouds had thinned, and the rain had finally stopped.

She left her car and read the board that explained fares were collected onboard the ferry. She checked the schedule. Twenty minutes to wait, and the air was fresh, with the crisp tang of salt. She felt stiff from the drive, so she walked the area.

To the left of the pier was a half-full parking lot. Foot passengers sheltered under a bus awning. A small building that looked like it might sell coffee was shuttered. On the other side of the pier, hundreds of small boats were packed into a marina that ran as far as she could see. There were floating boat houses, white buildings with roll-up doors, for the more expensive craft.

The wind whipped breakers to white foam crests suggesting a choppy crossing, but the island looked barely a mile away.

Her phone rang. Mandy's name appeared on the display. Jess answered. "What did you find?"

"I sent you an email with the address. According to the tax records, the Whitings lived in Vashon for four years before moving to Bamford."

"Sure?"

Mandy sighed. "I mean it could have been a mistake that I copied down four years of tax records, payment dates, and zip codes. Typed them up and sent them to you. Along with a screenshot, I might add."

"Okay, okay," Jess grimaced. "So, when did they move to Bamford?"

"Fourteen years ago."

Jess walked in a small circle. "Fourteen years?"

"Fourteen years and three months to be exact."

"When Peter was born."

"Seems like."

"Is that when they sold their Vashon place?"

"Yep. And it's when they bought the Bamford place. Sold one, bought the other."

"According to tax records."

"Don't scoff. You know how careful cities are with their taxes. Don't want to miss a penny."

Jess took a deep breath. "So, fourteen years ago, they are living in Vashon, they move to Bamford, and she gives birth to a boy in Portland."

"It happens."

"And three months after his birthday, the parents can't remember their son's age."

"That happens, too."

"It does, but in this case, the neighbor in Bamford said they turned up with a boy. He wasn't born in Bamford, they arrived with him."

"Well," Mandy said. "Because he was born in Portland?"

"I think the neighbor would have remembered that. I mean, you don't go away for the weekend and come back with a baby."

"Maybe they stayed over in an apartment for a while."

"But why? They had a perfectly good house."

"Maybe the house needed work? They could have stayed in an apartment. Would have made sense with a baby. And no, I can't look up every apartment in Washington to see where they lived."

Jess thought about the information, trying to make sense of it. "I can try the next-door neighbor. He'll probably remember if they did renovations before they moved in."

"That the forgetful guy?"

"He's not that forgetful. He remembered Vashon."

"Eventually. Look, I've gotta go. Got a line at my desk. Call me if you need anything."

Jess ended the call.

Nothing stacked up. The Whitings might be good people, but the dates weren't right, the places weren't right, and the stories weren't right. Nothing. She took a deep breath. Somewhere there was a simple explanation. Something that would make everything click into place.

She looked across the water to Vashon Island. The ferry was heading toward the pier. She returned to her car, and turned on the heated seat, surprised by how cold she'd become. The ferry docked, and moments later cars began streaming off in a single lane toward Tacoma. She looked up the address from Mandy's email while she waited.

When the last of the cars was off the ferry, the red and white barrier across the entrance lifted, and the waiting cars rolled on. Staff waved vehicles forward until the bumpers were within inches of each other. The car deck was filled within minutes. The boat shook, and the engines roared. Her balance swayed. The crew wasted no time setting off.

A ticket collector worked his way through the car deck, collecting fares. Jess paid with her credit card and left the receipt on the dashboard for the return journey.

She took the steps to the upper deck. A girl served snacks from a counter. Jess bought a black coffee and cold bagel and found an empty window seat. The marina swung by as the boat turned for the island. Small craft bobbed in the big boat's wake. The thrum of the engines grew louder as the ferry struck out across the open water.

The coffee was strong and hot, but the bagel had seen better days. She had little confidence in the food on the island, so she ate it after dipping pieces in the coffee to make them soft enough to chew without breaking her molars.

A middle-aged woman took the seat next to her. She propped a shopping bag on her knees, folded the handles over, and hugged the bag to her chest.

Jess smiled at her.

"Don't like this boat," the woman said.

Jess shrugged. "Seems okay."

The woman shook her head. "Rhody was better." She stamped her foot on the floor. "Didn't shake as much."

Jess raised her eyebrows. "Rhody?"

"Rhododendron."

"Unusual name for a boat."

The woman laughed and pointed to the sign on the side of the wall. "Any more unusual than Chetzemoka?"

"Guess not." Jess smiled. "You live on the island?"

"Coming on twenty years. Not born there, though."

"You like it?"

"Would you spend twenty years somewhere you didn't like?"

"No." Jess shook her head.

The woman gestured to the island with her head. "Why you visiting?"

There wasn't much to lose by telling the woman. "I'm looking into someone who used to live here."

The woman grunted. "Rob Hotchkiss."

"Er…"

"Musician. Lead guy in Train. Or used to be."

Jess shook her head. "The Whitings on Rainier Road."

The woman pursed her lips. "Don't know them."

"Moved away about a dozen years ago."

She shook her head. "Still don't think I knew them."

"What about Rainier Road?"

"Nice place. Some expensive houses down that way."

"What do people do?"

"Do?"

"For work? On the island."

"A few small businesses here. Shops and things. Difficult to commute. Quite a few people do financial stuff over the Internet. That's big now."

"Do the ferries run all night?"

The woman shook her head. "Start at five and stop around ten."

The boat's engine roared. Jess looked up to see they were almost docked. The engines roared again, and the boat lurched this time.

"Rhody didn't do that either," said the woman. "Don't like this boat."

Jess downed the last of her coffee and threw the paper cup in a large open trash bin.

"If you want something better, there's Chelsea's Place on 99th Avenue. Good seafood."

Jess thanked the woman, said her goodbyes, and worked her way to the lower deck and found her car. The vehicles rolled off moments after the boat docked. The whole process was handled like a practiced, regular routine. Which it was.

She followed the Vashon Highway north toward the center of the island before heading due east, and finally turned left near the small sign that marked Rainier Road.

The road was picturesque. A ribbon of tarmac with no curbs. Lines of trees were set back from the edges, fences even farther. Even in the flat light of a cloudy Washington day, it had the look of something from a movie or the cover of a romance novel with a happy ending. The tree limbs spread over the road. In a few more years they would touch, and the street would be postcard worthy. It would become a haven for photographers and nervous suitors proposing marriage.

She stopped on the side of the road and checked her phone. The Whiting house was almost at the end, on the right. Number 1823.

She pulled into the driveway. The brick, two-story house was well back from the road. The driveway led to the front door, sweeping in an arc around an ornamental pond before looping back and rejoining the drive. The grass on either side of the drive was lush and perfectly trimmed. Decorative fences ran along both sides of the property.

Jess slowed to a halt. Whoever lived here must spend every waking minute in the garden. She leaned forward. The Whiting house in Bamford had none of the trappings of wealth she saw here.

She eased the car up to the front of the house, stopping just beyond the sidewalk to the front door. She checked her hair in the mirror and stepped out.

"Help you?"

She turned to the side of the house. A man in jeans and a work jacket stood with a trowel in his hand. He waved the trowel.

"I'm Jess Kimball." Jess smiled and put a friendly tone in her voice. "I'm looking for the Whitings."

The man frowned. "John and Barbara?"

"I thought they lived here?"

"Not for years." He shook his head. "You know the Whitings?"

Jess shrugged. "Do you?"

"John and I used to work at the same place. Vashon Life and Casualty. Before he and Barbara moved away."

"Why?" She looked around. "Seems like a lovely place to live."

"Long story. They okay?"

Jess gave a slow nod. "John and Barbara are fine. Their son was hurt recently."

The man inched forward and cocked his head. "Son?"

"Yes, that's right."

"Well," he shrugged, "I kind of lost track of them, I guess."

"When they moved?"

He nodded. "They were in a bad way when they left here."

"Financially?"

The man shook his head. "After they lost the first one."

"Oh. I didn't know," Jess prompted.

The man nodded. "A boy. They had the place ready. Nursery decorated. Tons of clothes. You know how people are with their first one."

She nodded. "Yes."

"Even had a name picked out," he said. "My middle name." He pulled off his right glove and wiped his hand on his pants before he extended it to her. "Sorry. I didn't mean to be rude. I'm Joseph Peter Sandler. People call me Joe."

She accepted his handshake.

"Peter," she said. "Their boy is called Peter."

"No." He drew the word out, not in denial, but in disbelief. "Well, well."

He drifted off for a moment, shaking his head slowly. Jess let him work through his memories and waited until he lifted his head up. "Are you related?"

He shook his head. "We were friends. Good friends. They just…well…turned to each other after they lost their first."

Jess nodded. "Is that why they moved?"

"They were devastated. You can imagine. Especially Barbara. The loss really hit her hard. Put the place up for sale just a couple of weeks after."

Jess nodded. "Horrible."

They stood in silence a moment. Joe stared at the ground. "They were desperate to move. That's why I bought their place. They were practically giving it away for a quick sale."

"I'm sure they appreciated that the place went to a friend who would take good care of it."

He lifted his head. "Their son's going to be okay, right?"

"Hopefully." Jess nodded. "When did they move?"

Joe shrugged. "Fourteen years ago."

"Really?" She cocked her head and put a puzzled expression on her face. "Fourteen years? You're sure?"

He nodded. "Fourteen years and…well…it would be maybe two or three months. I remember because it was Mother's Day weekend when they lost the baby. They had a romantic evening at home planned, but she went into labor and, well, it didn't turn out that way. They moved a month or two after that."

Fourteen. Not thirteen. That jived with what she'd learned from their neighbor in Bamford. Not like the Whitings had said. A year different. An important year. A year that made sense of Peter Whiting's birth record in Portland. A year that matched up with their moving dates. There was just one more domino to fall.

"How far along was she?" Jess heard the tremor in her own voice.

The man grimaced. "The baby was full term. Nine months. She went into the hospital for the stillbirth and stayed a day or two afterward. They had a memorial service a couple of days later." He paused. "She was depressed. Couldn't talk to anyone. I mean, I tried. We all tried. But… Then she went to visit her sister, and she just couldn't bring herself to come back. Too painful, John said."

Jess's skin tingled. Full term. Fourteen years. Not thirteen. So Peter couldn't have celebrated his first birthday in Bamford. The last domino. She took a deep breath. "Where did they go? When they moved?"

He cocked his head again, thinking about it. "Portland, I think. John said it was a big enough town that he could find work. Similar to here, but different enough."

Her stomach was churning like a cement mixer. She needed to think. She turned away as if to look at the front garden, and cleared her throat. "You put a lot of effort in here."

He stepped forward, his hands on his hips, admiring his handiwork. He seemed relieved to change the subject. "Yeah. I'm retired now. Got to have something to keep me going."

"What kind of work did you do?"

"Me? Same as John. Insurance. All kinds. Medical, property, casualty, life. You name it. But I'd been at it a bit longer than him. Which is a polite way to say I'm a lot older."

Jess smiled and checked her watch. "I have to be going."

He nodded. "Well, say hello to John and Barbara for me when you see them."

"I will." Jess returned to her car and fell into the front seat. She turned the key in the ignition with a shaking hand.

Joe waved. "Tell them to come by one day." He called. "And bring their son. Like to see them again after all this time."

Jess waved and rolled out onto the road.

CHAPTER NINETEEN

JESS TURNED OFF RAINIER Road, drove back to the center of Vashon, and parked in the first empty space she found. Her hands were still shaking, and her heart pounded like a drum.

The facts were tumbling over themselves to contradict each other.

John and Barbara Whiting had lost a baby boy. A boy they intended to call Peter. They'd been so devastated that they'd sold their home at a loss and left this beautiful island.

They'd run away. Made a clean break with the painful memories of the past. They'd moved from the place that would have tormented them. Faced their grief and come out on the other side.

A tough transition. Doable. But never easy. And in the process, they'd abandoned friends and co-workers, and even the man whose middle name they intended to honor by naming their son.

Except they had used his name. They'd named their second

son Peter. They'd filled the void the loss of their stillborn baby had created with another.

Except he wasn't theirs. Not biologically.

Barbara Whiting's full term baby was stillborn on Mother's Day, always the second Sunday in May. Peter was born in Portland on June 15 the same year. Two dates, just six weeks apart. Not enough time for a second pregnancy and a live birth. Not even close to thirty-nine weeks. Not enough time for the premature birth of a second, healthy child.

It wasn't possible. Not even remotely.

Jess took several deep breaths to calm her pounding heart and wiped the perspiration from her forehead. She stopped her mind from making that giant leap that connected her with the boy in the hospital. She fought it back. Her rational intellect clung on to the need for one hundred percent proof, but eventually the thought formed.

The boy in the hospital was the right age. He *could* be hers.

After fourteen long years, maybe, just maybe, she had found Peter.

CHAPTER TWENTY

JESS DROVE STRAIGHT SOUTH, down through the middle of the island, and back to the port where she'd disembarked earlier. She sat in the line waiting for the ferry. Her cramped fingers gripped the steering wheel too tightly.

Reason had reasserted itself.

That the boy was named Peter meant nothing. That he'd seemed unsupervised in the early morning hours and abandoned at the Randolph hospital, meant nothing. But if it was true that the Whitings were not his biological parents, that meant something. And that they had appeared in Bamford with a male child so close to when her boy had been taken? She took a deep breath. That really might mean something.

Rain splatted on the windows. Fat drops. Distorting her view of the cars ahead and the water she had yet to cross. Mist formed on the windshield. She pried her hands from the wheel and turned on the defroster.

There was a fine line between love and obsession. On one

side were all the good things in the world, and on the other? She shook her head. She had her toes on the edge of that line. She was on the side of love, but she could see into the pit that lay beyond. A pit she had fought off every day since her Peter was taken. She took a deep breath.

Feelings and guesses and unexplained calendar dates were all a good start. But not nearly enough. She needed evidence. Hard evidence. DNA would do the job, but Stevenson wouldn't have the report for a while.

Jess called her office. Mandy answered, slightly breathless, on the third ring.

"Yes?"

"I need Peter David Whiting's birth certificate."

"I sent it."

"A photocopy of the original. With the signatures."

"Er… Why?"

"I just need it. I need to see the handwritten original."

Mandy sighed. "Okay, but I'll have to find someone in the area."

"I know."

"You're in the area…"

Jess's patience snapped. "Just find someone, will you?"

There was a long silence on Mandy's end of the line.

Jess swiped fingers through her curls and sighed. "I'm sorry."

Mandy's voice softened. "What's up, Jess?"

Jess bit her lip. She took a deep breath. "I can't tell you yet. I'll fill you in when I can. But I need that birth certificate."

Mandy paused a moment before replying. "No problem. I'll get it."

"There's something else. The Whitings lost a baby. When

they lived here on Vashon. A month or two before they moved. Find me anything you can. Okay? Anything."

"Okay."

"It's important, Mandy."

"I know. I'll get it… You know, if you want to talk—"

"Not now. I can't. Just find everything you can." She hung up before the conversation moved into areas she didn't want to discuss.

The ferry arrived. She crossed back to the mainland and escaped Tacoma. Diving fast. Passing trucks. Her gaze locked on the tarmac, the miles fleeing by, registered only by her subconscious.

She was on the outskirts of Randolph before she realized how far she'd traveled. She took what felt like her first deep breath in several hours as she passed the Welcome to Randolph sign, and cruised into town.

She turned onto Main Street and pulled into the police department parking lot.

She left the engine running, and stared at the sign over the station's door. The small print said "To protect and serve." It was the same sign posted by a thousand police stations in towns and cities all over the country. But she hoped these were more than empty words.

She took another deep breath to steady her nerves, fighting off the numbing mist that had settled on her consciousness. It had served its purpose. It had kept her soul from fragmenting and saved her from falling into an emotional pit from which she might never escape.

Her phone showed two emails. Mandy had been as good as her word. Somehow, she had obtained a scanned copy of the original entry in the register of births. The signatures were there.

John and Barbara Whiting. Peter's name was recorded. The place of birth was Kids Own Medical Center in Portland, Oregon. June 15. Fourteen years and three months ago.

She opened the second email. Two scanned documents this time. The first was a copy of an entry in a register of the stillbirth of a baby boy on May 9, fourteen years ago. It listed John and Barbara Whiting as the parents. The second was a page from a newspaper, announcing the death of their baby and a memorial service at a church on Vashon Island on May 17. Less than a month before Peter David Whiting was born.

Jess killed the engine, and sat in the car, listening to the tinkling sounds of the cooling engine. She had to do this right. She had to keep calm. She had to be professional.

There were a thousand ways she could be wrong. Any one of those ways could pile more suffering onto the Whitings' already painful ordeal.

She'd spent a decade searching for Peter. To think that he might be right here, right now, was almost beyond comprehension.

A Randolph PD cruiser looped around the building, coming to a stop near the exit, a lone officer inside. He began typing on a keyboard, probably clocking in for his shift.

She climbed out of her car, straightened her back, and walked into the police station.

The reception area floor was covered with hard vinyl. A high wood-veneer counter with a gate at one end ran the length of the room, dividing it in half. Behind the counter was a door. The walls were covered with the usual array of posters and public announcements. Fluorescent lights gave the room the cold-hearted feel of a building designed with a challenging budget.

Officer Charlene Mackie was behind the counter, leaning on

it like she was expecting company. She stared at Jess. "My, my. This is a surprise."

Jess ignored the sarcasm. "I need to see Captain Nelson."

Charlene nodded and drew back the gate in the counter. "I'm sure he'd be delighted."

Jess walked through. Charlene flashed an almost simpering smile. The woman was annoying as hell, but Jess couldn't think about that now.

The door opened. Nelson stood there. He moved to one side and gestured for Jess to walk by. He closed the door after her and pointed to one of the offices. Jess stepped inside.

Nelson's office had the same budget feel as the reception area. The same fluorescent lighting, and the same wood veneer. Underfoot the cheap vinyl had been replaced by carpet tiles, and on the walls were pictures of baseball stadiums. Nelson's clean desktop was littered with a few sheets of paper. Small cursive penmanship on notepaper.

There were two chairs in front of the desk and one behind. Jess took a chair to the left of the desk, away from the door. As she sat down, another officer walked in. He carried a hard folding chair, which he opened and set by the door as if she might try to make a run for the exit and he intended to stop her. He looked like the guy who'd followed her in the cruiser on her trip to Bamford.

Jess ignored him and turned to face Nelson. "I need to speak with you privately."

Nelson held up his hand. "Whatever you have to say to me, can be said in front of Officer Gardner."

"I don't want this information getting out. Uncontrolled."

"He's a police officer. He's capable of discretion." Nelson settled in his chair. "He stays."

She took a deep breath. "A lot of things about this situation don't make sense. I couldn't understand why Peter had traveled thirty miles to climb a tree."

"You said that before," Nelson nodded.

"Still doesn't make sense. There's something we don't know about that yet." She shook her head. "And then the Whitings couldn't remember if their boy was thirteen or fourteen."

"Who told you that?"

Jess gave a flat smile. "They eventually decided he was thirteen. We all forget things from time to time, but to forget your only son's age just three months after he'd celebrated his birthday? It seemed odd."

Nelson nodded again. "And?"

"I visited their home this morning. Met a neighbor. He told me the Whitings moved to Bamford from Vashon Island with their son. He was a toddler then. So I obtained the birth certificate. Peter was born fourteen years and three months ago." Jess opened up her email and held out the birth certificate for Nelson to see. He leaned forward, squinting slightly to read the small text. "He's fourteen. Not thirteen."

Nelson nodded. Gardner leaned closer.

"The birth certificate was signed by John and Barbara Whiting. Peter was born in Portland. That's a long way from Vashon, and when a woman goes into labor, she doesn't usually drive several hundred miles to give birth." Jess put the phone in her lap. "So, I visited Vashon Island. I found the person living in the Whiting's previous home. He was a good friend of theirs until they left the island. He never heard from them again."

Nelson said nothing. Gardner remained quiet, too.

She pulled up the second email. "This is why."

She held out the certificate of stillbirth and the newspaper announcement. "John and Barbara Whiting lost a child. On Mother's Day. One month before Peter Whiting was born."

Nelson took the phone, and studied the two documents.

"Six weeks' time after losing the first baby to birthing the second isn't possible," she said.

Nelson looked at her. "Vital records are not always accurate."

"Something could be wrong with the birth certificate." Jess paused, took a deep breath, exhaled, and stared back. "But the more reasonable answer is that Peter is not John and Barbara Whiting's biological son."

Nelson pursed his lips and placed her phone on his desk. "Do you have anything else to say?"

Jess shook her head.

"How did you know the parents had trouble remembering the boy's age?"

"That's not relevant. These documents. The dates. You can confirm everything yourself."

"I intend to."

"One month. No human pregnancy on earth has resulted in a viable child after one month. It's simply not possible."

Nelson frowned. It took her a moment to realize he wasn't looking at her. She followed his gaze. Gardner had removed his chair from the doorway, and the door stood open. Charlene waited there, Jess's big green jacket in her hands, the white trimmed cuffs hanging down.

"What's going on?" Jess turned to Nelson. "You broke into my car?"

Nelson stood up and adopted a formal tone. "Jessica Kimball, you are under arrest for second-degree arson in connection with the burning of the unoccupied home of John and Barbara Whiting in Bamford, Washington."

"What are you talking about?" Her eyes widened, and she whipped her head around to see Charlene's hard expression and back to Nelson.

"You have the right to remain silent," Nelson said. "Anything you do say can be used against you in a court of law." He recited the Miranda warnings she'd heard dozens of times before. She tuned them out.

What the hell was going on?

CHAPTER TWENTY-ONE

THE AIR IN NELSON'S office grew cold. Charlene stepped back into the corridor, the coat folded over her arm, her lips pressed tightly together. Gardner took hold of her arm, easing her out of Nelson's office. Nelson watched her go.

Gardner led Jess into an interview room. He started a video recorder and repeated the warnings for the record.

"I'm aware of my rights, deputy. Yes, I want to call my lawyer." Jess had been arrested before. More than once. Her high profile work with *Taboo Magazine* was usually the cause. Refusals to reveal confidential sources, misunderstandings with law enforcement, even false accusations from witnesses were the most common charges. She knew the drill.

Gardner nodded his understanding. Charlene came in and patted Jess down. They took the contents of her pockets and her bag and left the room. She heard the lock click behind them.

A fire at the Whitings' property? When? She'd been at the

Whitings' house in the morning, and she'd been nowhere near since then. Her alibi should be easy enough to establish.

Not only that, but she hadn't used anything while she'd been there that might have started a fire. And there'd been no fire before she left. The elderly neighbor would verify that, she hoped. Now she wished she'd asked his name. But he hadn't offered, and she hadn't wanted to pressure him.

The house had been unoccupied when she left, too. Probably explained the second-degree arson charge instead of first-degree, which would apply if someone had died in the fire. She'd covered arson cases for *Taboo*. She remembered a few of the legal niceties.

Criminal arson didn't require total destruction of the building. A deliberately set fire that damaged a portion of the Whitings' home or outbuildings on the property would be enough. Nelson hadn't said exactly what was burned.

But the bigger question, of course, was why Nelson thought she might want to set fire to the Whitings' place?

The most common motive for arson was money. Usually insurance money. Jess wouldn't get any insurance money for burning the Whitings out, but presumably, the Whitings would. Peter's hospital bills were bound to be significant. Could John Whiting afford to pay them on his salary from working at the chemical plant? Would Barbara Whiting's job at the call center make up the shortfall?

If money wasn't the motive, what was? Since the Whitings weren't home at the time, the motive couldn't have been to kill them.

She shook her head. The whole thing didn't make sense. Nothing about this whole damn situation made sense. Which meant she was missing something. But what?

The door opened. Nelson walked in and sat at the table, opposite her. "Do you want to talk?"

"Actually, I do. But I can't." She shook her head. "*Taboo Magazine* policy. I'll lose my job if I talk about the charges before my lawyer arrives. Doesn't stop you from telling me what the hell is going on here."

He cocked his head. After a moment, he nodded. "Fair enough. The Whitings' house was burned down. Totaled. Everything they owned, gone. A hideous act at any time, but while they're keeping vigil at their son's bedside…" He shook his head and took a deep breath. "If you were anywhere else, anywhere that could be verified. Time and place. Speed things up if you'd tell me."

"I gave you enough in your office. When did this happen?" Jess asked.

"A few hours ago. The neighbor, Arthur Urso, called it in." He nodded. "He told us you were there this morning, so you know where they lived."

Jess said nothing.

"We found a hotel room key in the rubble at the house, Jess. The key to your hotel room. The key's got your prints on it. Your prints are in law enforcement files because you've been arrested before. Confirms you were there." Nelson leaned in and rested his forearms on the table. "Urso said he saw the arsonist running away across his lawn. He saw a green coat with white cuffs. Just like yours."

Jess nodded. She had more information now. She knew the evidence against her. But she knew something Nelson didn't know. She knew she hadn't started that fire.

"The evidence against you is circumstantial, Jess. But it's enough for probable cause. You have no ties to the community.

You're a flight risk. Judge says we can hold you while we sift through the forensics looking for more." Nelson stood. "If you're not going to help me rule you out as a suspect, you'll have to stay here. So you'd better call that lawyer."

Jess nodded again.

Nelson stood up. "Do you know the number?"

"Yes." She nodded. "Or you could just check my movements today and confirm for yourself that you've got the wrong person locked up in here and let me go."

He sighed. "Of course I'm doing that. In the meantime, I'll get the phone."

He left the room and returned a moment later with an old gray plastic beast, push-buttons yellowed with age. He trailed a cord across the room and plugged it into a socket. He switched off the video recorder and unplugged it from the wall.

"Fifteen minutes is customary, but I'm not counting. I'll knock when I come back. Just say if you need more time." He left, locking the door after him.

She took a deep breath, and picked up the handset and punched in the number.

CHAPTER TWENTY-TWO

JESS COULD HAVE CALLED the magazine's legal department directly, but she dialed Carter Pierce instead.

Carter's voice was rich, full, relaxed, like an old-fashioned crooner or late-night radio host. "Jess. Unexpected pleasure. Got something for me?"

"Oh, yeah." She took a deep breath.

"I'm all ears," he said.

She heard a noise. Part metal, part plastic, all quality. She'd heard the sound dozens of times, on the phone and while she sat in his office. Carter's expensive Mont Blanc pen was being prepared for action. The owner of *Taboo Magazine* was a man who thrived on records and notes.

"I've been arrested."

"Excellent! Something exciting we can use, I hope?" She imagined his ear-to-ear grin. Carter had been in the media business for a long time. He believed nothing sold magazines like controversy. One of his most prestigious reporters wrongfully arrested? That was a story sure to sell thousands of copies.

"Not so exciting, actually. The charge is second-degree arson."

"Not much we can do with a charge like that. Not sexy enough." He sighed. "I'll have Miller come and get you out. Where are you?"

"Randolph, Washington. Small town south of Seattle." She heard paper on a pad being flipped over. Carter was writing everything down in his sturdy script. As usual. "He won't have any trouble finding the police station. Officer in charge is Captain Joshua Nelson."

"And exactly what are you doing in this place?"

She shook her head. "I heard about an injured boy. The only thing the hospital knew about him was his name. Peter."

"Peter?" Carter's chair creaked like he'd sat up a little straighter. "Do you have reason to believe this boy is your son?"

"I don't know yet." She swallowed. "Police found people claiming to be the boy's parents, but the facts don't add up. He can't be their biological child."

"I see," Carter said. "Is this boy related to the charges filed against you?"

"Yes. The destroyed building is the parents' home."

"I see," he said again. This time, his tone was somber. "Where and how did the boy get injured?"

"Here in Randolph. On the edge of an estate owned by Senator Meisner."

"As in Alistaire Meisner?" Surprise tinged the question.

"Do you know him?"

"I know of him. Been around a while. A high-society senator on the verge of bankruptcy who marries into big money? That sort of thing always interests *Taboo* readers. There was a hint of scandal when he left the Navy, but I could never get anyone to talk about that one." She could hear the Mont Blanc's nib flying over the paper. "Maybe there's something we can use here after all. Oh, you are innocent, aren't you? Of the arson, I mean?"

"Of course."

"Good. Don't worry, Jess. Miller's the best. Sit tight, keep your mouth shut, and listen to everything they say so you can brief him when he arrives in the morning."

"Will do."

Carter was silent a moment. "I know you've got Mandy running errands for you, but is there anything else we can do while you're detained?"

She shook her head again, even though he couldn't see her. "I don't think so."

Carter's chair creaked once more. "I believe it's the Africans who say it takes a village to raise a child, and we're the closest thing you've got to a village, Jess. You don't have to do this on your own."

She took a deep breath and blinked away the tears that glazed her eyes. "I know, Carter. Thank you."

She heard him snap the lid of his Mont Blanc back into place. "And if he's yours, we'll do everything possible to get him back."

This wasn't the first time she'd been grateful to him, and it wouldn't be the last. "Thank you, Carter. Truly."

"Everything possible." He paused. "I mean that."

"I know you do," She hung up before she embarrassed them both with tears. *Taboo* wasn't only the closest thing she had to a village, Carter and Mandy and the others were the only family she had. She'd never have made it through without them.

CHAPTER TWENTY-THREE

JESS PACED THE SMALL interview room. The blind eye of
the video recorder stared at her. She double-checked the machine
wasn't recording. Satisfied, she resumed her pacing.

She bit her lip. Charlene Mackie had searched her car.
Illegally, *Taboo's* lawyer, Miller, would rightfully say. She'd
been holding the green jacket. Nelson hadn't said anything about
the arrest until he saw the jacket. Which might mean his
evidence was weaker than he'd said.

There was a knock at the door. Charlene walked in with a
clipboard and a plastic tub. She put the tub on the table and
handed the clipboard to Jess. "You have to sign for your
possessions."

Jess looked through the few items in the tub. They were
all on the list attached to the clipboard. Names, colors, and even
her phone's model and serial number. Charlene had been
thorough. She pointed to the bottom of the page. "Sign and
date."

Jess dashed off her signature and handed the clipboard back. Charlene put the clipboard in the tub. She held out Jess's phone. "I don't suppose you're going to give us the password."

Jess rolled her eyes.

Charlene nodded. She turned the phone over in her hand. "Then at least show me the birth certificate you showed Captain Nelson earlier."

Jess stared at the phone. Should she? Miller wouldn't like it. But Miller wasn't the one staying overnight in jail, either. She wasn't giving away anything that might incriminate her. She'd already shown it to Nelson, and the birth certificate was a public record. They'd have their own copy soon enough.

Charlene stood with her arm out, Jess's phone in her hand.

Jess took the phone. She held it under the table, out of sight of the camera, and entered the passcode. As she pulled the device from under the table, a string of messages glowed on the display. She dismissed them with a swipe of her finger and brought up the birth certificate.

She held it out. Charlene made notes on her clipboard. She wrote down the record locator number. With that, she should be able to get the certificate quickly.

Charlene leaned closer, staring intently at the screen. Jess angled the screen toward her. The computer generated information was easy to read. A large font with each detail clearly laid out.

She considered asking Charlene what she was so interested in but decided against it.

Charlene made one last note on her clipboard, her writing slow and deliberate. Peter David Whiting's birth date. Charlene drew a line across the page. Separating the date from the rest of the page. Clarifying the most important detail.

Jess clicked her phone off. Charlene stared at the screen. Jess placed her phone in the tub.

Charlene nodded slowly. She looked at the clipboard. "I'd better go." She didn't move.

Jess leaned forward. "You okay?"

Charlene tucked the clipboard under her arm, picked up the tub, and cleared her throat. "I'll be back. Couple of minutes."

But she didn't come back. It was Officer Gardner who returned a few minutes later to escort Jess to her cell.

CHAPTER TWENTY-FOUR

THE POLICE STATION HAD two cells. Neither of them looked heavily used. Gardner placed Jess in the first one.

Someone had etched a stylized CK into the polished sheet of metal that did duty as an unbreakable mirror above the sink. Jess doubted Calvin Klein had ever heard of Randolph, let alone stopped by the police station to leave his famous initials.

The bedclothes were freshly laundered and left folded on the mattress. She took exaggerated care unfolding them and making the bed.

In a metal cup by the sink, she found a plastic-wrapped toothbrush and toothpaste. Through the thick glass of a narrow window, she could see it was twilight outside. She lay back on the bed and closed her eyes to think.

An hour later, Gardner returned with her dinner. A sandwich, a bag of plain chips and a bottle of water on a tray. She ate the sandwich and chips and drank half of the water, keeping the rest for later.

She slept poorly and woke early, the questions she had wanted to ask Nelson rolled around the edge of consciousness. She visualized her trip from Randolph to Bamford to Vashon.

Nelson said three pieces of evidence had led him to arrest her. Her visit to the Whiting house in the morning, the hotel key, and the green jacket.

She sat up in bed, leaning against the wall, and pulled the bedclothes up around her knees. She had visited the Whitings' place. She'd talked to Urso. She'd dropped her bag twice when the buckle came loose. The key must have fallen out at the house.

The green jacket had been seen at the fire. But the jacket wasn't unique. There had been several on the rack when she'd bought it, and with mass production, there had to be thousands across the country. Miller would make short work of that issue.

But the timing was tight. That's what bothered her. She rubbed her forehead. She'd bought the jacket in the morning, and by the afternoon, it was already being used as evidence against her.

Officer Gardner knocked on the door and entered the cell, holding another tray. Two breakfast burritos wrapped in silver foil and a paper cup of coffee. She took the tray.

"More coffee if you want," he said.

She nodded. "Thank you."

He stared at her, his eyes a fraction wider than normal. She realized she had just said her first words in twelve hours.

"You know, if you'll take some advice, you may not have burned down the Whiting place, but you don't need to be here. We'll figure out what's happened, but it might be better for you if you left town. No need to tempt fate. You know?"

She said nothing, and Gardner locked the door as he left.

She breathed in the steam from the coffee. Her senses tingled at the smell, like an addict craving a caffeine fix. The fast food place must have been close by because the coffee was piping hot. She ate one of the burritos. The coffee was still too hot to drink, so she finished her second burrito, and licked her lips. The burritos were surprisingly good.

The coffee had finally reached drinking temperature. She huddled on the bed, her back against the wall, and sipped on the restorative black liquid.

The green coat. The last straw that had led to her arrest. She'd bought it in the resale shop, and promptly driven to Bamford. She'd worn the coat at the Whitings' place. Urso saw it and her. There was only one more person who might have seen her wearing the coat. She couldn't be sure, but Gardner looked awfully similar to the officer who had tailed her into Bamford.

CHAPTER TWENTY-FIVE

OFFICER GARDNER RETURNED WITH another paper cup of coffee. Jess didn't speak. She sipped her way through it. An hour had passed before she heard another knock.

When the door opened this time, Nelson stood there. Behind him, she recognized Roger Miller, *Taboo Magazine's* outside legal counsel. Nelson opened the door wider and stepped aside. "Miss Kimball, you're free to go."

She looked at Miller and raised her eyebrows. He nodded.

She turned to Nelson. "So, I'm a free citizen again?"

Nelson nodded.

She leveled a steely gaze in his direction. "What did you find out?"

Nelson crossed his arms. "You drove to Point Defiance, took the ferry to Vashon, and talked to Mr. Joseph Sandler. After that, you drove, by my estimation, directly back here."

"No time for a spot of arson somewhere in all of that?"

"Arson is no joking matter."

She sighed. "Of course it's not. I'm sure you'll find the arsonist. I'm sorry for the Whitings. As you've said, they've been through enough."

Nelson nodded.

"What about the dates I showed you?" she said. "The Whitings are not Peter's biological parents. There's no question about it."

"You might have stumbled onto something." He shook his head. "There is an inconsistency that we can't yet explain. But we don't have the whole picture."

"We can definitely agree on that."

"Getting that picture is a police matter."

"Perhaps."

"I know you think you could have a personal interest in the boy." Nelson pressed his lips into a thin line and blew air out of his nose. "But there certainly is a boy clinging to life, and his loved ones are grieving."

"And someone burned their house down." Jess nodded. "Something is going on here, Nelson, and I'm as entitled to know the truth about that boy as anyone."

Nelson said nothing.

"So, you're not going to tell me anything more?"

He shook his head. "Nothing to tell you at the moment. Unfortunately."

She smiled flatly. "Time to go then."

She collected her things at the front desk. Miller shook hands with Nelson.

Charlene Mackie watched as Miller followed Jess outside.

Miller gestured to his rental car. She sat in the passenger seat and thumped the door shut. He drove down the road about half a mile, pulled into a gas station, and left the engine running.

"Carter is worried about you, Jess. He asked me to make sure you're okay here." Miller frowned. "This isn't the kind of case you usually work on. And you're too emotionally involved. How can I help you?"

Jess swiped both hands through her hair. She really needed a shower. "I'm not sure what's going on here. That boy is definitely not John and Barbara Whiting's biological son if the birth certificate is accurate."

Miller said, "Which opens up the possibility he could be yours. DNA testing would help, but given the boy's status and the information you've found, getting consent would not be easy or quick."

"I recovered a rock with his blood on it from where he fell. I'll get the results in a couple of days."

"Might give you personal assurance, but it'll be difficult in court."

"So? Even if he's not my son, there's still something wrong with this picture."

"A couple bringing up a child that is not theirs biologically? Happens all the time. Nothing necessarily illegal."

She jerked her thumb toward the police station. "They just arrested me on the flimsiest of evidence for burning down the parents' house. That doesn't happen all the time."

Miller nodded. "True, but they did their work and released you. Nelson is a good man. You can trust him."

"You think so?"

Miller took a deep breath. "I looked him up. In case we needed leverage on the guy. He's an orphan. Left at a fire station when he was a couple of months old. Lived his life in an orphanage until he went into the police academy straight from high school. Philly. Well respected. Took on difficult cases in the worst parts of town. Right up until two of his buddies got killed in a hostage situation.

"One of my contacts tells me he went to pieces. His wife insisted on the move out here. They left a lot of friends behind, but it probably saved him from himself."

"In what way?"

"His buddies said they were worried he might eat his gun."

They sat in silence for a moment.

"So, he's protecting the child at all costs," she said. "I can understand that. But if Peter's my son? I can't stop until I know. Surely you understand that?"

"I do. And I'm sure he does, too." Miller drummed his fingers on the steering wheel. "But stay within the law, Jess. The last thing you want is to discover that boy is yours, only to have a court decide you're unfit to be his legal guardian."

Miller's advice was solid. Jess would have offered the same advice to anyone else. "I'll call you if I need anything more, Roger." She placed a hand on his arm. "And really, I appreciate you coming all the way out here. I'll do my best not to need rescuing again."

"I'll tell Carter you're doing fine." Miller grinned. He drove her back to the Randolph Police Station and dropped her off at her car.

CHAPTER TWENTY-SIX

JESS DROVE TO THE Montpelier Hotel. The big man with the white beard was at the reception desk. He stared at her. She didn't know if he was just curious about where she had been all night, or if he knew she'd been in jail. Randolph was a small town, and she was a mini-celebrity. The news probably traveled fast.

She took a deep breath. "I'm afraid I've lost my key."

"You'll need to find it." He raised his eyebrows. "Our keys are expensive replicas of the originals, Miss Kimball."

"I'm sorry. But I've lost it for sure. I'll pay for a second one. But I need to get into my room, please."

"Wait here." He shook his head. "I'll be back."

A few minutes later he returned with a second key. "I'll add the cost to your final invoice."

She went up to her room and showered. She called for room service, but the kitchen was having problems, and she had to settle for coffee. When it arrived, it was a single cup and just lukewarm. She downed it anyway.

Nelson might have been doing what he thought was the right thing. The coat might have been a stupid coincidence. There was no denying the fact that someone had burned the Whiting house down. But who and, more importantly, why?

Nelson didn't know Jess from Adam. Until he finished thoroughly checking out her movements yesterday, circumstantial evidence would be enough to keep her on the list of suspects. In Jess's mind, though, the motive for the crime most likely pertained to the Whitings. But she dismissed the Whitings as suspects. If they had been caring for Peter all these years, why burn down their house now? Then again, if Peter wasn't really theirs, someone could have a definite ax to grind.

There was only one answer—Peter's fall. Either it had moved him into the limelight and, perhaps, stirred old grudges. Or what he had been doing was important.

She gazed across the perfect green lawn.

What had Peter been doing?

She checked the map on her phone and found Randolph Path, the trail that ran alongside Meisner's property. It began on the eastern edge of town and ran for three or four miles, only a mile of which looked to be on Meisner's land. Still, a mile was an awful lot of land. Randolph Path terminated near a cluster of terraced houses.

She brought up a satellite picture on her phone. There were several parallel rows of homes. A paved road ran down the length of each row, with sidewalk spurs leading to each front door. There were no driveways. At the end of the road, she saw a final line of buildings which looked like a separate garage block.

She stared at the layout. She'd seen it before in New York and other cities where land was scarce and expensive. It was the most efficient packaging. The optimum density that could be achieved without building a high-rise. In New York, it was expected. But in the rolling fields of Washington State, it looked incongruous. A label on the map indicated the area was called *Sunshine Estates*.

A few minutes later, she rolled out of the hotel parking lot and headed east, toward the entrance to Randolph Path.

CHAPTER TWENTY-SEVEN

JESS STOPPED ON A side road, locked the car, and put on her jacket. There was a bus stop on the main road not far away. If the boy had taken the bus from Bamford, he could have easily found the lane from that stop.

The entrance to the trail was between two houses. The path was paved for the first fifty feet, and then it progressed into the woods and turned into a country trail. It headed away from the houses and the road, snaking around in a curve. She crossed a modern wooden bridge that ran over a tiny stream. The width and height of the bridge suggested the water became more than a stream at certain times of the year.

The light through the trees waxed and waned. From time to time, she could see the edge of the woods. After a few minutes, she spotted the manor house. She took pictures with her phone, noting the curve of the hill and the barely visible rooftops of the stables behind the house.

The trail widened into a clearing, a hole in the uniform

woods. There were saplings and long grass, and the trail clearly continued to an exit, fifty feet away on the far side. She stuck to the path, and in a few more minutes arrived at the tree. Exertion made her hot under the jacket. She undid the zipper and flapped the sides to cool off.

The undergrowth around the tree had retained its trampled look, but the grass and weeds were recovering from the experience. In a few days, there would be no sign left of the tragedy.

The tall grass slapped at her boots as she worked her way from the path to the tree. The ankles of her jeans grew wet with the dew and the damp.

She pushed through the trees and undergrowth to the edge of the woods. She pulled back some branches. The Meisner house was there, lit by weak streams of sunlight. Straight up the hill, the front almost facing her. There were no people milling around today and no horses. Only a dark blue Cadillac parked by the side entrance.

Around the back, she knew there were more buildings. She pulled out her phone and studied the pictures she'd taken. She zoomed in. Two buildings. A large stable and another building further away. She held up her phone and tried to imagine the view from forty feet up. She looked back at the tree. Even from four stories up, the view of the rest of the estate wouldn't be any better than she'd seen earlier on the trail.

She put her phone in her pocket. On the top floor of the house, something moved. She stared. A window. The square of glass had flashed white and back to black. As if a curtain had been drawn, or someone had retreated from view. She was too far away to be sure. As she lowered her gaze, she glimpsed a flash. A glint. Light glancing off a hard surface. She stared at the window. Nothing moved. No colors changed. There were no more flashes. There was no one there.

She walked back to the tree, and surveyed the area of trampled grass. She worked her way through the grass, sweeping it from side to side with her foot.

The broken tree limb had been pushed into the undergrowth. The branch was thick. The broken end was yellowing with exposure to air. A long strip of bark curled around the yellow gash, pulled away when the limb separated from the tree. She ran her hand around the circumference of the break. It was substantial. Strong. She sighed. Peter Whiting couldn't have been unluckier.

She turned back to her car. All she had learned were negatives. He had climbed the tree for a reason, but it was hard to believe that reason was to see the Meisners' land. He could have done that anywhere along the trail without the risks of climbing so high into that particular tree.

She walked through the clearing and back into the woods on the other side. The ground was soft. It made walking harder than usual. Her calves ached. It was a familiar ache. She liked the feeling of her muscles burning. She never had enough time to become a regular at a gym, so exercise during her day was a good thing.

She unzipped her waterproof jacket. The morning's clouds had held their rain in abeyance. She slipped the jacket from her shoulders and wiped her hand across her forehead. Despite the cool air, she was sweating. She sat on a fallen tree trunk. The woods were thick and quiet. Leaves were falling from the deciduous trees, leaving a patchwork of deep greens and bare branches.

There was something else, too. Her skin tingled. Her heart missed a beat. Forty feet away. Between the tree trunks. She cursed herself for leaving her Glock in the car.

Staring at her through the thorny undergrowth was a pair of eyes.

CHAPTER TWENTY-EIGHT

THE EYES WERE SIDE by side. Pointing forward. A predator.

Jess moved slowly. She brought the jacket up in front of her. It would work well as a shield. She flexed her feet in her boots. Checking they were tight. She eased off the tree trunk. The eyes kept up their stare, lit by the thinnest of leaf-filtered light. She took a step along the trail. There was no movement in the bushes. She took a deep breath, her mouth open, and walked on. Slow steps. Putting her weight down deliberately. Avoiding broken branches. Keeping to the quiet of bare earth.

She walked, and the angles changed. She lost sight of the eyes but kept track of the bushes where they had been. She alternated, looking back and looking forward. Keeping up her breathing, keeping herself oxygenated in case she needed to run. She scanned the trail and the bushes to either side.

She heard no telltale cracks from the twigs breaking underfoot. The end of the trail was half a mile away. She had a good lead, and she was a runner. She took a deep breath. If it came to a straight chase, she could prevail. She rolled the jacket under her arm.

The trail twisted and turned, opening up new sightlines. She saw a figure. Ragged clothes and long hair. A gray beard. He moved away. She breathed a sigh of relief. A vagrant. Probably as scared of her as she had been by him.

She made it to her car, started the engine, and ran the heater.

A vagrant? He certainly had the weathered skin of someone who lived outdoors. She frowned. He hadn't seemed dangerous.

She drove into town and stopped at a burger chain. She bought the largest meal they had, and five minutes later she was back, walking through the woods to where she had seen the eyes.

There was no sign of him. She followed the direction he had taken. There was no real path, but there were telltale signs he had passed that way.

Black plastic glinted from under a mountain of vegetation. She moved around the mound until she saw an opening. "Hello," she called.

"Don't want no visitors," called a man's voice that was deep and rough, as if it had been steeped in smoky bars and hard liquor.

She poked her head under the exterior of the shelter. It was a small space lined with plastic bags and old clothes. He was huddled on a log in the corner. He stared at her.

He had thick eyebrows, a wild gray beard, and matching gray ponytail. He looked to be wearing three coats and woolen gloves. The gloves were different colors.

She kneeled down and held out the bag from the burger chain and a large coffee, steam curling from the lid into the damp air. "For you."

He moved forward an inch.

She placed it on the ground between them and backed away.

His eyes darted between Jess and the brown bag.

"Better get it while it's hot," she said.

He shuffled forward and opened the bag. The scent of fried food filled the air. He removed his gloves and wedged the palms in his pockets, the fingers waggling comically.

She waited as he unwrapped the burger and fries and ate his way through what she guessed was his first hot meal in a long time. In a couple of minutes, the food was gone, and he sat cradling the coffee in his hands.

"What's your name?"

He eyed her a moment. "Max."

"I'm Jess." She thought better of explaining who she was. "A boy fell from a tree in these woods—"

"Don't know nothing about it." His gaze darted around, refusing to make eye contact.

"I was wondering—"

"I said, I don't know nothing."

"He must have passed your home."

He shrugged.

Jess smiled. "You saw me earlier."

"Maybe."

"I saw you watching me. But you didn't see the boy?"

Max shuffled the leaves under his feet. He inched back into the vegetation. "No."

"Max, this could be—"

Max pointed. "He was that way. On the ground. Must have been early. I didn't see 'im fall. I was here. He was a long way away."

"What was the boy doing out there Max? Before he fell from the tree?"

Max shrugged.

"It's important, Max."

He shifted his weight and looked away.

"You did see him, didn't you?"

He shook his head, slowly. "No…but I heard him."

"Heard?"

He kept his head down. "It's cold, see. An' I don't like to get up so much no more. But there was a noise. He were flying a kite or something." He jerked his thumb toward Meisner's mansion. "That way."

"Did you see it?"

He shook his head. "I stayed here until after he fell."

"What kind of kite, Max," Charlene said.

He shrugged, keeping his gaze down.

"Do you have the kite, Max?"

He shook his head very slowly.

"Really?"

He sighed and placed the coffee on the ground, checking it for stability before letting go.

He dug his hand into a pile of leaves and produced a small black and silver object. He licked his lips before holding it out.

Jess took the object and frowned. "A remote control?"

Max shrugged.

The buttons on the remote were smeared with mud. The antenna was broken. She flipped the power on. A red light glowed.

"Doesn't work," Max said. "Doesn't do anything."

"Was it his?" Jess asked.

Max slunk back. "I found it. After the doctors took him away."

"Near the tree?"

"In the weeds."

"What does it control?" Jess asked.

Max shrugged.

Jess pushed buttons and moved the small joystick. Nothing moved around them. She turned the remote off.

"The police didn't find a remote control toy."

Max nodded. "I didn't neither. Must have gone."

Jess gestured in the direction of Meisner's place. "Up there, maybe?"

"Could be."

"Did you find anything else?" Jess asked.

Max shook his head.

"Sure?"

He nodded. He kept eye contact with her this time. He knew he'd been caught lying and might have been sorry for it. She couldn't imagine living his life, but perhaps finding the remote had been a moment's excitement in his world. Whatever his reason, he was telling the truth, now.

Peter had left a clue, but there was more to be uncovered. She would have to find the rest on her own, and she had an idea where she needed to look. She held up the remote control. "You've been a big help, Max."

He shuffled back into the corner of his shelter and hugged his coffee. He nodded toward the food bag. "Thank you."

CHAPTER TWENTY-NINE

JESS DROVE BACK TO the resale shop. A different woman occupied the checkout desk. Her name tag said Camilla.

Jess headed for the table filled with toys. The box she wanted was still there. She dug it out of a jumble of phone chargers and set it upright.

It was a big box. The picture on the front was a boy with a broad smile on his face holding a small white drone with four propellers. A quadcopter. Under the picture was a list of selling points, including the built-in camera capable of recording full HD video. The screen for watching the camera's view was on the remote.

"You have a child who might like this?" said Camilla.

"Yes," Jess said as she handed the woman the box.

Camilla placed it on the checkout. "It works good. The manager tried it out the other day." She pointed upward. "Flew it right over the roof. The video is real clear."

Jess paid with her credit card, thanked the lady, and returned to her car. She plugged the drone into the electrical socket and drove back to the trail.

By the time she arrived, the display on the top of the drone had indicated the battery was three-quarters charged. Maybe that would be enough.

She moved her Glock from its protective case into her bag. She didn't have a license, but she didn't care. Sleepy Randolph was turning out to be a more dangerous place than it first appeared.

She put the remote control in her pocket, tucked the drone under her arm, and headed back to the tree.

She walked inside the tree line, keeping her back to the woods, facing Meisner's estate and his mansion up the hill. She paid closer attention this time and noticed that this was one of the most open areas of the forest. She could see side to side across his estate.

She pulled the drone from under her arm. It had two tiny switches on top, one marked on, the other video. She clicked them both. A light on the top glowed red.

She laid the drone on the ground and took two steps back. Despite the comparative openness of the woods at that point, this wasn't a great place to fly a drone, either. She should have conducted her first flight in a big, open space

She switched on the remote. There were two joysticks, one for height, the other for direction. The tiny screen on the remote displayed a view of grass and leaves. The camera was underneath the drone.

The drone stayed on the ground. She leaned forward and tapped it. It didn't move. She shook the remote control. The drone remained stationary.

She turned the remote control over in her hands. There were no instructions. She pushed the direction lever forward. The drone buzzed but didn't take off. *Of course.* She rolled her eyes and pushed the elevation joystick.

The drone shot upward. She took her hand off the joystick, and the drone dropped to the ground.

Gingerly, she pushed the joystick again. The drone rose ten feet in the air. She eased it forward, stopped, and reversed it back to her. She pushed the joystick left, and the drone banked around in a tight circle. The picture on the tiny screen became a blur of green and brown.

She stopped circling and pointed the drone at the tree. The camera focused on the trunk.

She stepped closer to the tree and pushed the joystick. The drone rose up slowly. The camera lens remained fixed on the tree, even though she needed it to look in the direction the drone was moving. She walked backward, reaching a compromise between losing sight of the drone in the tree's foliage and her ability to judge the proximity of the branches.

She eased the drone left and right, working for higher altitude. The drone reached the gash on the tree—the long strip of bark and wood that had been torn away as Peter's weight overcame the tree's ability to support him.

She stopped the drone and stared for a moment. He certainly had guts to climb that high. He must not have been looking down, or he might have turned back as she did.

She returned her attention to the drone. It jerked to different angles. The remote's screen showed the fields around the mansion then, as she continued to turn the drone and the camera, the mansion itself.

There was no great revelation in the views. The cheap camera had a wide-angle lens. The mansion looked tiny compared to the surrounding green.

She rotated the camera back to the tree and pushed upward. Once or twice the propellers gave a loud buzzing noise as they clipped overhanging leaves. The drone shook, but always regained its level.

The elevation joystick reached the end of the drone's travel distance. She pushed it hard into the end stop, but the drone didn't climb any higher. She guessed it had reached twenty feet above the point Peter had climbed. Sixty feet. Six stories high.

The remote buzzed. She took her eye off the drone. A red light flashed on the handset. The batteries were almost exhausted. The drone's propellers buzzed. She looked up. The drone was barely visible. She pulled back on the joystick. The tiny screen showed leaves and branches and a glimpse of clouds. The buzzing stopped. The screen showed a jumble of colors before coming to a stop.

Jess recoiled from the image before realizing she was looking at a black plastic, insect-like creature. The creature had legs that extended forward and aft, and on the ends of the legs were propellers.

She drew the remote closer, studying the picture on the tiny screen. She looked up. Peter had been flying a drone.

Jess cycled the joystick back and forth. Far above, her drone made short, weak buzzing noises. The drone's camera inched closer to the artificial insect.

In the distance, an angry gas engine roared. She looked toward the mansion. A four-wheeler was heading her way.

She pushed forward and up on the remote's controls, the drone buzzing with each effort. The black insect's proportions became wildly distorted as the drones closed the distance between them. The insect lurched with each push she made from her drone. She glimpsed the edge of a branch.

The sound of the four-wheeler angled to her right, still closing, but not headed directly toward her.

She pushed her drone on. The last vestiges of its tiny battery thrusting it and the insect toward an edge.

She heard the four-wheeler stop near the fence a couple of hundred feet away.

She looked up. There was no sign of either drone. She kept up the steady pressure on the joysticks. Each successive push resulting in a weaker and weaker buzz from high above.

She heard shouting and the crash of a gate onto the metal fence.

The screen on the remote showed nothing but trees. She pushed forward and upward. The camera's view became a blur.

A knot of black and white plastic tumbled through the air. She ran hard and caught it before the drones touched the ground. The big black plastic insect was as unpleasant up close as it had been the first time she'd seen it on the screen.

The shouting grew closer.

She pulled the memory card out of her drone, but the black plastic insect wasn't so easy. She turned it over twice before ripping a panel off the top of its back. There was a small socket to charge the battery and a slot with a memory card poking out. She ripped the card out and swiftly tucked both cards down her collar and into her bra.

Fifty feet away, two men appeared between the trees. The first of the two shouted, "Halt!" He pointed a long gun in Jess's direction to back up his demand.

Jess eased the panel on the black plastic insect closed and tossed the pair of drones to the ground. "What's this?"

The two men approached quickly, gazes sweeping the area. They wore black ski jackets that made them seem even bulkier.

One man circled the area, the other stood in front of Jess, his gun lowered. "What are you doing?"

"Who are you?" Jess said.

"Senator Meisner's security team. You're trespassing on private property."

"I thought this was a right of way."

The man kicked at the drones with his boot. "The right of way is for crossing the land. It doesn't extend to spying."

"I wasn't spying…I was trying to recover a toy caught in the tree."

The man turned over Jess's drone with the toe of his boot. The camera's lens clearly visible. "Toy, huh?"

"You can't—"

He pointed his gun at her bag. "Open it."

She released a long, exasperated sigh and held her bag open. "I have a license for the Glock." She just hoped he didn't demand to see it since it wasn't legal for Washington State.

The man pointed a micro beam flashlight into her bag. He pulled the Glock and clicked the magazine out. "I'll return this back on the main road."

"You don't have—"

"Put your arms out."

Jess glowered. "If you think you're going to search me, think again."

The man glowered. He looked her up and down. "You're the reporter, aren't you?"

"I'm a reporter."

"You're on private property." The man scooped up the drones. "You've no right to be here."

"Give me my property."

The man gestured along the path, toward her car. "Tough

luck. We're confiscating it. You want pictures, you ask the press office."

She glared at him another moment, but he clearly held the upper hand. She turned and walked back to her car. Both men followed.

She stood by the car with her hand out.

"Take a hint. Don't come back." The man returned her Glock's magazine. "Next time, we'll have you arrested and charged."

She saw them in her rearview mirror, watching her until she drove away.

CHAPTER THIRTY

JESS DROVE TO THE Montpelier and went up to her room. She slipped the memory card from Peter's drone into a slot on the side of her computer. The insect drone's recorded video was far superior to the grainy image she'd seen on the remote control's tiny screen.

The images were shot in the early morning. Very early. Not yet sunrise at the beginning of the video. The video had no time stamp, but she guessed the time was before seven o'clock.

The drone soared across the grounds around Meisner's mansion, sweeping left and right over the ankle deep verdant grass. Definite trails crossed the fields, early morning animals tracking through the dew.

The big building flitted in and out of view. The drone swept around the structure at roof height, frequently turning sideways, and staring in through windows. Jess could easily see how a resident might get upset at such an intrusion.

A watery sun began to peek through thin clouds close to the

horizon. The camera turned down. The chalk white gravel that surrounded the building glowed. A dark blue Cadillac was parked by the main entrance, a chauffeur stood beside it. He looked up.

The drone banked away. The green fields came into view again. There was no soaring this time. The drone traveled straight, the grass whipping by below. Peter must have been spooked by the chauffeur.

The fence came into view. The drone pitched up, using its thrust to brake. It did one last 360-degree sweep. The mansion was far off, the man and the Cadillac barely visible. The sun glinted off the damp grass and the metal fence.

The camera pointed into the forest. The drone descended before twisting right. The camera spun. Fleeting images of ground and sky raced by, a blur of leaves and trees then a static image of a thick tree limb. The image appeared frozen, but after a few moments, a bird flew by. The drone was stuck.

Jess fast forwarded through the rest of the video. The picture didn't change. The image ended abruptly when the drone's battery ran out.

She exhaled slowly. Peter had flown his drone more than half a mile from where he stood. He'd circled Meisner's mansion, far beyond visual range. He'd swooped and soared over the fields. He was an expert pilot.

He must have loved flying his drone. It was obvious now why he'd climbed the tree to find it. He would never have left it behind.

Which left one question unanswered. Why had he chosen to fly it around Meisner's mansion?

CHAPTER THIRTY-ONE

JESS'S PHONE RANG. A local number appeared on the display. "Jessica Kimball."

"This is Charlene Mackie." She cleared her throat. "Where are you?"

"Why?"

"Because I'm heading down to Portland to check on the details on Peter Whiting's birth certificate. I wondered if you want to come along?"

Jess frowned. "I already have the birth certificate."

"Yeah…but we want to corroborate it with the hospital records."

It was a tempting idea. On the other hand, Charlene had produced the green jacket for Nelson, which got Jess arrested.

"I don't—"

"I'm sure you're not happy about last night. For what it's worth, I didn't expect Nelson to arrest you." Charlene paused.

"But the Whitings are homeless. We need to find out who's responsible. We didn't have much choice."

"I do understand. It's…"

"I thought you were interested."

Maybe getting in a car with Charlene was a little reckless, since she'd so gleefully broken into Jess's car and retrieved the jacket that got Jess arrested. But she probably wasn't dangerous. The woman was a cop, after all. "Give me ten minutes."

She dashed off a text to Mandy. *On my way to Portland with Charlene Mackie. If you don't hear from me in a couple of hours, call in the Marines! LOL!*

Mandy texted back immediately. *Will do!*

Jess checked her bag. The Glock rested exactly where it should be. Just in case.

She was dressed and standing outside the hotel when a ten-year-old Ford Crown Victoria backed into the parking lot and honked. The car looked rusty but trusty. Cops had told her that the Crown Vic was the best cruiser ever built and lamented that it was no longer in production. Maybe Randolph PD had thought so at one time, too.

This one had served its purpose. The black paint was faded, and a few dents marred the lines here and there. The Crown Vic had seen better days. The old tank probably got no more than ten miles to the gallon, at best. Charlene beckoned to her through the rear window. Jess trotted out to the driveway and entered the massive sedan on the passenger side.

Charlene wore her uniform shirt and pants, but none of her badges. She still looked like a cop, albeit less official. She eased the big boat out of the parking lot and onto the road. She glanced at Jess. "Kid's Own Medical Center is on the south side of Portland."

"Why didn't you just send them an email? Or make a phone call?"

Charlene shrugged. "I wanted to see the originals, and it avoids email ping-pong."

Jess pulled out her phone. "Should I call Nelson and thank him?"

Charlene glanced briefly away from the road. "Thank him for what?"

"A couple of hours ago, he told me to stay out of his investigation."

"He's a good man. At least I think he is. You can never tell until they're under pressure. I mean captains, well, and men in general, I suppose." She took a deep breath. "But I wouldn't tell him you're with me."

Jess twisted around in her seat. "He doesn't know that you called me?"

"He's trying to do what's right. He should, he's an officer of the law. But I'm a mother, too. And… You lost your kid, didn't you?"

"Yes."

"Everyone's different, and I don't know what you went through with the emotions and everything." She shook her head. "But a mother has a right to know. So let's see what we find and take it from there."

The old cruiser ate up the miles. A straight shot south on I-5. Through woods and forests. The sides of the highway blurred into an almost continuous line of trees, a few reds and golds of early fall mixed with determined evergreens.

Everyone's different. The words echoed in Jess's

subconscious. Charlene wasn't empathizing, she was sympathizing. Jess broke the silence. "When I first met you, you said you had written to me."

Charlene nodded. "Years ago. I heard you were making a name for yourself at *Taboo*."

"You know I get far more mail than I can ever read."

"I know." Charlene took a deep breath. "I wrote because I had...I have a daughter. Crystal. She...well, we didn't always see eye to eye. I was a young mother," Charlene glanced at Jess. "Like you."

Jess waited.

"She disappeared. When she was twenty-three. Fourteen years ago. June 22. Seven days after the date on Peter Whiting's birth certificate. Just like that. One minute she was living in Randolph, the next she was gone."

"She ran away?"

"Some folks think so. Happens often enough, I guess." Charlene shook her head. "I really don't know. We didn't always have the best life, but...I don't think she would have. Not without telling me. I mean, we were family, no matter how we got along."

"Who saw her last?"

"An old lady saw her walking through the area where she lived. It was late. Dark."

"There was an investigation into her disappearance, right? You tried to find her?"

"To start with, everyone just thought she'd run away. She'd left debts behind. She was living with a guy who," Charlene shook her head. "They call him Spud, but his name is Johnny Yukon. Scum of the earth."

Jess had heard the same tale many times. Sometimes she had

been able to help, but oftentimes, no one could. "You've been looking ever since then? Fourteen years?"

"What mother would stop?" Charlene glanced away from her driving to look at Jess. "You know?"

Jess nodded. She knew all too well.

"So what made you write to me?" It seemed like an obvious question, and she expected the obvious answer—that Charlene had run out of viable options. People who wrote to Jess at *Taboo* were usually desperate. They'd exhausted all other avenues and hit nothing but brick walls.

"The last time I saw her," Charlene took a deep breath and held it a moment before she continued. "Crystal was pregnant."

Jess nodded. Not uncommon. Charlene had said she was living with a man her mother didn't like. Maybe Charlene had flipped out when her daughter came home pregnant. Maybe she'd wanted the girl to have an abortion. Girls had run away from home for a lot less.

"Very pregnant." Charlene nodded and glanced at Jess again. This time, her look seemed heavy with meaning. "Her due date was June fifteen."

Jess leaned forward. The tingle ran over her skin again. "Why didn't you say that when you looked at Peter Whiting's birth certificate on my phone yesterday?"

"People are sick of hearing from me. I talked about it so much. I questioned everything. I've chased after every single thread, and hoped so many times." She ducked her head and smiled weakly. "Nobody wants to hear about Crystal Mackie's disappearance anymore and…I mean, I can't…I have to keep my hopes in check."

Jess rubbed the tips of her fingers against her thumb. "The woman who last saw Crystal. Did she say if—"

"The old lady's gone, but thought Crystal didn't look pregnant when she saw her that last time."

"You think she delivered around her due date?"

Charlene breathed in and out several times. Her voice was a little stronger when she replied. "There's no good way to say this, but Crystal's baby was a boy. She told me that much."

Jess eased back into her seat. "But if, and it is a big if…"

"I know. And I know what you're hoping. And I understand what you want. But Peter Whiting might be my grandson."

Jess stared through the windscreen. "Or…"

"Or he could be your son. Or he could be another boy entirely." Charlene nodded. "But there's no question he is not Barbara Whiting's natural child."

"There's only one way to find out."

"Yes," Charlene said as she pushed the Crown Vic's accelerator a little closer to the floor.

Both women fell silent, staring through the windshield.

Jess wondered whether either of them would be returning to Randolph with confirmed suspicions or both would still carry the sting of haunting loss.

Light rain sprinkled the windshield. The wipers created grimy arcs on the glass, and the world became a blur as the Crown Vic ate up the silent miles to Portland.

CHAPTER THIRTY-TWO

BLACKSTAKE FOLLOWED THE AGING Crown Vic out of Randolph. His frame-up hadn't worked, and now his GPS locator on the reporter's rental was useless while her car was parked in the lot at her hotel. He'd keep eyes on her the old-fashioned way.

Following wasn't difficult. The Crown Vic was a distinctive shape, and its tired black paint made it stand out among the nameless foreign imports that filled the roads.

The only mystery was why the Mackie woman had collected the reporter and where they were headed. Kimball was unpredictable, and she had a big national megaphone, which made her dangerous. But Mackie had been passive enough. He didn't expect her to change. People rarely did.

He traveled four cars behind the Crown Vic. Occasionally he would pass and cut the separation down to three cars, but then he would slow, falling back a couple of car lengths. It broke the pattern. Not one car, always the same distance behind. If they saw him, they'd probably think he was some grouchy old guy, complaining at everything on the road. He grinned, not so far from the truth.

The Crown Vic wheezed along. Blue-gray smoke trailed from the exhaust on the inclines. Its loose body wallowed on the suspension as it rolled over expansion joints and potholes. His rental had a firm ride, not harsh, but none of the gyrations the Ford exhibited.

He laughed to himself. A decade ago, he'd have been happy to be in the Crown Vic. Plenty of power, miles of leg room, and a spacious trunk for those times when trunk space was essential. These days he preferred soundproofing and heated seats.

The freeway skirted alongside the Columbia River and narrowed into Vancouver, Oregon. The Crown Vic crossed the river, and traffic grew thicker as they entered Portland city limits. After almost three hours, he was tired of following, but now wasn't the time to relax or make a mistake. He closed the gap on the duo and wondered again where in the hell they were going.

CHAPTER THIRTY-THREE

JESS WATCHED THE WELCOME to Portland sign pass by. They crossed the Columbia River and continued south on I-5 through Portland past the high-rises that populated downtown.

Her phone buzzed with a message from Stephenson. *Been out of the office. Just sent rock for full DNA testing. Results in 3 days. Will forward soonest.*

She sighed. An unfortunate delay, but she knew whatever results he obtained she could depend on one hundred percent.

The city was thinning out when Jess saw a small green sign for Kid's Own Medical Center. Charlene took the exit. The side road swept around to a Y-split. Local traffic to the left, hospital traffic on the right. Charlene veered right and slowed as they pulled into the lot. She worked her way around until she found an empty parking space.

The building's main doors led into an atrium. The gray sky filled the interior space with the same dull glow they'd left outside. Six-foot-tall teddy bears stood guard at the elevators.

Yuccas and small trees were planted at regular intervals, and clusters of soft chairs were filled with patients and visitors.

A large Reception sign hung over a broad, elbow-high counter. Two women were dealing with a line of visitors.

Charlene approached one of the women and asked, "Which way to the records office?"

The woman pointed to the oversized bears. "Elevator's over there. Fourth floor."

Jess weaved through the foliage and stuffed animals and Charlene followed. The elevator announced each floor in a calm female alto as they ascended.

"Do you have a contact here?' Jess asked, finally breaking the silence between them.

"Dr. Nepovim," Charlene responded.

Jess frowned. "They have a doctor working in the records department?"

"Records are a lot more complicated these days, what with all the legal issues and coordination of care and such, I'm told." Charlene shrugged. "We hear Nepovim is not very well liked, either. Maybe records was the only department that would have him."

The records office was identified by a small sign held in an aluminum frame attached to the door. They walked through the doorway straight into two rows of desks and a half dozen busy people. No receptionist.

A clean-cut young man at the first desk removed his headset. Oscar Platte, according to his name tag. "Help you?"

"Dr. Nepovim?" Charlene didn't display her badge, but her question carried the official, off-putting tone used by cops everywhere.

Platte's nose wrinkled and he nodded toward a glassed-in

office at the far end of the room. He replaced his headset.

"Thank you." Jess smiled and handed him her business card. She figured she might need a source before this case was over and young people were sometimes more enamored of *Taboo*, according to the magazine's market research.

Platte looked at the card. Smiled like he recognized the *Taboo* logo.

A man stepped out of the far office and called across the distance. "Officer Mackie? Dr. Nepovim." He gestured into his office. "Come this way."

Platte grimaced and shrugged. Jess smiled at him. He put her card in his shirt pocket and returned to his work.

Jess and Charlene walked back to the office.

"Take a seat." Nepovim gestured and closed the door behind them.

They settled into uncomfortable tubular steel chairs facing Nepovim across his cluttered desk. He held his hands wide. "How can I help you?"

"As I mentioned on the phone, we're interested in a boy who was born here fourteen years ago. Peter David Whiting," Charlene said, sounding even more official than she'd been with Platte.

Nepovim put his hands together, interlacing his fingers. "You're asking for personal medical information on the boy and his family without a court order?"

"We're not looking for confidential medical treatment details," Jess shook her head and tried to avoid the problem she knew was coming.

Nepovim looked at Jess. "I'm sorry, I didn't get your name?"

Jess held her hand out. "Jessica Kimball."

Nepovim shook her hand briefly. "Are you related to the child?"

"We are trying to identify an accident victim," Charlene said. "Basic information that doesn't contravene medical privacy laws."

Nepovim's smile faded. He leaned back in his chair.

"We need Peter David Whiting's exact date of birth, along with the names and addresses of both parents, as noted on the official delivery record at the time of the actual delivery." Charlene continued as if she couldn't see the disapproval on Nepovim's face. "We'll take things from there."

"And this is in conjunction with some sort of," Nepovim waved his hand, "police investigation?"

"It is," Charlene said. "I can get a court order, but we're trying to speed things up here. The boy is in the hospital now with a serious injury."

He scribbled a note on an official Kid's Own Medical Center prescription pad, signed it, wrote his medical identification number under his name, tore it off, and handed it to Charlene. "One copy is enough?"

Charlene looked at the paper then handed it to Jess. Nepovim had neat, readable handwriting. Unusual for a doctor, in Jess's experience.

He'd written *Peter David Whiting, Caucasian male. Father, John Whiting. Mother, Barbara Whiting.* Followed by *June 15*, the same date of birth reflected on the official birth certificate Mandy had obtained. The exact information Jess and Charlene knew to be biologically impossible.

"You have these details memorized for every birth at this hospital?" Charlene asked.

"You called ahead. I looked it up for you." He shrugged.

"We transferred this data to the official birth certificate at the time, which is where I found it. You can obtain a certified copy from the state quickly enough."

"We already did," Jess said.

Nepovim frowned. "So why are you here?"

"As I said on the phone, the boy's unconscious. We can't get information from him." Charlene said. "We need to see the original hospital delivery record created at the time of the birth."

"We'd also like to speak with the attending physician and the labor and delivery nurse who was primarily responsible at the birth," Jess added.

Nepovim looked at a computer printout in front of him. He bit his lip and then folded the paper several times, presumably to hide confidential information before showing it to Jess. The attending physician was listed as Dr. Melise Youree and the attending labor and delivery nurse's initials were N.F.

Jess leaned back. "Is that all you have?"

"A birth of a healthy boy, full term, with no complications, from fourteen years ago?" Nepovim arched both eyebrows. "What more do you think you need?"

"Were your records all digital back then?" Charlene asked.

"Mostly paper." Nepovim shook his head and plastered an expression on his face that was probably meant to be regret but looked more like a satisfied smirk. "Old records are stored off premises. We have a procedure in place for requesting the originals. You need consent from the patient or a subpoena from the appropriate court. Usually takes about six weeks."

Jess's lip curled. A doctor with zero concern for an unconscious boy barely ranked on her personal scale of people who deserved respect.

"We'd like to see the original now," Charlene said, in her most official tone.

"I can't justify using our limited resources for a time-consuming search at this time." Nepovim shook his head again. "You go through proper channels. Make a formal request. I've provided what you asked me for based on our electronic records. Get a court order or consent from the family and we'll pull the original records for you." He stood up, walked around and opened the door. "If you'll excuse me, I have other matters to attend."

Jess resisted the urge to glare at him on the way out, but Charlene was less cautious. "We'll be back, Dr. Nepovim." Charlene's words were a definite threat. "If there's any irregularities with these records, you'll be answering not only to a judge but also to the licensing board and your malpractice carrier."

"You do what you have to do, Officer Mackie." Nepovim's tone was smarmy.

Jess shoved her hands into her pockets, tempted to slap that smug smile off his face. Before she had the chance to commit battery, he closed the door firmly behind them.

Charlene walked swiftly across the large open room toward the door. The edges of her mouth curled down. "We didn't get much."

"What a jerk." Jess followed along two steps behind. "What is Nepovim hiding?"

"Hard to say. He's right about releasing the original hospital records. We do need consent or a court order." Charlene swiped a hand through her hair. "I was hoping he'd be a decent human being, willing to help us, and let us take a quick look if we were standing right here in front of him. I should have known better."

They'd reached Oscar Platte's desk, and he overheard. An almost involuntary bark of laughter escaped his lips.

Jess stopped walking. "Mr. Platte?"

"Oscar," he replied, shaking his head. "Sorry you made the trip for nothing, Miss Kimball. I don't know where you got your background information, but no one around here would ever accuse Nepovim of being a decent human being."

"Yeah. We kind of got that vibe." Jess frowned. She'd coaxed information from many witnesses who'd offered such a slim opening. Maybe the trip could be salvaged after all. "Hard to believe he'd be like that with us, though, Oscar. We're trying to identify the parents of an injured boy who's lying in a medically induced coma over in Randolph. Nepovim says he can't show us the original records. He says they're in storage somewhere or something."

"That so? Maybe I can help." Oscar grinned in the way of all rebels seeking to stick it to the man and clicked a few keys on his keyboard. "Today's my last day. What's Nepovim going to do to me? What's the boy's name?"

"That's part of our problem," Jess shrugged, figuring maybe Oscar had looked her up while they were in with Nepovim. Anyone who knew her work and was on what she considered the right side of justice was usually willing to help her. "We think his name is Peter David Whiting."

Oscar pulled up a blank screen and typed the name. "Date of birth?"

"We're not sure. As I said, he's unconscious, and we can't get anything directly from him," Charlene said, biting her lip.

Oscar looked up and nodded. "Got a general idea of the birth date, at least?"

Jess said, "We think it's June fifteen."

He clicked the keys. "Year?"

"Not sure." Charlene shrugged. "Between thirteen and fifteen years ago, the docs estimated."

"I can use a date range." Oscar nodded again and clicked more keys. He pushed the search key and looked up as the system did its thing. "Nepovim didn't exactly lie. Computerizing the old records *is* an ongoing project. But even if we don't have everything online yet, we should have some records as far back as twenty years scanned into the system already."

Jess's heart skipped a couple of beats and then pounded too fast. She might be one computer search away from finding out the truth. Peter David Whiting could be her son. Or not. She held her breath while she struggled to prepare herself for the outcome, either way.

She glanced at Charlene. Her face had blanched completely white. She looked like she might faint.

"Uh-oh," Oscar said when his computer completed its search. "Looks like we could have a problem."

"What kind of problem?" Jess asked, feeling like she'd been given a small reprieve.

"We've got a lot of births during that time frame. We could have one for your patient. But," he paused to run his tongue over his lips. "There's a flag on all of these babies."

"A flag? What does that mean?" Charlene squeaked out.

"I wasn't working here back then." Oscar cleared his throat and lowered his voice when he spoke again. "During those three years, and for about ten years after that, Norah Fender was one of our most active delivery room nurses."

"Norah Fender?" Charlene shook her head.

Oscar looked up from his screen. He glanced from Charlene to Jess and back again. "You don't know who she is?"

"I guess we don't," Jess said. "Why don't you fill us in?"

CHAPTER THIRTY-FOUR

BLACKSTAKE SAT IN THE Kid's Own Medical Center parking lot and watched the two women walk in through the main entrance. After an appropriate interval, he followed them inside, breaking to the right when he reached the atrium. He grabbed a leaflet and stood as if he was reading.

The space was filled with children. The noise drowned out the reporter's words. He watched them circle around the reception desk and head for the elevators.

The stairs were to his right. He took them fast, up two floors, and looked into the corridor. He dashed up two more flights and emerged on the fourth floor. The elevator doors were closing behind the two women, and he glimpsed Mackie's black uniform as she disappeared into an interior office.

As he walked down the corridor, he passed the door the Mackie woman had used. The words "Records Office" were printed on a plaque on the door.

He reached the end of the corridor. Could mean anything,

but with Mackie involved and that reporter in tow, his senses were on high alert. Mackie's meddling heightened his concern about this trip from tedious curiosity to serious worry.

The medical world was foolishly steeped in myriad privacy concerns. Any hacker worth his salt could hack any health record anywhere. Why they insisted on making life harder for legitimate information seekers while criminals ran amok in their records was only one of health care's absurdities.

The misplaced secrecy might work in his favor today. Whatever Mackie and Kimball were looking for, the hospital might refuse. Plenty of legal mumbo-jumbo they could hide behind if they wanted to. Even if Kimball was pushy. He'd let Meisner know, there would be time to thwart them if they kept digging.

But only if Blackstake learned what, exactly, Mackie and Kimball were trying to find.

He walked back to the Records Office, pushed open the door and stepped inside. Desks were lined up on either side of a walkway. At the far end was an office enclosed by frosted glass walls.

"Help you?" asked a clean-cut young man with a well-trimmed goatee at the first desk.

Blackstake ignored him and stared at the back office. The overhead strip lights glared off the frosted glass. He saw movement, but little else. He took a step closer. There were figures inside the frosted glass room. Three figures. He glimpsed blond hair. The reporter.

The young man stood up. "Sir, can I help you?"

Occupants at the other desks looked up and began to stare. Blackstake wanted to punch him. Hard. He wanted to shove his holier-than-thou look right down his throat until he choked on it, no matter how much attention it attracted.

He flexed his fingers at his sides. For a moment, his professional cool battled his desire to maim the nosey young pest for life. He regained control and breathed out. "Sorry. Wrong room, I think."

Blackstake turned and strode past the cretin before he had a chance to speak, clicking the door closed behind him.

He walked to his car, cursing under his breath.

He was done with this nonsense.

He used his regular phone to dial the boss's burner, answered to open the connection, and placed the burner's speaker on mute. He turned up the burner's microphone to the max.

He tested the open line to be sure he could hear normal voice tones through his cell.

From the glove box of the Chrysler, he pulled out the roll of duct tape he'd stashed there. He never traveled anywhere without it.

He wound a gray strip around the plastic phone, doubling the tape back on itself to leave a section of the adhesive free.

He opened the Chrysler's trunk and found the spare tire under the cheap carpet flooring. In the middle of the wheel was what the manufacturer laughably called a toolkit. But it would serve his purposes.

He grabbed the heavy, eight-inch steel jack handle.

The parking lot was relatively quiet. No pedestrians or arriving or departing vehicles in the immediate vicinity. He ambled through the rows of parked cars, the metal bar in his pocket and the duct-taped phone in his hand. He knelt at the rear of Mackie's Crown Vic, fussing over his shoe, pretending to tie his laces.

He slid the jack handle from his pocket and rammed it into the gap between the Crown Vic's trunk and the body. Right by the lock. He levered up and down, leaning forward, his weight grinding the steel jack handle into the gradually expanding gap.

When he had two inches of the handle inside the trunk, he levered downward, pressing the trunk lid out and bending the body inward. The Ford's metal creaked and squealed.

With a half-inch of deflection, the lock no longer reached the retaining striker. The trunk lid began to rise. He had grabbed the lid before the springs lifted it more than a few inches.

He ducked his head down, his arm outstretched, and leaned into the Crown Vic's trunk, slapping the taped burner phone against the rear parcel shelf, near a gap that opened into the body of the cabin. He ran his hand along the tape, fixing the phone to the shelf as tightly as the tape would allow.

He backed out of the trunk, gave the lid a good wrench and pushed it closed. The latch clicked. Not a firm click. He pulled on the lid. It didn't open. He'd just have to hope it didn't spring up with the stresses and strains of Mackie's driving all the way back to Randolph.

If the trunk lid popped open while she was driving, she'd find the burner. He shrugged. He'd handle that problem when and if it arose.

He returned to his rental, dropped heavily into the driver's seat, and clicked the door closed. He'd learned nothing useful inside the hospital. Mackie and Kimball were seeking some sort of records, but which records and, more importantly, why, remained to be discovered.

He smirked. Mackie talked too much. He remembered that from the few encounters he'd had with her over time. Whatever they were doing inside, she'd talk about it in the Crown Vic on the long return trip to Randolph.

As long as his connection stayed open, he'd hear every word. He picked up his cell phone and waited.

CHAPTER THIRTY-FIVE

OSCAR PLATTE CONTINUED SEARCHING through his computer files even as he glanced over his shoulder to be sure Dr. Nepovim wasn't on his way to throw them all out or call security or something worse.

"Dr. Nepovim showed us a computer printout. It listed Peter Whiting's attending physician, Dr. Melise Youree. The labor and delivery nurse's initials were N.F." Jess sensed that Oscar was more than willing to answer questions, but she didn't know what to ask. "So that must have been Norah Fender? What should we know about her, Oscar?"

"You can look her up online. Get more details." He glanced over his shoulder again.

Jess looked toward Nepovim's office. He was seated behind his desk, busy with his own computer keyboard.

"Give me the broad strokes. So I know what to look for." Jess was good at cajoling witnesses.

"Dr. Youree was only here for her residency. She returned to her home country. Somewhere in Asia, I think?" Oscar lowered his voice and glanced over his shoulder again before he continued. "A few years ago, Wollenstone General Hospital caught a nurse selling babies."

"Norah Fender?"

Oscar nodded. "She was arrested and tried and convicted. Served only a couple of years, I think."

"Really? I'd have thought she'd get a tougher sentence." Jess frowned.

"It wasn't like that, I guess." Oscar shook his head and returned his eyes to the screen. "The judge gave her maybe five years. Revoked her nursing license. Some of the jail time was suspended and then she got out early because of good behavior or something."

"Was she selling babies from here at Kid's Own, too?" Charlene's tone was too hard, too cop-like. Oscar shrugged again and returned to his searching.

"I've run across this kind of thing before. Finding homes for unwanted babies is not as sordid as people sometimes think, Charlene." Jess put some sympathy into her tone. She moved closer to Oscar's desk and leaned in as if to engage in confidential conversation. Her heart was pounding wildly, and her legs felt weak. "The birth mother needs the money to get back on her feet. She can't take care of the baby. The families who want to adopt the baby have the financial resources to help out."

Charlene seemed skeptical, but she didn't argue.

"Norah Fender was selling unwanted babies to families who wanted to adopt them." Jess tried to sound sympathetic. "She wasn't a bad person. She was trying to help everyone involved, wasn't she Oscar?"

"Maybe. I didn't know her. That's what I heard." Oscar ducked his head briefly. He pointed to his screen. "But look, I found Peter David Whiting."

"What records do you have there?"

"It's like Nepovim said. The full hospital record is still in hard copy and in storage." Oscar scanned the information on his screen. "His mother was our patient. Barbara Whiting. On the system, we only have scanned and searchable copies of the admission record, a summary of the delivery record, and the birth record."

"Would you be able to print those for us?" Jess asked as if her request wasn't completely outrageous.

Oscar shook his head. "The printer is close to Nepovim's office. If I did that, he'd call security in a hot second."

"We really need to find this boy's parents, Oscar." Jess took a deep breath. "Before it's too late."

Oscar gazed directly at Jess and nodded. "I have to run to the men's room. Watch my desk for me while I'm gone, will you?" He stood and walked out into the corridor.

Jess quickly pulled her phone out of her pocket and moved to an unobstructed view of Oscar's screen. The overhead fluorescent light cast a glare on the monitor. She turned it to the left slightly before she opened the camera on her phone and shot a photo of the screen. She hit the "next" button and shot a photo of the second screen. Again, for the third screen. She slipped the phone back into her pocket.

Charlene stood behind her and read over her shoulder. Jess flipped back to the first screen. A hospital admission form. John and Barbara Whiting's names were typed on the form along with their address on Vashon Island. The bottom of the page was signed in John Whiting's familiar script as the guarantor of the bill.

The second page was the delivery summary, a series of notes about the birth. Attending physician, date and time of birth, hospital room number, length of stay. Norah Fender's name was listed as the attending labor and delivery nurse.

The last page was the birth record. Peter's full name, his weight, length, sex, and other vital information was listed. And prints of his tiny feet.

At the bottom of the birth record were two typed names and above the typewriting, two signatures, John Whiting and Barbara Whiting. The signatures were witnessed by Norah Fender.

Jess had studied Peter's official birth certificate until the image was practically seared on her retinas. She looked hard at the handwriting on the scanned images on Oscar's screen.

John Whiting's signature looked identical to the one on the official birth certificate.

But Barbara Whiting's signature on the hospital record didn't match the official birth certificate. Not even close.

Charlene had seen the discrepancy, too. She gripped Jess's arm. Wrinkles crept across her forehead. Her eyes glistened. Her lips curled down. Her hand shook.

"Charlene?" Jess turned to look at her. "Are you okay?"

But Charlene didn't answer. She dissolved into tears. Great gulping sobs.

Charlene's reaction drew attention. People were starting to look up from their desks. It was only a matter of time before Nepovim would notice and call security.

Jess grabbed Charlene's arm. "Come on. We need to go. Right now."

She led Charlene toward the door and grabbed a box of tissues off one of the desks on the way out. In the corridor, she stuffed the tissue box into Charlene's hand and pushed her toward the elevator. Charlene continued to sob all the way down in the elevator after they reached the lobby and walked outside.

Charlene wiped her nose on another tissue and threw the wad into the trash barrel by the door. She took a few breaths, fighting for control. "Barbara Whiting's signature," she wiped her nose on another tissue, "It's Crystal's handwriting."

Jess bit her lip. She looked at the ground and blinked away the glassy tears that had sprung to her eyes. If Charlene was right about the handwriting, it meant Peter Whiting was not Jess's missing son. She'd never allowed herself to believe this boy was her Peter. Not really. She hoped. Dear God, she'd hoped this boy was her child. She'd allowed herself to think it was possible. That he could be hers. And it could still be true. The DNA wasn't back yet. Charlene could be wrong. This boy could be hers. But the visceral reality had never settled into her heart.

In her dreams, when she found Peter, he was as she'd last seen him, still a toddler. She was outside, in a park. He came running, laughing, brown eyes flashing, a tussle of blonde curls and plump legs and soft roundness, bounding into her arms and hugging her in a fit of sweet giggles. She wasn't prepared to give up that dream.

She wanted to find her son. Desperately. But she wanted him to be alive and healthy. She wanted a joyous reunion. And she would have that. But maybe not this time.

She looked at Charlene. Her tears were real and heartbreaking.

"Are you sure?" Jess said.

Charlene nodded.

"What do you want to do now?"

Charlene shrugged. Tears continued to stream down her

face, but the hard sobs had subsided. "Peter Whiting is my grandson." Her voice was raw and husky.

"It seems likely." The air outside was still cold and the sky still gray. "Come on." They walked to the Crown Vic. She took the car keys from Charlene and placed her in the passenger's seat. Jess settled behind the wheel, started the engine and ran the heater.

She knew what she wanted to do next, but she wasn't sure about Charlene. "When you said your daughter disappeared, exactly what did you mean?"

It seemed to take the question several seconds to sink in. Charlene remained focused on the dashboard in front of her for a while.

"Was there a search for her? There must have been. Anyone open an official investigation?"

"She disappeared. Never came back." Charlene's eyes were wet and her nose a bright red. "We searched every inch of Randolph and the other towns nearby. The previous police chief questioned everyone. Searched all over. He worked very hard trying to find Crystal or at least to figure out what happened to her."

The conversation seemed to be helping Charlene. "Didn't they find anything at all?"

Charlene nodded. "Her car. Two months later. At the Greyhound station in Tacoma." She reached out and gripped Jess's sleeve. "I know you came to Randolph hoping Peter Whiting would be your son." She hung her head down.

Jess took a deep breath. She didn't know exactly what to say. Charlene had traded one set of heartache for another because she believed now that Peter Whiting was her grandson.

Jess patted Charlene's hand. "You recognized Crystal's signature, but there's a lot of open questions here."

Charlene nodded. "I know."

"If you feel up to it, we need to talk to Norah Fender. She can tell us what happened with Crystal. Why and how Crystal gave up her baby." Jess paused. She didn't want to promise too much. "Maybe Norah Fender has some idea about where Crystal went."

Charlene's eyes widened. "Do you think we might be able to find her, even though it's been such a long time?"

"I don't want to get your hopes up. Let's take it one step at a time." Jess sent a message to Mandy, and a few minutes later Mandy replied with Norah Fender's address. Ten miles south in a small town called Castleford. Jess put the address in her phone's GPS and followed directions to I-5 south.

CHAPTER THIRTY-SIX

BLACKSTAKE STARTED HIS ENGINE as the Crown
Victoria backed out of its parking space. He waited for another
car to insert itself between him and his target and followed them
to the freeway.

His trick with the burner phone had worked better than he'd
expected. The rear parcel shelf had made a good surface,
vibrating with the pitch of the voices and amplifying their words.
He'd barely had to turn up the volume on his end to hear the
entire conversation.

Which was the end of the good news.

Something they'd seen at the hospital had proved Peter
Whiting was Crystal Mackie's son. Blackstake couldn't
believe his luck. He'd been looking for that boy for years, and
all the time, he'd been living in Bamford. Thirty miles from
Randolph. The boy who fell out of the tree. The one
Blackstake might have, and probably should have, killed two
days ago.

He sighed. He needed to call the boss, but he couldn't hang up on his burner.

He followed the Ford as his mind raced to figure out how he'd handle all of these problems with the media spotlight glaring brightly every day. Plans for the fundraiser were well underway. Meisner's timing sucked. He'd certainly picked the wrong time to run for President.

CHAPTER THIRTY-SEVEN

CHARLENE REACHED INTO HER pocket and pulled out a snapshot. She looked at the photo for a few moments. "Crystal. Six months before she disappeared."

She handed the picture to Jess.

Crystal looked relaxed and happy. Shoulder length blonde hair glistened in the sunlight. High cheekbones and bright eyes like a runway model. She was leaning against a maple tree. She wore expensive blue jeans and a fitted black T-shirt with a heart-shaped American flag on the front. Centered above the heart, was the letter "I" and below it were two letters, "DC." The message was meant to be read aloud as, "I love DC."

She didn't look even five minutes pregnant.

Jess kept to the speed limit as she drove into Castleford. The welcome sign said the population numbered 8,971, and in her experience of the area, the smaller the town, the more vigilant the traffic cops.

The GPS led her past a couple of strip malls and then into

residential housing. Sidewalks lined the sides of the road, and leaves lined the sidewalks. Broadleaf trees hung over the road. The houses were small two-story affairs, not the McMansions that ringed many larger cities.

The GPS announced they had arrived at their destination. Jess pulled up to the curb. The street was quiet, no barking dogs or kids riding bikes.

The house looked freshly painted. A brass knocker gleamed on the front door. The garden was fading, sticks and twigs remained where summertime flowers had once bloomed. Upstairs and downstairs, the drapes were open. Jess could see inside the rooms. She saw no movement.

"Wait here," she said, turning off the engine.

She walked up to the front door. She had a good view into the tidy living room. Sparse, but in a stylish way, the result of preference, not forced economy.

Jess knocked on the door. The sound reverberated back to her. She looked through the windows and the mottled glass of the front door. She heard no movement inside. No dog barked, and no curious cat strolled into view.

She waited half a minute and knocked again. Louder this time. Gripping the brass knocker firmly, hammering it against the striker. The sound reverberated again. No creaking floor boards or moving shadows.

She waited a full minute before returning to the car.

She sat in the driver's seat and closed the door with a thump.

Charlene stared at her. "What now?"

"No one is ever waiting at home anymore. We'll come back later."

She started the car, drove back to the strip mall, and parked in front of a local donut shop. "We'll give her an hour, and try again."

CHAPTER THIRTY-EIGHT

BLACKSTAKE FOLLOWED THE CROWN Vic all the way to a residential neighborhood.

He saw the Ford stop on the right-hand side of the road. Through his phone's speaker, he heard the reporter tell Charlene to stay in the car. He needed to get closer without being seen. He looped around the next street and stopped at the far end of Dominion.

Kimball stood at the front door of a house that looked freshly painted. After a couple of minutes, Kimball returned to the Ford. She told Mackie they'd come back in an hour to see Norah Fender as they drove away.

He ducked as the Crown Vic passed by.

His blood ran cold. Norah Fender was a name that he remembered. For years, she had made a good living working with lawyers to organize private adoptions for unwanted babies. She'd done some freelancing, too. Where biological or adoptive parents required an illegal deal for whatever reasons, she did more than organize. She'd made a much more significant profit on those outright sales.

She'd been in the news, but despite a big scandal with national media attention, she'd faded fast from the public eye when she went to prison. She was released after a few years and dropped out of sight.

Norah Fender was a good explanation for a lot of things. Crystal Mackie had been pregnant at one point. The last time he saw Crystal, she'd delivered the baby.

That was fourteen years ago. He'd spent a lot of time and resources to find that infant. He'd failed. He didn't fail often, and the failure still rankled. Now he had a second chance to contain the situation.

Mackie and Kimball might spark renewed interest in a frigid cold case. A case he intended to keep cold.

He hung up his phone.

From where he was parked he could make out the house number stenciled on the curbstone. Twenty-four seventy-six.

He ran a few searches on Norah Fender and a string of predictable articles scrolled by. Had she been involved with the Mackie tramp? Had she sold the Mackie baby? Or had she, as was another rumor, aborted that child? Was that what Kimball was digging into now? A possibility. Also a risk. He didn't like risks.

He stared at the house. When they found out Crystal Mackie was no longer pregnant, he had spent weeks searching public records, trawling hospitals, and talking to doctors. He'd tracked down every associate she knew. He'd watched her white trash mother for weeks, in case she returned. Despite his efforts, he'd never learned what happened to Crystal Mackie's baby. Any open question was a serious threat.

He should have trusted his instincts. He knew from the moment he first saw Kimball that she'd be trouble. He should have dealt with her at the first opportunity. Now, making her disappear would be more difficult, and bring far too much police attention. He swore. He liked a challenge, but he hated risk.

He looked back at the Fender house. He unclenched his teeth. The faintest sliver of a smile crossed his lips. He might not be beaten after all. A woman in a fawn coat was opening the front door. A woman he recognized. Older, sure. But he recognized her all the same.

Norah Fender returning home.

CHAPTER THIRTY-NINE

JESS'S SEARCH FOR COFFEE was unsuccessful because the doughnut shop was closed. She had finally relented and bought a weak concoction at a drive-through burger joint. One mouthful told her all she needed to know about it. The cooling brew temporarily occupied the cup holder between the front seats when she pulled back into Dominion Street.

She parked a few doors down from Norah Fender's house. The street was strangely silent, but she saw a sliver of light around the edges of a curtain.

Jess patted her bag. Her Glock was still there. Charlene leaned to her side and slid her holster into view. Jess hadn't seen it before.

Charlene popped the cover and tapped the grip.

Jess recognized the grip's dimpled surface.

"Charlene." She licked her lips. "How about I go and meet with her? She's not going to want to talk to us, and—"

"You think I might shoot her? I just might." Charlene said. "She deserves killing. After all she's put me through."

Jess raised her eyebrows. "You've had a shock. I know you want to find out about—"

"You *think* you know. Do you know I spent years crying myself to sleep cradling a photograph of my daughter? Or that I spent every penny I had on private investigators? Or that I keep every scrap of paper my daughter ever wrote on just to keep her memory alive in my heart?" Charlene's tirade had left her temporarily breathless. She inhaled. Coldly calm, teeth clamped hard together, she said, "You don't know any of that. You have no idea."

Of course, Jess knew how a mother felt when her child went missing. She wanted to push back. Fight against Charlene's thoughtless accusations. But she didn't.

She'd been accused before. By other mothers. Other fathers. Other cases. Losing a child means losing a parent's normal sanity. She understood.

When she'd chosen this work, finding justice for victims like Charlene instead of burying her own grief, she'd donned the tarnished armor necessary to withstand the blows. Some cases were harder than others, but keeping her name and her search for Peter in the public eye could mean she'd find him one day.

Someone knew what had happened to her Peter. A conscientious citizen might come forward. She forced herself to remain tough every day. She stayed as hard on the outside as she could possibly be. It was the only way she could continue her mission, which she would never give up. Not until she found her son.

"I know you want answers, Charlene. You're entitled to them. But you have no jurisdiction here." She took a deep breath and let it out slowly, but her tone was firm. "Let me do my job. We need to find out what happened. To your daughter and to her baby. I've done this before. Let me help you. Let me talk to her first. Whatever happened at that hospital fourteen years ago is too important to go in there, guns blazing, threatening Norah Fender, and losing this chance to get the truth."

Charlene glared a moment longer before her tears began to fall again and she lowered her head. She moved her hand away from her weapon.

"You're a cop. Don't let this take away your livelihood along with everything else you've already lost. You know justice doesn't eliminate the pain or turn back the clock." Jess nodded and exhaled slowly. "But it does bring some measure of closure. That's the best justice can do. The best I can do. The best you can do." Jess put her hand on Charlene's arm. "I promise you I'll do everything in my power to see justice is served here."

Charlene swallowed, her teeth clenched, the veins on her neck bulging.

Jess didn't say anything about Charlene's grandson. That situation might not turn out well, either. Reminding her of the boy now could set her off again.

"People will say things to a reporter that they would never say to a police officer. You know that." She offered a sympathetic smile. "We need Fender to talk. We need her to relax. We need her to run her mouth."

Charlene breathed deep. She nodded. Slowly at first. She licked her lips. "I just want to know. My daughter, and…"

"I understand." Jess patted Charlene's hand, opened the door, grabbed her bag, and slipped out of the car before Charlene changed her mind. "Wait here. I'll be back."

The light was fading as Jess walked up to Norah Fender's

front door. The upstairs windows were dark, but the warm yellow of an incandescent light escaped around a heavy drape in the front room. The house looked freshly painted.

She noticed a gleaming brass doorbell this time. When she pressed it, chimes rang out, too deep and sonorously old-fashioned for this modern house. The sound echoed through the walls.

She checked up and down the street. Charlene's Crown Vic hadn't moved. A delivery truck barreled down the street, veering around a parked car and shaking tree limbs in its wake.

Jess turned back to the door. Despite the distortions in the glass, she saw no changes inside the house. No doors had been opened, no additional lights switched on.

She counted to ten and rang the bell again. The same sound reverberated through the house. The same stillness followed.

No surprise that Norah Fender didn't answer her door to strangers. She'd probably been hounded by every reporter, anxious parent, and crazy crank in the state. Not that she didn't deserve such treatment. The truth behind her motives would probably never come out, but lining her own pockets was no doubt a big part of her reasoning. Selling babies was a lucrative business.

Jess looked into the house through the glass again. Something inside was different. Nora Fender must have come home.

She'd come this close. She wouldn't leave until she got some answers.

CHAPTER FORTY

WHEN NORAH DIDN'T ANSWER the front doorbell, Jess followed a well-worn path around the side of the house. A six-foot stockade fence blocked the entrance to the back yard. She tried the latch, and the gate swung open.

The stockade fence ran around the perimeter of the back yard. There was no other way in or out. She closed the gate with a distinct push. She wanted Norah Fender to know she was there. Invading a private home in a country with a high level of gun ownership wasn't a wise course of action. Intruders had been shot for less. Legally so. Jess had no problem with that. She was a gun owner herself.

The back entrance was covered with a storm door. The hinges squealed as she drew it back. Another good way to announce her presence. The top half of the rear entrance door was clear glass. She could see into the kitchen. Steam billowed from two large saucepans on a gas stovetop. One looked to be boiling over.

The kitchen surfaces were polished and uncluttered. There were no dishes on the draining board. A single note she couldn't read from this distance was held to the fridge door by a magnet.

Jess clenched her fist and rapped hard on the glass with her knuckles. Three hard impacts, evenly spaced, glass rattling. Unmistakable.

Jess waited, holding the spring loaded storm door back with her heel.

No one appeared. Steam continued to billow from the saucepans. Sauce oozed over the top of one.

She put her hand on the door handle. Miller's cautionary words ran through her mind. An armed home invasion would definitely be one of the things *Taboo's* lawyer would disapprove of. Most judges would, too.

The clear sauce turned brown. Black smoke wafted into the air. She hammered on the door. The glass shook. The door rattled in its frame. The kitchen door remained closed.

The sticky mass bubbling from the saucepan caught fire. Yellow and blue flames flickered and danced.

The situation had become what lawyers call "exigent circumstances." Enough to justify breaking and entering. She hoped. Regardless of the legal outcome, this was one of those times when she should seek forgiveness instead of permission.

She rocked her weight back and forth on the door handle. The old wood creaked. Black soot spiraled from the burning sauce forming a black stain on the ceiling.

Jess swung her hip at the door, close to the lock. The wood protested.

She repeated the action. Harder. All her weight. Leaning inward.

The wood gave way. Crashing and splintering.

The door sailed back in an arc, crashing into a metal trashcan standing at the end of the row of cabinets. She fell sideways, stumbling inside, off balance but upright.

She caught a whiff of sweetness under the burning smell.

Jess stopped to listen. The house remained silent. She might have believed Norah Fender had gone out and left the light on to fool intruders. But no one leaves home with two saucepans cooking on the stove.

She ran to the range and turned off the gas burners. She grabbed a kitchen towel off the rack, doused it with water, and threw it over the flaming saucepan. It crackled and spat. She found another towel, soaked it, and threw it on top of the first.

Black smoke billowed out in suffocating clouds.

She held her hand over her nose and mouth and breathed as infrequently as possible while she threw cups of water over the cloths until the flames finally spluttered out.

She waved her hands, making an effort to disperse the smoke.

Jess pulled her Glock from her bag, placed the bag on the counter, and readied her weapon.

"Norah?" she called out, loud enough to be heard throughout the house. "I'm Jess Kimball. I let myself in because I saw your cooking catch fire."

She stood and listened. The refrigerator whirred, and air breezed from the ventilation ducts, but she heard no voices nor creaking of floorboards or anything else to indicate where Norah was inside the house.

Norah Fender wasn't a young woman. Maybe she'd had a stroke or a heart attack or something. She could be incapacitated somewhere.

Or she could be hiding from an intruder with a loaded gun, prepared to shoot.

Jess moved carefully into the hallway. One door on the right and two on the left. Stairs led upward on the right.

She stood to one side of the first door on the left and knocked. No response.

She pushed the door open with her foot. An overhead light illuminated the room. A reading light on a side table, beside a paisley print armchair. A book lay on the chair's arm, upturned so the reader didn't lose her place. A sofa faced the armchair, decorated in the same paisley fabric.

She saw that the second door from the hallway led into the same room. Someone must have knocked down a dividing wall to enlarge the living room at some stage in the home's history.

Jess backed out of the living room. She moved carefully down to the door on the right and pushed it open. This one accessed a dining room. The table was bare. A cabinet displayed a collection of bone china plates adorned with birds.

Jess looked along the corridor. Kitchen, living, and dining room.

She looked up the stairs. Fender couldn't be gone. Not with the stove on and food cooking. She'd been a nurse. Surely, she was more careful.

Jess looked down the corridor to the rear door. She couldn't walk out. She'd searched half the place. If Fender had collapsed for some reason, she'd need immediate medical attention. Charlene would want to know every possibility had been checked.

She'd take a quick look and then call 911.

Jess put her foot on the first step. It creaked. She walked up, keeping close to the wall to reduce the creaking noises.

The landing was small, with three rooms leading off to each side. Two bedrooms and a bathroom, Jess guessed.

She opened the first door. The bed had been used, but the table surfaces were clear. No makeup or perfumes. No pictures, no keys, no phone.

No Norah Fender.

She looked out the window. No traffic on the street and no one walking past. The Crown Vic hadn't moved. Charlene would be getting antsy.

Jess opened the closet. The clothes were bunched at one end of the rail. Odd. She moved them, but there was nothing behind. Three pairs of shoes were neatly arranged on a rack. A space for a fourth was unoccupied. Jess closed the closet.

While she was here, she worked her way through a cabinet. Like the closet, the contents were pressed against one end of the drawers. Decidedly odd. She returned the drawers to their original positions.

The second door on the landing was a bedroom, unused. She glanced around inside the closet, which was empty.

She walked back to the landing to check the last door, presumably the bathroom. The handle turned easily. The door swung inward. Weak light entered through a long, thin frosted window. She glimpsed white tiles and flipped the light switch.

She jolted backward at the sight.

Legs sprawled out of the tub. A woman's body. The ankles bound.

Jess spun around, training the Glock along the landing and down the stairs and back to the bathroom. She stepped forward, into the bathroom.

A man's gloved hand shot out from behind the door, grabbed her wrist, and pointed the gun down.

She wrenched her arm back.

The big hand gripped harder and pulled her forward, smacking her face into the corner of the door.

Pain ran up her nose and across her forehead. Stars twinkled in her vision.

She twisted her hand, struggling to break free.

The gloved hand repeated its maneuver, shoving her back and forward, slamming her face into the corner of the door. The door creaked with the impact. More stars and twinkling lights danced before her with glee.

Adrenaline flooded her system. She was alive, alert, running on pure fear. If she stopped fighting, if she gave up, she would die. She knew it.

She tried to curl up her hand, twisting the gun in the man's direction behind the door. A second hand joined the cold iron grip of the first. It twisted the gun downward. The first hand wrapped around her trigger finger.

"Help!"

The man's shoulder banged against the door, pounding it into her body. Searing pain shot through her nose. Her lips were wet with the metallic tang of blood.

The gloved hands squeezed. Crushing her fingers. Curling them around the Glock's trigger.

She pushed back.

He had the advantage. Overwhelmingly.

The Glock fired. A single shot. Loud. Stunning in the small, tiled space. She wouldn't let go.

The gloved hands levered her fingers back and forth until the Glock boomed again. The gun shook in her hands.

The world went silent except for a distant whistle. She shouted, but heard nothing.

She had no choice. Offense was her only defense. She threw herself forward into the bathroom, twisting the gun in the direction of the space behind the door.

She glimpsed a long black coat. One of the gloved hands let go and curled into a fist. She leaned left, but the fist stabbed toward her, slamming into her shoulder. She barely felt the impact as her body jolted back. The bathroom spun around her. Blacks and grays swirled. Diffuse blooms of color mixed with pinpricks of the brightest light.

She stumbled. Her knees gave out. She fell forward, trapping one arm under her.

She was on the edge of darkness. Trapped in her silent world. Warmth welled up to meet her, to scoop her up in its arms. She welcomed its embrace.

The man swept past her.

More sensation than sight. She waved her gun upward, but he was gone.

She rolled onto her knees and curled over, her head close to the floor. She felt thumping. Footsteps a long way off. The staircase.

She forced her head up with a grunt. The room spun. The sink and shower curtain spun wildly around her. The tub curled into the air, the lifeless legs flashing by. She braced herself with both hands on the ground, willing the world to still itself.

The distant, muffled footsteps reached the end of the stairs.

She took a deep breath. Her brain vibrated in her skull. Her nose throbbed. She grabbed the door handle and levered herself up.

She stumbled for the stairs. Muffled sounds as wood crashed and glass rattled. The backdoor. She grabbed the handrail and stumbled down the stairs. Her knees trembled as if they could give out at any moment. Adrenaline and determination kept her going.

She kept her eyes down. Focusing on the carpet. Directing her feet. Watching for the end of the steps. Twinkling lights continued to dance in her vision. All of them blinding white. She twisted her head to one side to reduce the ache in her left shoulder and keep the blinding light from spearing pain in her skull.

She turned one hundred eighty degrees at the bottom of the stairs. He'd run out the back door. To the back yard. With the tall fences. She tightened her grip on the Glock. He'd be trapped.

No. That's not right.

She shook her head, and the pain and lights sparkled again.

The only way out led to the front of the house, toward the street.

She'd get ahead of him.

She staggered to the front door, grabbed the lock, and twisted it open.

The door was heavy. It swung inward, pushing her back.

She clung to the handle to keep upright. The door slammed against the wall. The security chain whipped around and slapped the backs of her hands.

She stepped out. Two doors down, a man in a black coat was hurrying away.

Jess lifted her Glock. "Stop!" she screamed, but she barely heard her own voice.

The man ducked into a white car.

She squinted, trying to focus. The car's engine roared, and the tires squealed. She staggered to the middle of the front lawn.

Her stomach heaved.

The man and the white car raced by.

She held her gun out, fighting to level her aim on the moving target.

She lowered her weapon. She couldn't fire. Not wildly. Not in a neighborhood where bystanders could be hit.

Her sight line followed the Chrysler.

Charlene. In the street.

Charlene stood by the Crown Vic, her gun in her outstretched arms, pointing at the fast approaching white Chrysler.

The car fishtailed around her, the rear end striking a fence before roaring off down the street.

Charlene came running to Jess. "What happened? You all right?"

Jess lowered her Glock, and sank to her knees. The taste of blood filled her mouth.

Charlene knelt beside her. "You okay?"

Jess looked up. "Call 911. We need an ambulance."

Charlene pulled out her cell. "Have you been shot?"

Jess rolled backward, twisting her legs underneath her, slumping onto the ground. Shot? The world danced around her.

Charlene dialed 911 and held the phone to her ear with her shoulder while she patted Jess down. "Have you been shot?"

Jess rolled her head from side to side and clamped her teeth together to hold back nausea. "No. Face. Shoulder. Punched."

Charlene ran her hand over Jess's forehead. "That man?"

"Yeah."

"I heard gunshots."

Jess gripped Charlene's arm and pulled herself to an upright seated position. "There's a body. In the bathtub. Upstairs."

Charlene spoke into her phone. She gave her name and the street address, and she reported a shooting with injuries.

Jess grabbed Charlene's hand and struggled to her feet. Her balance rocked, and her shoulder ached, and her head felt as if her neck had turned into a spring. She wiped the back of her hand under her chin. It came away bloody.

But she was alive. She'd be fine. Sore. Bruised. But fine.

Sirens sounded in the distance.

Jess labored her way to the front door. "We have to check. She could be alive."

Charlene took Jess by the arm and steered her inside the house. Jess grabbed a handful of tissues from a box on a table in the hallway and patted them around her nose and mouth. The sight of giant blots of blood surprised her. The door had mashed her face, but the adrenaline had been an anesthetic.

Jess put a foot on the first step. Her knee trembled.

Charlene renewed her grip on Jess's arm. "You going to make it?"

Jess grabbed the banister and lurched up the stairs.

The bathroom door was half open, the bathtub visible, the legs where she'd first seen them.

The chemical residue of gunfire was pungent in the air. Jess pushed the door open with her cuff. Her prints were already all over the house, but she didn't need to make things worse.

But things were already much worse.

She sagged backward.

The body in the tub was female. The head was wedged between the taps at a right angle to the rest of the body. Her legs were too long for the bathtub and draped over the side. One arm was tucked under her, the other wrapped over her head. Long hair was matted and stuck to her face with dried blood.

Large blooms marred her floral dress. Ruby red. Blood on pastel.

Jess's breath escaped her. She swallowed hard. "Gunshot wounds," she muttered.

Charlene stared. Her eyes rigidly fixed on the body. "Fender?"

"It's her house."

Charlene stared.

Jess shook Charlene's arm. "You okay?"

Charlene didn't move. Jess shook her arm again. Charlene turned and hurried from the room.

Jess looked back at the bathtub. Her shock was wearing off, and welcome clarity was slowly returning to her mind.

Her attacker had twisted her hand until her gun pointed at the body and fired. He'd left her with the Glock. She had run into the street brandishing it like a mad woman. Witnesses were likely. Simple forensic tests would establish her gun had shot Norah Fender and Jess had been holding it at the time.

Jess's hearing was coming back, too. She heard the wail of sirens and the screeching of tires out front as if from a great distance. And an almost constant ringing in her ears.

She put her hand on the wall for balance, and wobbled down the stairs to the front door. She laid her Glock on the table and walked outside.

CHAPTER FORTY-ONE

A TRIO OF POLICE cars pulled onto the street. They split, two parking in front of Fender's house, the other on the far side of the road. Jess walked toward the pair of cars, and the officers jumped out, drawing their weapons.

Jess held her hands up by her shoulders. "I'm Jessica Kimball. I found the body."

Three of the men entered the house, the other approached Jess. His name tag said Gonzalez. "You made the call?"

She shook her head. "Officer Charlene Mackie did. There's a body in the bathtub. Upstairs. I was attacked—"

An ambulance arrived. Its siren warbled into silence. A man and a woman jumped out and ran for the house, large medical bags in their hands.

Jess shook her head. "She's gone."

"We'll see," said the female medic, and they bustled past into the house.

"There was a man…"

"Is he still inside?" Gonzalez asked, hand on his radio.

She shook her head again. "No. He ran out. Drove away." She pointed in the direction the Chrysler had gone.

"Okay. Take it easy. We'll find him." Gonzalez placed a steadying hand on her right bicep. "Let's get you some medical attention. And you can tell me all about it."

"My bag is in the kitchen. My ID's in there." Even with her injuries, she recognized the problems. And she knew she wasn't thinking straight. She could have a concussion. Or worse.

"Okay. We'll get it." Gonzalez sent a man to fetch the bag. He waved one of the paramedics over. "Go with him. He'll take a look at you. Stay there while we sort this out. Then we can talk."

The paramedic led Jess to the ambulance and helped her climb inside. She sat on a gurney. The paramedic cleaned the blood off her face and shined a penlight into her eyes. Jess winced and reflexively squeezed her eyes shut until he moved the light away. The paramedic made a note.

"Did you lose consciousness at any time?"

"No." A loss of consciousness wasn't necessary for a concussion diagnosis.

"Dizziness? Visual problems?"

"A little dizziness. Vision seems to be okay now. No vomiting." The fewer symptoms of concussion she exhibited, the better. She didn't want to be admitted to a hospital in Oregon today.

"How about confusion or amnesia?" The paramedic seemed to be reading from a list and looking for items to check off.

"I'm very clear on what happened back there. No confusion at all."

"Headache?"

"Not yet. Unless you count the throbbing from where he slammed my face into the door."

The paramedic nodded and wrote that down, too. "You were in an enclosed space where two gunshots were fired. How's your hearing? Any ringing in your ears?"

"Some. It'll get better."

"If you're lucky. The damage can be permanent. You should be tested." The paramedic made a few more notes and cleaned the rest of the blood off Jess's face. He prodded her sore nose, feeling both sides, checking for fractures.

He put two butterfly bandages across the bridge of her nose and handed her an ice pack. "Hold this on your forehead and nose for a few minutes. Then take a break and hold it there a few minutes more. Let's try to keep the bruising and swelling down."

Jess did as she was told.

"You'll need X-rays. Probably an MRI, too." He made a few more notes. After a while, he left her alone. He took a medical bag and walked over to check on Charlene.

She was seated inside the Crown Vic talking to Gonzalez. Jess pulled out her phone. She was halfway through dialing her editor when she hung up and dialed Nelson.

He answered the phone himself, which was a little surprising. "Randolph Police."

"Jessica Kimball. We're in Castleford. South of Portland."

"Who is 'we'?" He didn't give any hint that he'd heard from Gonzalez.

"We have a problem here." She took a deep breath, ignoring his question.

"What kind of problem?"

"We went to Kid's Own Medical Center. Turns out one of

their nurses was charged with selling babies. She was convicted. Served some time."

"You're not making a lot of sense here, Jess," Nelson said. "You think all of this is relevant to Peter Whiting?"

"The nurse's name was Norah Fender. She signed Peter Whiting's original birth record. She was the labor and delivery nurse."

"I see," he said again, although he didn't seem to understand. "And you think that since Barbara Whiting can't be Peter's biological mother, this Norah Fender arranged a private adoption?"

"Maybe that. Or maybe an outright sale."

"You still think that Peter Whiting might be your son?" He paused as if to think through the implications.

"We're at Norah Fender's house." Jess took a deep breath. "There's a body in the bathtub. We think it's her."

"You've called the police."

"Yeah. They're here now."

"Natural causes?"

"No." Jess bit her lip. "What do you know about Charlene's daughter, Crystal?"

Nelson skipped a beat. "She went missing before my time. There was an investigation. I read up on it when I arrived. A lot of rumor and speculation, but no results."

"Rumor and speculation about what?"

He sighed. "Charlene's not an easy woman. Some folks say it's no surprise that Crystal ran away and never came back."

"People don't just disappear into thin air." Jess pressed the ice pack over her eyes to stop the twinkling lights. "Charlene told me Crystal was pregnant."

Nelson took a deep breath. "Why is this important right now?"

"Because Charlene thinks it's her daughter's handwriting on Peter Whiting's original delivery record. Charlene thinks Peter Whiting is Crystal's baby."

"I, uh, see." He paused almost a full second. "Crystal was pregnant around the time she went missing, but the last witness to see her wasn't sure whether she'd given birth. But if she did, I'd be amazed if that wasn't discovered at the time. Portland isn't that far from Randolph, and it's one of the biggest cities within driving distance. Someone would have checked hospitals there. People looked for her for quite a while. Her name was all over the local news."

"The birth mother checked into Kid's Own using Barbara Whiting's name. But Charlene says it's Crystal's handwriting on the delivery record."

"How do you know what Charlene says about that?"

Jess blinked. Maybe she wasn't making herself clear enough. "Charlene's here with me."

"You took her along?"

"I didn't. You sent her."

Nelson uh-huh'd. "I didn't send her anywhere. She went home sick this morning. Haven't heard from her since."

"Well, she's here."

"Let me give a word of warning, Jess. Crystal's disappearance has played on Charlene's nerves for all these years. She's wound pretty tight. Just be careful you don't set her off."

CHAPTER FORTY-TWO

JESS WATCHED THE PARAMEDIC head toward the house and another officer approach Charlene in the Crown Vic. They talked for a few moments and then Charlene got out. The officer took her gun.

Their discussion continued, but Jess's concentration was broken by Captain Gonzalez's approach. "That your gun in there? On the table in the hall?"

"Yes."

Gonzalez nodded. "We'll have to take it, but if everything checks out, you'll get it back."

She'd expected as much. She nodded.

A large white truck arrived and parked behind the ambulance. A crime scene investigation unit. From Portland, not Castleford. Gonzalez looked at it and back at Jess. "We'll need your elimination prints, too."

She nodded again. "My prints are on file lots of places."

"It'll be quicker if you give us an elimination set. Any problem with that?"

"No."

"We found your bag. We'll catalog it and then you can have it back, too."

"Did you find my ID?"

"Journalist with *Taboo Magazine*, but they tell me you're on the side of the victims, not looking to make victims out of the criminals. That true?"

"Absolutely."

"FBI database says you're licensed for concealed carry in Colorado, but not here in Oregon." He gave her a stern look but didn't say he planned to arrest her for unlawful possession of the gun. "No outstanding warrants. Quite a few arrests in several states. Charges usually dismissed. No convictions. Most recent arrest two days ago in Randolph, Washington. I've got a call into Randolph PD."

"Captain Nelson. I talked to him a few minutes ago." She pointed toward Charlene in the Crown Vic. "Officer Mackie is one of his."

Gonzalez cocked his head. "What are you doing here?"

"I came to interview Norah Fender." She nodded to the house.

"Can you give us a positive ID? Was that her in the bathtub?"

Jess shrugged. "I've never seen her before, but that makes sense."

"Why'd you want to talk to her?"

"Her name came up in a case I'm investigating. About selling babies."

"We checked her prior criminal history." He seemed

satisfied with her answers. "So tell me what happened here."

"There was a man standing behind the bathroom door. Very strong." She took a deep breath. "He twisted my gun to point at Norah Fender, and pushed my finger against the trigger."

Gonzalez nodded. "Who let you in the house?"

She paused.

"Anyone invite you in?"

"The lights were on. A saucepan on the stove was on fire. I was concerned that the fire might take down the whole house." She swiped a hand through her curls. "Where I come from, lawyers call that exigent circumstances. It's as good as an invitation."

"Yeah, for cops and first responders. Not for civilians." Gonzalez glanced back at the house. An officer by the front door made hand signals.

She looked at Gonzalez. He had big brown eyes, a buzz cut, and a square jaw. He didn't look like the sort of person who worked in anything but facts.

"The case I'm working on?" Jess pointed at Charlene again. "The disappearance of her daughter and her grandson."

Gonzalez's eyes locked on hers. "Sounds like a police matter."

"It was." Jess nodded. "Crystal Mackie disappeared more than a decade ago."

He grunted. "You think you have a new lead, you hand it over to the police. That's our job."

"We didn't know we had a lead until we got here."

He looked over at the officer talking to Charlene. "Stay here. I'll be back."

Gonzalez and Charlene talked for a while. Charlene gazed down. She nodded from time to time. Jess was too far away to hear the conversation.

Three crime scene technicians in white overalls exited the truck. They carried bulky cases of equipment into the house.

Jess was sore, and a dull ache had settled in the front of her head, but she was fine. Fit enough. She wasn't under arrest. She could move.

She'd known entering the house was dangerous. She'd done it anyway. The only thing she'd accomplished was stopping the fire before it got out of hand.

She lifted the ice pack to her face again. It was cold and damp, and it felt good against her bruises. Gonzalez was right. If she'd phoned the police instead of going inside, the house would have sustained more damage, Norah Fender would still be dead, and her killer might still be in the wind. But Jess would have been a lot better off right now.

She closed her eyes. The woman had been in the tub when she'd opened the bathroom door. It might be hard to prove Jess hadn't shoved Norah into the bathtub first and then shot her.

Jess hadn't been arrested, but she probably should have called Miller already. He'd be reading her the riot act when he found out about all of this. Too much cooperation could produce evidence that ended up being used against her. She knew that, too. But she wanted to get out of here, and the only way that was going to happen was if Gonzalez agreed. Stonewalling definitely wouldn't produce the desired result.

As if he'd read her thoughts, one of the white-coated crime scene techs came out of the house and asked to swab her hands for gun powder residue. Jess held out her palms. Gonzalez watched from the Crown Vic.

The tech took two samples from each hand. Different types of swabs with various pungent chemical odors.

"Better chance of positive detection," he said. The tech left, and she saw Gonzalez walk toward the house again.

Jess lifted her head. She'd done the right thing. In fact, if she'd been a few moments earlier, Norah Fender might still be alive.

She drew in a sharp breath. She felt like slapping a palm to her head, but she had been slapped around enough today. In fact, her brain must have been bruised or something. Otherwise, she'd certainly have recognized the improbable coincidence a lot sooner.

Just exactly how did she manage to arrive at exactly the same time that man decided to kill Norah Fender? She could think of only one answer.

CHAPTER FORTY-THREE

A GRAY-HAIRED WOMAN wearing a white coat approached the ambulance. She was tall and rail thin, emaciated almost. Her face and neck had no hint of fat. Gonzalez was with her. His square jaw set. His gaze trained on Jess.

"I'm Doctor Edna Alison," the woman said. "And you're Jess Kimball?"

Jess nodded.

"You found the body, right?"

"Yes."

Alison nodded toward the house. "There were two close-range gunshots. Both went into the body, through the plastic bathtub, and into the floor. We haven't found either bullet yet."

Jess nodded, listening carefully.

"Which means she was already in the tub at the time she was shot. The first shot didn't kill her. It hit her in the abdomen. Second shot was to the chest. Each entry wound, exit wound, and bathtub hole lines up. Which means she didn't move between or after the two gunshots."

Jess looked at Alison. "That seems extremely unlikely. Somebody's shooting at me, I'm scrambling to get out of the way."

The woman held out clenched fists. "Grip me."

Jess didn't move.

Alison smiled. "It's not a trick."

Jess looked from Alison's fists back to her face and nodded. She reached out with both hands, wrapped them around Alison's fists and squeezed.

"Harder," Alison said.

Jess squeezed harder. She could feel the bones in Alison's hands clicking over one another to absorb the force. Alison uncurled her fingers, enlarging her fists. Jess squeezed harder trying to crush the doctor's hands back into a clenched fist.

The doctor smiled. "Enough."

Jess let go. The woman was strong. Far stronger than her fragile appearance implied.

Jess shrugged, questioningly.

"Thank you." Alison and Gonzalez turned and walked back into the house, heads bent together.

Jess pulled out her phone. She dialed her editor.

"Carter Pierce, here." His warm tone exuded confidence, as always.

"Carter, I'm afraid I need help again."

"Why is it that I only hear from you when you're in trouble?"

Her mind searched for a witty rejoinder, but her heart wasn't in it. "I found a nurse who was selling babies, but a man overpowered me and used my gun to shoot her. Now it seems I'm suspected of murder."

"That's a bit more interesting than arson now, isn't it?" She heard the cap on Carter's Mont Blanc pen click. "You think this is all somehow connected with Peter, right?"

Jess closed her eyes and sighed. "A boy named Peter, yes. But it looks like he's not my son."

She heard the pen land on Carter's mahogany desk as he laid it down. Followed by a long silence before he exhaled. "Are you sure?"

"Believe me, no one is more upset by that reality than I am."

"Yes, of course." He sighed. "I'm sorry, Jess. I really thought you might be onto something this time."

"I did, too." Jess squeezed her eyes shut and swallowed hard.

Carter remained quiet for several moments. "Tell me what you need, Jess."

She looked over at the Crown Vic where Charlene remained seated with one of Gonzalez's team leaning on the door. She needed to find out what had happened to Crystal Mackie. She needed to find out if Peter Whiting was Charlene's grandson. She needed to get back to work, back to looking for her own Peter.

She took a deep breath. She wasn't going to find the answer to her son's disappearance here, but she was going to do everything she could to find out about Charlene's daughter.

And she wasn't going to do that by sitting here.

"I need Miller."

"No problem." The warm tones of Carter's voice took on a new quality. Satisfaction. "Thought he might come in handy. I had him camp out in Seattle. I'll call him now."

CHAPTER FORTY-FOUR

JESS WAITED WHILE THE crime scene techs walked boxes in and out of the house. Gonzalez returned to his squad car and sat in the driver's seat. She couldn't see what he was doing there. After a few minutes, he came over to talk with her again.

"You've been in touch with your legal people? Miller, right?"

Jess nodded.

"He's been making phone calls all over."

She said nothing.

"I have a dead body and a suspect that admits shooting her. That's a tricky legal position for Miller, I guess." He cocked his head. "Me? I'm a cop. I don't deal with legal positions. I collect facts and make logical deductions and find the killer. Let the lawyers sort things out after I'm done."

Jess did not reply, but she sensed a different vibe coming from him now and she didn't know what that meant.

"I've got probable cause to hold you. At least until we've got more facts." He reached out a hand to help her down from the back of the ambulance. They walked toward his cruiser. "So I could take you down to the station. But I don't really believe you killed Norah Fender. And Dr. Alison doesn't think so, either."

She looked at the house. The front door was half open. She wanted to know what was going on inside. "We both want the facts, don't we?"

"We do," Gonzalez said.

Jess believed Miller would figure out a way to get her out of jail if she went back to the station with Gonzalez. But she couldn't wait the hours or days it would take him to accomplish the feat. She'd waited too long already.

"Let's go inside. Maybe we can help each other out," Jess said.

"You'll lead us through what happened? Complete blow-by-blow. Word for word."

"And you'll answer my questions. Sounds like a plan." She looked over at Charlene.

"We've got too many people in there already." Gonzalez shook his head. "Just you for now. We'll get her take on things later."

Jess could feel Charlene's eyes boring into her back as they walked into the house.

CHAPTER FORTY-FIVE

JESS FOLLOWED GONZALEZ TO the front door of the house. He handed her a pair of booties to slip over her shoes and a pair of latex gloves from his pockets.

When they walked inside, she noticed that her Glock was no longer resting on the hall table. Its outline was marked with fingerprint dusting powder.

"Don't touch anything," Gonzalez said. "We're still processing."

Jess nodded. "I put my gun there just before I walked out."

"Let's start in the kitchen." Gonzalez led the way.

Doctor Edna Alison was in the kitchen, examining the splintered wood around the backdoor lock with an eye loupe.

Jess stepped closer to the back door. "It opened pretty easily."

Gonzalez replied, "The chains on both the front and the back doors were cheap. Easily broken."

Jess turned to the stove. The burnt saucepan and scorched

towels were exactly where she remembered placing them. Black soot stained the ceiling. "There was a good risk of a bigger fire."

Jess could hear Miller's voice in her head, chiding her for talking before he'd arrived. She shoved the voice away.

"Show us how you broke the door," Alison said.

Jess motioned bumping it with her hip. Alison glanced at Gonzalez and nodded. "That's consistent with the damage."

"So you're inside. What then?" Gonzalez said.

"I called out to Norah Fender. There was no answer. No creaking floors. No radio or television." She pointed to the stove. "I threw a wet towel over the flames and shut off the gas."

Alison pointed to the controls. "What was the setting?"

"High." Jess looked at the black mass that had boiled over and was now welded to the stovetop.

"Did it smell in here?"

"Burned, slightly sweet smell." Jess approached the stove. "What was in these pots?"

Alison stood beside Jess. "Sugar and some sort of foaming agent. I'll get the results from the lab. Hydroxymethylfurfural."

Jess raised her eyebrows.

"Sugar doesn't burn well unless it's powdered or heated to high temperatures very quickly. This was a combination. High heat and foam to cover a large surface area. Makes a compound called Hydroxymethylfurfural, which does burn easily and can actually explode."

"He meant to burn the house down."

"What happened next?" Alison said. "After you put out the fire."

Jess led them to the living room. They stood between the

sofa and the armchair. Two table lamps had been switched on since she was last there, one on either side of the sofa. They gave the room a warm and welcoming glow. There were two plants and several sun catchers on the window and over the fireplace. There was no sign of dust.

She pointed at a cupboard. "May I?"

Alison nodded. "Don't use the handle."

Jess stooped and opened the cupboard door from the bottom. There were five shelves, all stuffed with books. Hardbacks filled the upper two shelves and paperbacks the lower.

"Alphabetical by author," Alison said.

Jess studied the names and nodded. She pointed to occasional books that were shelved spine-in. Their titles were hidden and the creamy white of their pages exposed. "Odd."

Alison nodded. "Leave them for us to examine."

Jess eased the cupboard door closed. She pointed to the book on the armchair. "She was disturbed."

"But she had time to put her book down so as not to lose her place," Gonzalez said.

"A knock at the front door, perhaps?" Jess said.

She walked back out into the hallway. The security chain had been ripped off the doorframe. The lock looked intact. "She opened the door."

Alison nodded. "Could have been someone she knew."

"But not well, because she had the chain on."

"So, someone she recognized. Like a police officer," Gonzalez said.

Jess stared. "If you mean Charlene, she was in the car. I asked her to wait. I thought Norah Fender might talk more easily to a reporter than a police officer."

Gonzalez nodded.

Jess turned back to Alison. "Either way, he definitely came in through the front door."

Jess led the group upstairs.

Two techs were crammed in the bathroom. Several boxes and machines were on the landing. Jess eased past the open bathroom door and into the main bedroom.

Alison pointed to the clothes bunched up at one end of the rail in the closet. "Did you move the clothes like that?"

Jess shook her head. "It was like that when I arrived. Someone searched roughly. The drawers are the same."

"You touched the handles."

"I did." Jess drew their attention to the alarm clock. "Five minutes fast."

Alison nodded. "The woman was a neat freak. Advancing the time on the clock goes along with that need for control and rule-following."

Jess looked under the bed. There was a power supply strip plugged into the wall. "She has a computer."

"No sign of it, nor her phone."

Jess looked around the rest of the room. "I can't remember if he was carrying anything when he ran outside."

Gonzalez said, "Are you sure?"

Jess frowned. "It wasn't a robbery gone wrong."

"How do you know?" Gonzalez asked.

"Because he forced me to shoot her." She shivered involuntarily. "It's not the sort of thing a robber typically does, is it?"

Alison and Gonzalez said nothing.

"I told you this already." Jess shook her head.

Gonzalez nodded. "The computer had been connected to the internet. But it was turned off two streets from here."

Jess scowled. "So you know there was someone else here." She waved her arm, pointing out of the window. "The man who ran off."

"Unless he was your accomplice," Gonzalez said.

"Seriously? You think I'd let an accomplice beat me up and then get away if I had a choice?"

Alison smiled. "She's right. I don't see that happening."

Gonzalez blew out a lungful of air. "All right."

Jess sighed. "One last thing."

Alison raised her eyebrows.

"Tell me your preliminary determinations about the body," Jess said.

Alison led them to the bathroom. The two techs shuffled out of the way, moving their equipment with them.

Jess stared at Norah Fender's body from the doorway. "Can I get closer?"

Alison shook her head. "We've got enough trace evidence to deal with already."

"She was lying there when I first saw her. I had my gun out." She mimicked holding her Glock ready to shoot. "There was a man behind the door. He grabbed my hands, twisted the gun down, and pushed my finger into the trigger."

"How many times?" Gonzalez asked.

"Twice. He pounded my face against the door."

"How do you know it was a man?" Gonzalez said.

"He was wearing a man's coat, and I saw him running out."

"Distinguishing features? Could you identify him?"

Jess shook her head slowly. "I was on the verge of passing out. I could barely see him." She touched her face carefully. "What about Norah's body? Any forensics that might identify him?"

Alison took a half step into the bathroom. "It's too early to say for sure, but we didn't find skin or blood under her fingernails."

"So she didn't fight her attacker," Jess said.

"People fight like hell when their lives are on the line if they can. It appears she didn't fight." Alison pointed to Norah's neck. "Those marks are consistent with her being dragged to the bathroom. There is only slight bruising around the neck, which could mean she was close to death at the time."

"She was strangled?" Gonzalez asked.

"I don't think so," Alison said. "I'd expect more evidence of a struggle if she'd been strangled."

"Blows to the head?" Jess asked.

Alison shook her head. "And the blood loss from the gunshots is limited. Consistent with gravity causing the drainage after the heart stops pumping."

Jess looked at the bloody corpse. "You'd call that mild blood loss?"

"Compared to what it would have been if her heart was pumping at the time, yes. She didn't lose much from the gunshots."

Jess tried to process this new evidence by talking it through. "So she was already dead?"

Alison nodded. "Autopsy will confirm it, but that's my best guess based on what I see now."

"So he didn't use me to kill her. He wanted to set me up."

"Possibly," Gonzalez said. "But why? It implies that he knew who you were, doesn't it?"

Jess nodded. "And I only heard Norah Fender's name for the first time about an hour before I arrived here."

"Who told you about Fender?"

"Doctor Nepovim, at Kid's Own Medical Center. He showed me a printout with her name on it." Which was only half true. He had shown her the computer printout with Norah Fender's initials on it. But she didn't want to get Oscar Platte in trouble. He was a source. She couldn't be compelled to name him.

Jess spelled Nepovim's name.

"Maybe he didn't want her reputation to damage his hospital and thought you might help to publicize that." Gonzalez wrote Nepovim's name down in a small notebook. "Hospitals are big business these days. Could be a lot of money at stake."

"But murder? To keep her quiet about crimes that took place at least a decade ago? That's pretty extreme, isn't it?" Jess said.

"I agree." Alison nodded. "Setting you up seems a crime of opportunity. The killer thought we wouldn't notice that she was already dead before you shot her."

"Assuming the autopsy agrees with your preliminary assessment," Gonzalez said. "This seems personal. Like he knew who you were and he wanted to get you as well as Fender tied up in one neat package."

"Did anyone else know you were coming here?" Alison asked.

Jess took a deep breath. She didn't want to open up that Pandora's Box, but she had no choice. "Charlene Mackie was the only one."

Gonzalez scowled and cocked his head. "You think your friend is responsible?"

"Charlene didn't do this. We were working together," Jess said. She shook her head and stopped abruptly when the pain pierced her skull. "She's been looking for her daughter for fourteen years. We found a link that led us to Norah Fender.

Charlene wouldn't have killed Fender without finding out what she knew first, at the very least."

"How do you know she didn't find out that Fender did something to her daughter?" Gonzalez gave a flat smile. "Mothers have killed for less."

CHAPTER FORTY-SIX

ALISON'S TECHS TOOK FINGERPRINTS from Jess and Charlene. They used a portable machine that read the results straight into a computer. The computer brought up both of their names with the word "matched" in a bright red font.

Gonzalez recorded Jess's and Charlene's mobile phone numbers in his notebook and pushed it into his pocket. "We've got enough evidence to release you now. But if we come up with something new that implicates either of you, we'll use those consent forms you signed to have you picked up no matter what jurisdiction you're in."

"It won't be necessary to come after us, Gonzalez. We didn't kill Norah Fender, and you know it," Charlene said.

"You know where to find us if you need testimony against the killer or anything," Jess said.

"I do." Gonzalez nodded. "And your lawyer, Miller? He's assured me that you'll cooperate to help us prosecute the killer when we find him."

"You bet I will," Jess said, shaking hands all around.

When they'd returned to the car, Jess fired off a message to Miller, thanking him for his help, and informing him she was headed back to Randolph. He replied a moment later with a smiley emoji and the words *I'll be ready for the next time.*

Charlene drove the Crown Vic back to the highway and settled into a seventy-mile-an-hour cruise, north to Randolph.

Jess waited until Portland was twenty miles behind them before she spoke. "Tell me about your daughter's disappearance."

Charlene seemed lost in her own thoughts.

"If you want," Jess said. "Maybe I can help."

Charlene cleared her throat. "Last time I saw her was about a week before she disappeared. She was pregnant like I said. Living with her no-account boyfriend. We had a big fight. Total blowout." She took another lungful of air. "You have to understand. Crystal and I, we didn't get along. I loved her. I loved her from the moment she was born. But she…she was difficult. We had a hell of a time through her teens. But we came out on the other side, basically undamaged. Until she got pregnant. And me? I wasn't the best for her. At times, you know? People in Randolph would be only too happy to tell you that if you asked."

Jess nodded. It was a familiar story for runaways. Particularly girls. Too often, they left because home wasn't a great place to be. The trouble was, they usually learned that home was a better place than living on the streets. Pride kept them from going back.

Charlene bit her lip. "She didn't tell me who the father was, either."

"Where was she going, after that big fight?"

"Don't know. Her so-called boyfriend went after her. Didn't find her. He says." She paused while she passed a slow-moving truck in the right lane. "He didn't know. He didn't even realize she'd come home or left again. So he says."

Jess looked at Charlene. "You don't trust him?"

"I wasn't the best of people at the time, but he's nothing but trash. Hated him then, hate him now."

"Why?"

Charlene snorted. "He was a bum. Still is. Booze, drugs, and a temper."

"Why did she stay with him?"

Charlene shrugged. "I asked her that question a thousand times."

Jess changed her approach. "When the neighbor saw Crystal that last time, was she on foot?"

"Don't know." Charlene shrugged again. "Two months later her car was found in a remote lot at a Greyhound station in Seattle."

"She was heading through the neighborhood, though? Meaning she was going from one place to somewhere else?"

"Her house was the first turn on the left as you go into Sunshine Estates. Crystal was walking toward the back. Toward the woods along Meisner's place."

"Could she have gone anywhere else if she walked along that route?"

"Sure. There're lots of options. She could have walked along the lane and out the other end. Could have gone to see someone else living at Sunshine Estates. Could have done a lot of things." Charlene turned her head to look at Jess. "But she didn't. All of that was checked out at the time."

"Where was her car? When the neighbor saw her, I mean."

"The houses have communal parking. Her car wasn't parked there by the time we started looking for her."

"But her car could have been there that last night?"

"Could have."

"When did the police get notified that Crystal was missing?"

"A week later. She worked up at the Meisner's place. They reported she hadn't been into work."

"A whole week before they contacted anybody?"

Charlene snorted. "The Meisners? They couldn't care less about the people who work up there. Hired someone to replace her right away. There's always a line of workers."

"And the boyfriend? Didn't he care enough to report her missing before she'd been gone a whole week?"

"He doesn't care about anything that he can't drink or shoot up." Charlene's tone was full of disgust.

"But he went after her, that last time? When she came back?"

"Depending on how much credibility you put in the testimony of a heavy drug user. I've seen him on days when he couldn't even speak."

Charlene drove on in silence for a while. They passed a sign stating ten miles to Randolph.

"Why was Norah Fender killed?" Charlene finally asked.

"My theory is that someone is trying to cover something up. Like the hospital, or someone else involved in Norah Fender's baby-selling operation. She can't have been working alone. She had to have help."

"There aren't many motives for murder, according to the police academy manuals. One of the limited choices is to conceal a crime. So I guess you could be right. It's happened before."

Charlene pulled into The Montpelier Hotel parking lot and let Jess out by the front door.

Charlene lowered the window. "Do you think Crystal is still alive?"

Jess blew out a long breath. "We haven't found anything that indicates she isn't."

Charlene gave a long slow nod. "So you don't know either."

"No. But now isn't the time to give up."

Charlene nodded and drove away.

CHAPTER FORTY-SEVEN

BLACKSTAKE ARRIVED AT THE gate to Meisner's estate after midnight. His entire body ached. He'd walked a long way to a bus station in Portland after torching the big white Chrysler. He'd taken a bus to another small town. A taxi and another long walk to another bus. The final leg of his journey backtracked to Bamford and a third bus that dropped him in Randolph. He'd walked the final distance from there.

He had made no phone calls since leaving the Fender house. Along the way, he'd disposed of his burner phones, a few destroyed pieces of more than twenty plastic components deposited in trash barrels as he came to them. No one would find the pieces or attempt to reconstruct the phones.

The boss wouldn't like it, but Blackstake had decided to wait until the morning to deliver his report.

The men at the gate said little to him. He'd arrived in unusual ways at odd hours many times before. They offered him a ride from the gate to the manor house. He accepted.

The driver dropped him at a side entrance. The door led to a corridor that led to his apartment. Four elegantly appointed rooms, one overwhelmed by his king size bed. He was getting too old for his chosen profession. His bed beckoned.

But the phone rang before he made it to oblivion.

Blackstake sighed and straightened his posture and blinked himself awake. Tomorrow, he would have made a more circumspect report. The boss craved plausible deniability for all of Blackstake's projects, and he made it a point to deliver what the boss required. But he couldn't muster the energy for clandestine ops tonight.

"I found a nurse who sold Crystal Mackie's baby," Blackstake said. "Eliminated her and framed Kimball for the murder. Got rid of my car and phone and…you get the picture."

"You're sure?"

"Kimball's hand was on her gun when she shot the nurse. Even those bumpkins in Podunk, Oregon, should be able to arrest her and keep her until she's convicted with that evidence."

"Well, well. And the baby?"

"A boy. In fact, the boy who fell from the tree. Peter Whiting."

"Hell." There was a long silence. "Better not be any blowback on this."

"There won't be." Blackstake shook his head and swiped a palm over his face. "It means nothing. You're fine. There is nothing to lead from him to you. Docs in Randolph say the boy isn't going to recover, anyway. Bad head injury. The Whitings don't want anyone to know, and the nurse is dead. Kimball was the one causing trouble. But now she's out of the picture…"

"Kimball was snooping around the tree where the boy was found. Security confiscated a couple of drones from her. No computer chips or anything in them. Nothing remarkable. One of the guys has them if you want to take a look." A deep sigh traveled across the line. "We'll discuss this in the morning. Call me."

The line went dead. Blackstake hung up thoughtfully. A drone. So that's what the kid had been doing. Flying a drone around the area. Some of those drones had cameras in them. The kid's drone could have snapped some damning photos. But if it had, where were the photos?

He shook his head. He couldn't deal with it tonight. He'd follow up with the security staff tomorrow.

He wasn't worried. Everything was under control. He was a professional. He'd handled the situation. Appropriately. Finally.

He would sleep easy tonight.

He'd sleep a lot easier than Jess Kimball that was for damn sure.

CHAPTER FORTY-EIGHT

Randolph, Washington
Thursday, September 29
8:00 a.m. Pacific Time

JESS WOKE TO THE sound of birds at her window. She'd slept fitfully. Her muscles ached. Her lips were puffy, and the side of her face was tender to the touch. She lay still, listening to the sound of nature, hoping the soreness would fade.

She reached for her phone. One missed call from FBI Agent Henry Morris. She didn't want to try to talk to him right now. Whatever he wanted to talk to her about had nothing to do with Peter Whiting. She'd deal with him back in Denver. No other messages. Probably not a bad thing.

She pried herself out of the hotel's soft white sheets and moved into the shower. The water was hot. She breathed in the steam and let the heat work on her aches and pains.

The issues that had roamed through her head all night resurfaced. She had come to Randolph because she believed Peter Whiting could be her son. When she started questioning

Peter's birth date, before she knew he had to have been adopted, the Whiting house was burned down. When she went to Kid's Own to find Peter's hospital records, his labor and delivery nurse was murdered.

Somehow, Peter Whiting's fall and her desire to find her son had collided and ignited something. The connection seemed too firm to ignore.

The steam fogged the top of the elegantly curved mirror. She turned the water temperature up to the hottest she could stand.

There were plenty of people who had been affected. John and Barbara Whiting, for starters. They'd gone to extraordinary lengths to conceal Peter's adoption, and Jess didn't understand why. Each and every day there were thousands of children adopted. Usually to great joy all around.

Jess worked conditioner through her hair, rinsed, and stepped out of the shower. She wrapped a towel around herself and sat on the edge of her bed.

Her mind had spent the night spinning ever more elaborate stories about Peter's adoption to explain the Whitings' behavior. She'd considered everything from blackmail to kidnapping and discarded those theories just as quickly.

Jess toweled off and dressed.

None of her late night imaginings could explain why the Whitings might murder Norah Fender, the woman who had helped them obtain the son they so obviously cherished.

Jess looked at the clock by her bedside. The hotel restaurant was open by now. She styled her hair using the big mirror in the bathroom. The right side of her face and her nose were puffy and red. A red gash crossed her mouth where the blood clotted over the cut. Her nose wasn't broken, but she couldn't breathe very well. Her forehead had an ugly purple hue. She did the best she could with her makeup to look presentable, collected her phone, and headed down to breakfast.

The hotel foyer was empty except for a vaguely familiar man standing with his back to her, one hand leaning on the counter. A woman stood with him. Senator Alistaire Meisner and his wife, Margot.

The owner was behind the desk, head forward, nodding as Meisner talked.

Jess crossed the marble floor. When she was close enough to hear the conversation, she slowed her pace.

Margot noticed Jess first. An instant frown shadowed her near-perfect features. A moment later, Meisner slapped the owner on the shoulder and turned around. His expression mirrored his wife's when he saw Jess.

"Mrs. Meisner," Jess nodded. "Senator."

Meisner paused ever so briefly and then flashed a false smile so broad his ears lifted a fraction. The practiced face of a career politician greeting people he had hoped never to meet again, while he shook hands and kissed babies for votes.

Jess shook his proffered hand, ignoring the feeling of something cold and slimy crawling down her back. "Jessica Kimball. We met in the woods near your estate."

"Yes," Margot said.

Meisner nodded. "I remember, of course. You work for my friend Carter Pierce. *Taboo Magazine*, right?"

A lie. Carter didn't even know the man. "Do you have a moment?"

Meisner looked at his watch.

"I just wanted to ask you about Crystal Mackie," Jess said.

The smile on Meisner's face inched down a fraction. "Please forgive my rudeness, but have you been in an accident?"

"Thank you for your concern." Jess touched her face. "It's nothing."

"It doesn't look like nothing. Looks like you ran into something."

Jess took a deep breath. "A door. Someone pushed me into it."

Margot gasped. Meisner raised his eyebrows. "I hope you filed a police report."

"Yes, of course."

"Your nose definitely needs some work. Maybe your forehead, too." Meisner cocked his head and flashed a smarmy smile. "I can recommend Doctor Eric Hewson. You'd have to go to Seattle, of course, but he's very good. Especially with cosmetic procedures."

"Thank you. I'll consider that." She paused, biting her tongue to keep the retort about Margot's obviously Botoxed facial lines in check. "About Crystal Mackie, she worked for you, just before she disappeared, didn't she?"

"That was a long time ago." Meisner frowned and wagged his ample chin as if he felt genuine sorrow. Which, Jess was willing to bet, he did not. "Tragic situation. Caused a lot of good people a lot of heartache."

"I'm helping her mother." Jess nodded. "She wants to know what happened to her daughter. Any mother would."

"After all this time? We all know what happened to her, surely. She ran away. She's never coming back." Meisner shrugged.

"A lot of young girls run away from home, Miss Kimball." Margot shook her head as if the truth was too much to bear. "It's sad and painful for the runaways and for those they leave behind."

Jess nodded. "You were the one who reported her missing, weren't you, Senator? After she didn't show up to work for a week?"

Meisner took a deep breath and let it out slowly. "All of these questions were answered years ago. I have issued statements that are available from my office. If you'd like to contact my assistants, they will help you get copies. I have no additional comments for your magazine at this time."

"I'm trying to establish what brought a girl's life to an end."

"To an end?" Meisner screwed up his face and made clucking sounds with his tongue. "She disappeared, yes. I suppose that was the end of the life she was living here. But no body was found. She had an abusive boyfriend, and her car was found abandoned at a bus station."

Margot nodded. "People make the decision to move on with their lives. To make a break from the old life to a new one. Hopefully, a better one."

"You think she left? Went somewhere better?"

"Why not?" Meisner shrugged. "From what I understood of her circumstances, almost any life would have been better than the one she had."

"Why did you wait a week before reporting her missing?"

He gave another fake sympathetic smile. "It was years ago. I went over everything at the time with the police. I tried to help everyone. I did everything I could to assist with the search. I'm sorry, but I don't have anything else to add after all these years."

"I'm not accusing you of anything—"

He held up his hand, palm out, and scowled. "I sincerely hope not. Your magazine's lawyer would be hearing from mine."

Jess nodded. "That's why we have lawyers on retainer."

He took a breath. "I have every sympathy for Charlene

Mackie and all those affected by her daughter's disappearance. It was a sad and emotional time for them, I'm sure. Yes, she was in my employ, as are dozens of others. I have an estate manager who deals with our personnel. As I said, you are free to contact my office for a copy of my official statements containing all the facts."

He held out his hand. She wanted to fire back at him, marshal her questions until she had the answers she wanted. But she wasn't prepared. There were too many moving parts, too many unknowns, and she had no doubt that she would lose any argument with him unless she held all the answers.

Jess smiled. "I hope to meet you again, Senator. Perhaps *Taboo* will cover your campaign. You're running for President next cycle, aren't you?"

He laughed. "Give my best to Mr. Pierce, will you?" He gripped her hand in a hard shake. She squeezed back and stared into his eyes. He didn't blink. She released her grip, and he held on for a full ten count before he turned away. His wife nodded and walked beside him.

Jess watched them go. He pulled out a phone as he left the lobby. The Meisners hustled down the front stairs heading for a large Cadillac with its engine running and a chauffeur waiting to open the rear door. The limo swept away, steam trailing from its exhaust, billowing into the cold, damp air.

Jess stared at the space where Meisner's car had been. Several uncharitable thoughts sprang to mind. What the hell was he hiding?

CHAPTER FORTY-NINE

JESS ATE BREAKFAST SERVED on a white linen tablecloth in the hotel dining room. The coffee arrived in a bright chrome pot. The aroma alone sharpened her senses. She was surprised she could smell the coffee at all, and she hoped it meant her nose wasn't permanently damaged.

She sent a message to Mandy to request Meisner's old prepared statements on the disappearance of Crystal Mackie. Meisner's lawyers would be calling Carter Pierce soon if they hadn't already. The old statements would be ammunition if he needed it.

As she finished her meal, her phone showed a message from Captain Nelson, requesting her presence at the station. She poured another coffee and savored every sip.

Thirty minutes later, her shoes clicked on the marble as she crossed The Montpelier Hotel's foyer toward the exit. The owner was still standing behind the reception desk. He smiled and beckoned to her. "Miss Kimball."

She walked over.

He grimaced. "I'm sorry to say that we are fully booked tonight through next week."

Jess frowned. "I already have a room."

"I'm sorry." He shook his head. "When you checked in, you said you were only staying one or two nights."

"Yes, but my plans changed."

"We'd have told you when you checked in if we'd known you wanted an extended stay." He held his hands out, palms upward. "A large party with a previous booking, I'm afraid. We must honor it." He pointed toward the south. "There's The Plum Inn. I'm sure they have rooms. Not that I'd really recommend the place. I could find you a lovely hotel in Seattle."

"Thanks." Jess exhaled. "I'll manage."

She settled her bill and gathered up her things from her room. When she crossed the foyer a few minutes later, the owner was nowhere to be seen. She put her bag in the trunk of her car and drove to the police station.

The sky was a uniform gray from horizon to horizon. There was no sun. Only diffuse light that cast no shadows. Water dripped from the eaves of the station as she walked in through the creaky aluminum door.

Charlene's gaze flicked to Jess and returned to her work. Officer Gardner stopped his hands on his keyboard and glowered.

Nelson appeared from the corridor that led to his office. She followed him and took the same chair she had occupied a couple of days earlier. Nelson closed the door and sat down behind the desk.

Jess smiled. "Do I need legal representation?"

"I'm hoping none of us do. I need to sort through these facts and report to the mayor. Depending on what you have to say, Charlene and I might both be out of a job by the end of the day." When she started to speak, Nelson put his hand up. "First off, Charlene is our most junior officer with the least amount of training. She's our dispatcher, and that's about the limit of her ability, frankly. She has no authority other than the very limited tasks I assign to her. And we have no jurisdiction outside of Randolph."

"Anyway, I'm the one who found the body—"

"After you broke into a private residence."

"With reasonable cause. The killer had set a fire." Jess squared her shoulders. "Charlene stayed in the car, so she's not to blame for the break-in. Captain Gonzalez has all the details. Call him and ask."

Nelson sighed. "They took Charlene's prints."

"We both gave them exclusion prints to speed up the crime scene processing. We'd been inside the building. We were cooperating with local law enforcement. There was no reason to refuse."

He held up a piece of paper. "The mayor's already had a letter from the Kid's Own legal department."

"About what?"

"A warning shot." He flipped it onto his desk. "Privacy concerns. They want some sort of data protection agreement signed. Promises not to talk to the press. Yadda, yadda, yadda."

"It's their job to protect their data. We don't owe them anything." Jess shrugged. "The lawyers can sort out whether records related to concealing a fraud and selling babies are covered by medical privacy. I'm guessing they're not."

"Hopefully, the mayor will be satisfied with that answer." Nelson shuffled through the papers on his desk and selected a half dozen pages held together with a bulldog clip. "Preliminary autopsy report on Norah Fender. Expedited. Got a courtesy copy about an hour ago."

"What does it say about the cause of death?"

Nelson flipped to the third page. "Victim died from asphyxiation. The subject had been heavily dosed with," he waved his hand, "some drug with a long name that caused paralysis. They found needle marks. Death likely occurred minutes before the body was discovered."

"No kidding. The murderer was still in the room when I found her." Jess paused to calm her breathing. "Killing Fender wasn't a spur of the moment thing. No one carries drugs that cause fatal paralysis, just in case they might come in handy."

He folded his hands on his desk. "Premeditated murder. The most dangerous kind."

"A professional killer. Definitely not Charlene Mackie and not me, either." Jess nodded. "Does it say how long it took for the drug to kill her?"

Nelson flipped through a few more pages of the autopsy report. "A large dose of sedative. Too large."

"We arrived about forty minutes earlier," Jess said, slowly. "Knocked and rang the bell, and got no answer."

"You think he was there already?"

"It was black inside the house. No movement." She shrugged. "I figured there was no one home. But he could have been around at the time, I guess."

"You see the guy's car?"

"Chrysler sedan. White."

"You or Charlene get the license number?"

She shook her head and touched the side of her face.

Nelson said, "Looks painful."

"It's improving."

He turned another page. "The front door was broken."

She shook her head. "Just the security chain. No damage to the door outside. Looks like Fender opened the door when he knocked or rang the bell. But she had the chain on. He pushed inside, busting the chain."

"And you entered through the back door?"

She shrugged. "There was a fire brewing on the stovetop, so I pushed the back door open."

Nelson nodded as he read on through the report. "So we're thinking he was faking an accidental death."

"Right up until he used my gun to put holes in her body. He went from faking an accidental death to setting me up in an instant."

"No way Charlene was capable of all of that without help." Nelson shook his head. "But you're a one-woman crime magnet."

"Someone's spooked. For sure." She paused. "But why? I haven't done anything to spook anybody."

"You've done something. We need to figure out what it is." Nelson cocked his head and then returned to the reports. "Fender's place was extremely tidy, it says here."

"She was a neat freak, but her place had been searched. I'm not sure when the killer found the time to search it. He rushed out when he left, for sure, because I chased after him." The timing was only one of the open questions about his behavior. She had a long list if she ever met the guy.

Nelson nodded and pulled out another report. "Crime scene techs concluded the same thing." He turned over another page.

Jess nodded and straightened herself in her chair. "She had lived in that house a while. If she was a danger to someone, why didn't they deal with her before now? I mean, why was she killed only at the point when we went to talk with her?"

Nelson shook his head.

She said, "Maybe whoever killed her didn't know about her before. He didn't know who she was and how she was connected to whatever has been spooking whoever it is that's spooked."

"Spooked enough to kill."

Jess cocked her head. "Maybe. Could be the spooked guy. Or it could be someone else. A hired hit. If the killer was a professional."

"Let's go about this a different way," Nelson said. "Who knew you were going to visit Norah Fender?"

"Charlene and I. That's all. Because we didn't make the decision until we got in the Crown Vic after we left Kid's Own." Jess took a deep breath and thought the question through. "But plenty of people could have figured it out. Doctor Nepovim from the Kid's Own records department, for sure. The Whitings have got to know I've been looking into them and their son. They knew Fender professionally and what she was doing. Probably others could have figured it out, too."

Nelson raised his eyebrows. "Someone from Kid's Own makes the most sense. Wouldn't be the first time someone figured saving a reputation was worth killing for."

"The timing's wrong, though." Jess shook her head. "Charlene and I went straight to Fender's from the hospital. No one from Kid's Own could have arrived faster than we did."

"How long from the hospital to her place?"

"Fifteen minutes. Tops."

He frowned. "Who knew you were going to the hospital?"

"Beats me." Jess shook her head. "I didn't even know I was going until Charlene called me, and I didn't tell anyone."

He exhaled. "So Charlene is pretty much the only link…"

"Wrong answer. Even if she was capable of doing something like this, she didn't do it." Jess shook her head. "First, she was completely shocked when she saw her daughter's handwriting on those medical records. She was barely able to speak, she was so upset. She couldn't even drive. There's no way she arranged a professional hit in the lapsed time between our visit to Kid's Own and an hour later." She took a deep breath. "Second, if she'd talked to anyone at all, I'd have known. She was in the car with me the whole time. She didn't make a single phone call. I can vouch for that."

He thought about what she'd said for a bit before he frowned and leaned forward, elbows on his desk. "How much do you actually know about Charlene Mackie?"

CHAPTER FIFTY

JESS LOOKED BEHIND HER. Nelson's door was closed. "Okay. Tell me what I don't know."

Nelson sighed. "I arrived here three years ago. The outgoing guy wasn't around to brief me, or anyone else for that matter." He tapped his chest. "Heart attack. So I reviewed the cases from the past ten years. It didn't take long. Randolph isn't exactly a hotbed of crime. Until I got to the Crystal Mackie case."

Jess raised her eyebrows, encouraging him on.

"Crystal disappeared. She was gone for six days, reappears at her house for," he shrugged, "minutes? Certainly not an hour. She's seen leaving. Heading toward the back of the Meisner estate."

"Toward the woods."

"In that direction. But there was no evidence found that she went into the woods, or even reached them."

"She must have gone somewhere."

"There were no more reported sightings. Her car turned up in a Greyhound station a couple of months later. No CCTV. No fingerprints." Nelson shook his head. "None. It'd been wiped clean. Inside, outside, the trunk, the gas cap. Thorough job."

"But it was her car. Why would she wipe it clean?"

"She wouldn't. There would be no point." Nelson nodded and took a deep breath, as if he didn't want to go further, but he did. "Which is where we need to start talking about Charlene. She made the same deduction. Everyone did. Up until then, it was a missing person's case."

Jess nodded. Made sense.

Nelson leaned forward. "From what I understand, that's when she started to fall apart. She'd been looking for every chance her daughter might be alive. But then? It was like her whole world collapsed."

Jess squeezed her lips together and shook her head. "It's understandable."

"Definitely." He nodded. "But she lost it. She became obsessive. She blamed everyone and everything. Every detail she could latch onto became a reason someone had killed her daughter. The boyfriend. People on the Meisner estate, and of course, Meisner."

"Meisner?"

"Well, he wasn't exactly a bundle of sympathy." Nelson nodded. "And he started a lawsuit to keep people off his property."

"The path?"

"The right of way. Long precedence, yadda, yadda. Big court fight. Meisner put up that fence, which is overkill if you ask me. Cut off people's access. It was a big inconvenience, but most people just put up with it."

"Except Charlene?"

"Oh yes. She went wild. Walking through the estate and the

woods had become a habit. Every day. More than once. The place was, well…like a shrine to her, I suppose."

"It's a mean fence. Built by a vindictive person. Who puts barbed wire on the top of a fence like that? It's not like he's worried about livestock." She paused. "He did it to keep people off his property. Overkill."

Nelson shrugged. "Guess he's entitled to his privacy. And he's a politician. On any given day, he's probably got half a dozen death threats. Half the voters are bound to hate him. The nature of the animal. His security detail probably insisted on the barbed wire."

"Are they Government security?"

"Senators who aren't members of leadership aren't entitled to constant protection, even though they need it." Nelson shook his head. "Meisner calls them aides, but they're former military and clandestine operatives. You wouldn't like to tangle with them unarmed."

Jess shrugged. "His security detail wasn't there when we met Meisner that day at the tree."

"Must have been nearby. Somewhere." He shrugged. "The point is, Meisner got a restraining order against Charlene."

"Why? What did she do?"

"She was accosting him everywhere. She's lucky he didn't sue her for slander. Or have her arrested or held on involuntary commitment to a mental hospital. She was relentless, apparently. Stirred up a lot of anger among the locals."

"I don't remember hearing about any altercations during his last election."

"Like I said, he's a wealthy politician. Lots of money and plenty of clout. He's good at handling the media." He grimaced. "No offense."

Jess shook her head. "None taken. Tell me about the restraining order."

"Still in effect. Meisner has it renewed regularly. Charlene doesn't protest. But he doesn't seem to enforce it now because she still walks along the lane." Nelson shook his head.

Jess thought about everything Nelson had said and everything she'd learned from Charlene. "Does she still blame Meisner for her daughter's disappearance?"

"Probably." Nelson shrugged. "She's blamed a long string of people. And she has no evidence against him. She feels Meisner waited a suspicious amount of time before reporting that Crystal hadn't turned up for work."

"Charlene mentioned that to me. And I think she's right, don't you?"

Nelson nodded. "Did she tell you they hired someone new the day after they made the report about Crystal?"

"Yeah, she mentioned that, too. But it's a big house. Maybe they needed the help. I mean, no one knew what had happened at that point, right?"

"A search started as soon as Meisner made the report, but she wasn't formally declared a missing person for another two days." Nelson nodded again. "But no one knows what happened to Crystal even now."

Jess shuffled in her chair. "Not exactly damning evidence, is it?"

Nelson shook his head. "It isn't evidence of anything. She just got obsessed." He sighed. "Her daughter had gone missing after all."

Jess bit her lip. "Is she clinically depressed?"

"Not diagnosed by a doctor, as far as I know." He drummed his fingers on the desk. "It's like she's on the verge of climbing out of it sometimes, but she never does. Which probably means she should be getting treatment."

"Explains why she's so focused on Peter Whiting."

Jess pulled out the memory card she'd kept from Peter's drone. She handed it to Nelson. "Peter Whiting climbed that tree to recover a drone. It was a higher-end toy, and it had a camera."

He turned the memory card over. "You didn't think to mention this before?"

She sighed. "I've been a little busy. I took that card from the drone before one of Meisner's *aides* took the drone from me."

He frowned.

"I didn't hand it over willingly."

"Where was the drone?"

"Stuck in the tree. A little higher than he climbed."

"He's in the hospital all because of this?" Nelson leaned back in his chair, the memory card still between his fingers. "Doctors say another couple of days before he'll regain consciousness. Even then… Damn."

"Kids do crazy things sometimes. Aren't you the one who told me that?"

He held up the memory card. "You've looked at this I guess?"

She nodded. "He was a good pilot. The drone went all the way around Meisner's mansion, but on the way back it crashed in the tree. High up. He fell before he reached it."

Nelson plugged the memory card into his computer. Jess watched the twisting and turning video. The drone's camera swooped over green fields, and animal trails marked the early morning dew. The images were bigger and easier to see on the computer screen.

"The video doesn't tell us why the boy was there in the first place." She shifted in her seat. "Have you talked to the Whitings?"

He nodded. "And they don't want to be interviewed."

She held out her phone with the two Barbara Whiting signatures side-by-side on the display. "Have you asked them about these signatures?"

He nodded again. "We're meeting with their lawyer this afternoon."

"So at least one of these signatures is actually hers, then."

"I'll keep an open mind until this afternoon." He took a deep breath and looked at the ceiling. "If this goes as I expect, there's a fifty-fifty chance Peter could be taken away from them."

"Maybe. At this point, all we know is that Peter isn't their biological child. Doesn't mean he was kidnapped or the adoption was illegal." Jess shrugged. "If Charlene is right about the signatures on the delivery record, looks like Crystal effectively consented to the adoption."

"My parents robbed a convenience store when I was six. A man died. I had no family, and the state put me in an orphanage where I stayed until I was eighteen. The only time I saw my parents after the conviction was through Plexiglas. They both died in prison. I've had to explain that all my life. From bullies in the playground to every job interview I've ever had, and now to you. If I can save Peter from that sort of life, I'm planning to do it."

Jess didn't know what to say. Peter was not the Whitings' biological child, but that didn't mean they'd kidnapped him. If they weren't his legal guardians, the potential quagmire could last for years.

They sat in silence a few moments. Jess stared at the signatures on her phone. "This issue isn't about Peter."

Nelson nodded. "It seems to be about Crystal Mackie."

"Does Meisner have an alibi for Crystal's disappearance?"

"We are not going there." Nelson waved his hand and shook his head. "We have absolutely no evidence linking anything to Meisner. It's going to be difficult enough cleaning up after Charlene's behavior yesterday. Adding an angry senator to the mix would just…" He shook his head.

"Doesn't stop me," Jess said. "I met him again in my hotel this morning. I asked him about Crystal."

Nelson slowly closed his eyes.

"He referred me to his office for an official statement."

Nelson opened his eyes. "I have a copy of his prior statement in the file. Doesn't say much. Nice words. Sympathetic. He refers to "the family," never Charlene. Denies knowing Crystal, denies knowing what happened to her."

"Everything you'd expect from a politician."

"Or someone who knows nothing about the disappearance." He slid a picture across the desk. "You've met Meisner. Do you think he's capable of that?"

Jess stared at the image. Not that she needed the reminder. Norah Fender. Her legs dangling over the edge of the tub, her head twisted against the wall. Large stains where the bullets from Jess's gun had pierced her clothes. Blood on pastels.

"The point is," Nelson sighed, "Nothing links Meisner to Crystal Mackie's disappearance or Norah Fender's murder. Nothing. So stay away from him. Please."

Jess pushed Norah Fender's photograph back to Nelson. "She died for some reason. If you look at the contents of her modest house in a downscale neighborhood, it's obvious she wasn't even the kingpin in the baby-selling operation."

Nelson didn't argue.

Jess curled her hands together, and folded her fingers backward, cracking her knuckles. "Maybe we're ignoring the elephant. Crystal's disappearance is suspicious. Who's the most likely culprit?"

Nelson grunted. "Usually, the spouse, or in this case, her significant other. Not that I'd call Johnny Yukon significant in any way."

"Surely he was interviewed at the time."

"Hell, yes. But he said very little besides a long string of cuss words."

"A DNA sample might clear up a lot of this."

"Confirm him as Peter Whiting's father? That certainly wouldn't help anyone. Least of all, Peter. And Charlene hates the guy."

"Is Johnny Yukon still in the area?"

Nelson frowned. "He's still in the same house, 46 Pine Street on Sunshine Estates."

She pulled out her car keys. "Let's go meet him."

He shook his head. "I'll drive."

CHAPTER FIFTY-ONE

BLACKSTAKE SAT IN HIS car on the side of the road, a hundred yards down from the police station. It hadn't taken long for word to reach him that Kimball was back in Randolph. He'd seen the drones and the boss was right—they didn't have memory cards inside. Kimball had probably removed them before security arrived to get her off the property. He'd get the photos from her and then deal with that damn reporter once and for all.

A police cruiser approached. He rearranged a paper map over the steering wheel and kept his head down. The cruiser passed by. Without moving his head, he saw the passengers in his peripheral vision. Two people. A man driving, and a woman engrossed in her phone. Nelson and Kimball.

They showed no interest in him or his car.

He waited until the cruiser took a side road before pulling out after it. He kept a safe distance back. Several cars between him and his target.

Nelson turned onto Sunshine Estates and took the first left again. Blackstake drove past. Half a mile later he found a fast food place and parked, his car pointed at Sunshine Estates, both for a quick getaway, and to watch for the cruiser to pass.

He pulled out his phone. The boss answered without speaking.

Blackstake cleared his throat. "Kimball is riding shotgun with Nelson. They're visiting Johnny Yukon."

The boss blew out a long breath.

Blackstake said, "They're opening it up. Starting again. They're going to go round the whole thing at the worst possible time."

"Recommendation?"

"Nelson's controllable." Blackstake flexed his scarred hand. "Limited options at this point for Kimball."

Blackstake heard labored breathing. "You're supposed to be the best."

"Doesn't mean I can work miracles."

Silence from the other end of the line.

Blackstake said, "I'll sort it."

"You do that."

CHAPTER FIFTY-TWO

NELSON PARKED OUTSIDE A two-story townhouse with a garage to one side. No fences separated the front lawns, but 46 Pine Street was easily distinguishable from the others on the row. Thistles had taken hold across the dirt that might once have been as lushly green as its neighbors. An unpainted square of plywood covered the lower half of the front door. Gray duct tape crossed the glass in the upper half.

The curtains were drawn. No light spilled around their edges. No shadows flitted across the windows. No movement inside. No recognition that the police had arrived.

Jess followed Nelson up the path to the front door. He pulled a foot-long metal flashlight from his belt, and rapped on the plywood. The door shook. The glass rattled. Nelson rapped again. The same force. The same shaking and rattling. He gave it a moment and repeated his actions.

"It's morning," he said. "Johnny'll be sleeping."

"A night owl?"

"Among other things."

A shout came from inside. Slurred words. Muffled.

Nelson rapped on the door again. The shouting was clearer this time. Jess caught the word "off." Nelson grinned. "If you put Johnny in your magazine, you're going to have to edit any quotes."

Jess smiled. "I've dealt with worse."

"Don't call him Spud. A nickname he hates." He grimaced.

Nelson rapped again. Johnny Yukon's response was unambiguous this time. The second word was definitely "off."

"It's Captain Nelson. I need to talk to you," Nelson's voice was loud and controlled.

The door opened.

A man with long hair and several days' beard growth hunched in the doorway. He cussed twice. He stared at Jess, and back at Nelson. "Ain't seen her before. Never touched her." He pushed the door.

Nelson held the door open with his boot. "Hello, Johnny."

Johnny shook the door in an effort to free it. "I ain't never touched her. No matter what she says."

"I never said you did. Nor did she."

Johnny stopped shaking the door. "Then what you here for?"

Nelson pointed down the corridor with his flashlight. "Inside."

Johnny sneered. "I ain't done nothing."

Nelson nodded down the corridor. "Inside, Johnny."

Johnny Yukon let go of the door and worked his way down the corridor into the house, using the walls for support.

Jess closed the door behind her.

Johnny led them into a kitchen at the rear of the house. He sat in a chair at a small table. Jess stood by the window. Apart from a sagging washing line strung between a pole and the side of the house, the back yard was no different than the front.

Nelson stood directly in front of Johnny, six feet away, downwind.

"What?" Johnny said.

"Crystal Mackie."

Johnny sagged and put his hand to his forehead. "I ain't got nothing more to say on that. Nothing."

"New details have come up."

Johnny lifted his head, frowning. "Like what?"

"Where have you been for the past two days?"

Johnny screwed up his face. "What?"

"Anybody to vouch for you? The last two days."

"Why would I need that?"

"Because something has happened in the last two days that you don't want to be arrested for. If you've got any sense, you'll answer my question."

Johnny rotated his head from side to side. Slowly. Trying to shake away the fog shrouding his mind without bringing down the wrath of whatever he'd been doing the night before. "I might. Maybe some of the time." He waved his hand in front of his face. "It's a bit hazy, see?"

"Well, unhaze it."

Johnny rocked his head back and forth and sighed. "Wait a minute."

He left the kitchen and thumped up the stairs. He returned a minute later with a young woman trailing behind. Her head was down, her long blond hair dangled limp, obscuring her face. Every step seemed like an Olympic achievement.

"This is Laurie." He held out Laurie's hand. "Tell 'em when you got here."

Laurie waved her head from side to side. "Um…"

Johnny rolled his eyes. "How many nights you been here?"

Laurie nodded. "Yeah, right. Nights. Yeah. Two. I think."

Johnny shook her arm.

"Right," she said. "Two. For sure." She lifted her head and parted her hair. Her mouth hung open. Her face was white. She had intense blue eyes that somehow had no shine or depth. A line ran down her forehead and carried on past her nose and over her lips. A crease line. Folds in the fabric of the bedsheets in which she had lain, face down.

"Good girl," Yukon said.

Jess squeezed her lips together. She breathed deep, clenching her fist. Her blood boiled. Chemicals charged her muscles and expanded her lungs.

She could absolutely understand Charlene Mackie's desire to pound him flat. To kick him so hard he never walked again. She breathed out. Hard. The only thing she could do that wouldn't unleash her anger on the waste of a human life that was Johnny Yukon.

Laurie's gaze drifted. Jess wanted to reach forward and take the girl from this snake pit. But Laurie turned and staggered back upstairs. A dull thump overhead. Probably her, collapsing on a bed.

Yukon shrugged. "Big night."

Jess's gaze bore into his miserable, greasy face. She took a deep breath, swallowed hard, pushing bile back down her throat. "We need a DNA sample."

Johnny frowned. "Who are you?"

"Jessica Kimball."

"You a cop?"

"I'm a reporter for *Taboo Magazine*."

Johnny's eyes widened. "Reporter?" He straightened his back and smoothed his hair down. "What you doing here?"

"Like Captain Nelson said, new details in Crystal Mackie's disappearance."

Johnny closed one eye, struggling to concentrate. "What details?"

"We can't say."

Johnny's open eye stared at her. "You found some blood or something?"

"Something like that."

He opened both eyes and looked at Nelson. "This what you here for, too?"

"DNA would clear some things up."

Johnny shook his head. "I know my rights. I didn't have nothing to do with her going missing. She up and walked out on me."

Jess clenched her fist. The jerk was infuriating. She forcibly relaxed her muscles. "Then you have nothing to worry about, and my magazine would reimburse you for the inconvenience."

"I don't know…"

"It's simple. Wipe a couple swabs in your mouth, and you're done."

Johnny snorted. "I'm busy. I got things to do."

"Right." Jess fought to keep her voice level. "Perhaps two hundred would help?"

"Two hundred?" He scowled.

"Dollars."

Johnny scoffed. "More like five hundred."

"Two hundred."

Wrinkles of concentration lined Johnny's forehead. "Four…no, five…no three hundred. Yeah, three hundred."

Jess put her hand in her bag and pulled out a roll of notes. She counted three hundred and wrapped an elastic band around the bundle.

Johnny reached for the money. Jess wrapped her hands around the notes. She looked at Nelson. "You have the DNA kit."

Nelson took out a small bag.

Johnny rinsed his mouth with water and swabbed each cheek twice. Nelson sealed the samples in sterilized bottles. He wrote the date and Johnny's name on each bottle in small capital letters.

Jess held out the roll of bills. Johnny snatched them away from her and wrapped his fist around the roll.

She glared at him. "You seem a little desperate."

"Money for old rope."

"You're not worried what we might find with your DNA?"

He shrugged. "You won't find anything. I didn't kill her or abuse her or anything."

"She was pregnant."

He doubled over with laughter.

Jess fought back the urge to reach out and punch him. "What's so funny?"

He slowed his laughter and leaned back in his chair. "You don't know, do ya?"

She stared.

He gestured to himself. "I'm sterile. An' you paid for my DNA for nothing."

"We'll see."

He shook his head. "Trust me. I got tested right after she told me she was pregnant."

"Why?"

"Ain't that obvious? I didn't trust her. Not an inch."

"Why not?"

"Hey, we were living life to the fullest. I didn't come back some nights, an' she didn't come back some nights. Days an' all." He shrugged. "We weren't exclusive or nuthin'."

"Where did she go? The nights she didn't come back?"

"Who knows? She never told me. I never asked."

"You never asked?"

Yukon shrugged. "She had her own life. We just…like…intersected sometimes."

"She had another lover."

He shrugged. "So? I ain't jealous."

"And you don't know who?"

He shook his head. "Only thing she ever talked about was her work up at Meisner's place. Work and Meisner, two things that don't do nothing for me."

"What did she say about Meisner?"

"Nothing. Just about the stuff he was doing. Politics. Another thing that doesn't do it for me."

Jess frowned. "But she was a maid, wasn't she?"

"So?"

"Did she talk to him a lot?"

"Nah. I don't think so. Anyway, she had a short attention span. The novelty wore off, and she stopped talkin' about him."

"Then did she start talking about anyone else?"

He shrugged. "That was about when she disappeared."

Jess cocked her head. It wasn't unusual for employees to talk about the boss. Being a senator made Meisner famous, if not really a celebrity. Some people liked to be near power. No matter what the job, they thought they gained some sort of prestige from it.

Yukon yawned. "Are we done?"

"Not quite," Nelson said. "Get Laurie."

Yukon frowned. "What for?"

"I'm taking her home."

Yukon's frown turned to a scowl. "She's a big girl. Don't need no big daddy to look after her anymore."

"You want me to search this place?"

Yukon glared.

"I'm pretty sure it would be worthwhile. Turn up some interesting stuff. Illegal stuff. Stuff with your prints all over it."

Yukon inched backward.

"Tell her to bring her things," Nelson said.

Yukon skulked out of the room. There were muffled voices upstairs and a few dull thumps. A few minutes later, Laurie was at the bottom of the stairs, one hand on the banister to hold herself upright, the other gripping two plastic trash bags.

Nelson led the way out to his cruiser. Jess guided Laurie into the rear seat and sat beside her. The girl sat with the bags crumpled on her lap and said nothing.

CHAPTER FIFTY-THREE

BLACKSTAKE WATCHED THE POLICE cruiser leave Sunshine Estates. The cop stared forward. Intent. Focused. The reporter was in the back seat with a girl who looked like she'd been on an all-night bender. They'd found something. He pursed his lips. Things were out of his control. Unacceptable.

He watched the cruiser disappear in his rearview mirror. It headed out of town, not toward the station. It wasn't an arrest.

He flexed his fingers. The cop would be back. That was the way with police business. Leg work and repetition.

He took a small bag from the glove compartment and checked the contents.

Whatever had happened in Yukon's hovel of a house was done.

He couldn't change history, but the future was in his own hands.

CHAPTER FIFTY-FOUR

NELSON DROVE OUT OF town to a small two-story house with a picture perfect garden. The front door had opened before he had come to a stop in the driveway. A middle-aged man and woman stood on the step.

"Laurie's parents," Nelson said.

They descended on the cruiser, helping Laurie from the rear seat and into the house. She didn't protest. Nelson talked up a rehab facility in Seattle, and they promised to take her.

A few minutes after they had arrived, Nelson was back on the road.

"Is Yukon a dealer?" Jess said.

Nelson shook his head. "He's too pathetic."

"But he's on drugs."

"Perpetually."

"And he hooked Laurie, too." She shook her head. "Isn't there anything you can do about that?"

"We've just done the best we can."

"But he has to be buying hardcore drugs from somewhere."

Nelson turned to Jess. "I'll work on it. He's been inside twice and sent for outpatient rehab at taxpayer expense at least three times already. What's the point of sending him back?"

Nelson stopped at the traffic light in the center of town. "I just try to make Yukon as unpopular as possible in the hope people won't go near him. There's no perfect solution."

"I can think of one." She took a deep breath. "But how long for the DNA results?"

"We can get preliminary results sufficient to prove paternity in about twenty-four hours." He shrugged. "But not much point if it's true that he's sterile."

The light turned green, and Nelson drove to the station. He parked in his space, right outside the front door.

"And if he was lying?" Jess said.

"We'll pay him another visit."

"Promise me you'll take me with you."

Nelson laughed. "You want to see the smile wiped off his face. Not a surprising reaction. Most of Randolph feels that way."

They walked into Nelson's office. The evidence boxes were lined up against the wall. Somewhere in the musty files was the answer to Crystal Mackie's disappearance. Someone knew the truth. Someone knew if she had abandoned her past, her family, and friends, and started life anew. Someone knew where she was now.

She pulled one of the boxes of evidence toward her. "The answer to Crystal's disappearance is here. It has to be. Your predecessor was thorough. He collected enough statements for a Presidential assassination investigation."

"And plenty of people have been over every word, multiple times, and found nothing helpful."

"But the person that knows what happened to her is mentioned in here, I'm sure of it. He must be."

"Or she."

"Do you think Crystal could have been headed to Meisner's house the last night she was seen?"

"She was one of the maids, but she hadn't been there in a week. Because of what you and Charlene found out, we now know she'd been in Portland at Kid's Own Medical Center delivering her baby." He shrugged. "It was late. I doubt she was going to pop over and catch up on what had happened in her absence."

"What if she was going to see someone? Maybe not Meisner, but someone at the house." Jess flipped through the stack of statements. "It's a big place. A friend? One of the staff, perhaps?"

Nelson looked over several boxes before picking one up, and placing it on his desk, in front of Jess. "This has all the statements from folks in the Meisner household at the time."

The box was filled with hanging files. Labels poked above the level of the green folders. Jess thumbed her way through the first few. "A lot of names."

"Like you said, it's a big house with a big staff. There's a stables and offices. His campaign staff and consultants of one kind or another are always coming and going, too. And the security team." He shrugged again. "Maybe more. I don't know if there were people doing work on the grounds back then, but it's likely. A place like that requires a lot of upkeep."

She pulled a random file from the box. It contained an interview with the Meisner's chief gardener. "Chief" implied they had more than one. Even a team, possibly?

"You really think she was headed to Meisner's house?" Nelson said.

"There aren't a lot of other options." Jess hummed and flipped through another file. A farm hand. A round, friendly face with character lines. From the length of the statement, he liked to talk.

Nelson settled into reading the papers on his desk. Jess worked her way through the statements taken at the Meisner house.

Everyone had been concerned for Crystal. Everyone asked to be informed of what the police found. Everyone seemed to be her friend. There were statements galore to back up their claim that she was fun and a hard worker. A responsible person.

No one mentioned that she might have been a different person outside of work. No one hinted that her idea of fun was a little beyond ordinary. No one suggested she was into anything illegal.

Jess shook her head. Crystal Mackie had been living with Johnny Yukon, practically the definition of a reckless streak, and yet everyone who knew her said she was as pure as the driven snow.

The statements were thorough. Consistent questions. An even tone. The answers recorded verbatim. Nelson's predecessor had been a good officer. Disciplined. A good listener and a good observer. He hadn't been able to find Crystal Mackie, but he had left everything he'd learned well organized for those that came after him.

She reached the last file in the Meisner box. A maid. Her statement echoed the sentiments of the rest of the staff. Jess squeezed the folder back into the box.

She frowned. "There's no statement from Meisner."

Nelson shook himself out of his reverie and waved at the boxes. "It's in another one. His prepared statement."

"Why isn't his statement in this box with the others?"

Nelson shrugged. "I probably moved it. Nothing much there. You know politicians."

She nodded. "Strange that everyone else in the house was open, helpful, and complimentary to Crystal. But Meisner gives a formal, attorney approved statement." Jess leaned back in her chair. "Why get so formal unless he knew something bad had happened? Something he needed to manage. Politically, at least."

Nelson shook his head. "He probably does that with everything. He got someone to handle it, and bingo, a formal statement rather than a casual chat."

"I still think it's worth following up with him," Jess said. "Crystal was pregnant. There has to be a father. We know it wasn't Johnny Yukon. Could have been someone she worked with."

Nelson shook his head. "I have enough to deal with. I don't need to add to my list. Come up with a good lead, and we'll chase it down. Until then, I'm not hassling Meisner."

Jess leaned over the box of statements and pulled out one with a familiar name. Alistaire Meisner. She slid the other papers into the box. "Okay. So what's next?"

Nelson shook his head. "Some of us have work to do."

CHAPTER FIFTY-FIVE

JESS LEFT THE POLICE station and drove to a store she had seen earlier. The windows were barred, and there were several stern notices on the door, warning would-be criminals of cameras and the full force of the law. They contrasted with the large neon sign that read "Wolfhound Willy's Guns and Ammo—Come and get 'em!"

Inside, the store was lit with powerful fluorescent lights. The walls were covered with racks of guns in wire-framed cupboards. She gravitated to the more expensive end of the display cases and the weapons she either recognized or had used before.

A man in sunglasses and a long white beard, who was a dead ringer for a member of a southern rock band, stepped forward.

"I need a gun," she said.

"Got your license?"

Jess held out her Colorado driver's license and concealed carry permit.

"No reciprocity here with Colorado." He shook his head.

"Arkansas, Louisiana, Michigan, Mississippi, Missouri, North Carolina, North Dakota, Idaho, Ohio, Oklahoma and Utah only." He recited the states with the same enthusiasm as a middle schooler on a geography test.

"How long to get a Washington concealed carry license?"

"First you've got to buy the gun. For non-residents, that's up to sixty days." He grimaced.

"Any way around that?"

He shook his head.

"I'm a lone female, I could do with something for defense."

He pointed to the opposite side of the store. "We have knives. Pretty good deterrent value."

He lined up several plain mid-length knives on the counter. Jess tried a couple in her hand. They felt cumbersome. She eventually settled for a switchblade. The retaining mechanism was strong, and the blade flicked cleanly into place. She might never use it, but she felt vulnerable without her Glock, so she paid and left.

She realized she was hungry all of a sudden. The easiest place to grab a quick bite was Biscuits. She drove on and parked by the front of the building. The lot was as empty as on Jess's previous visits. For the first time, she noticed the sign over the door said *M. Harvey*. Jess grinned. No wonder Elisha had wanted to support the place.

Jess grabbed her bag, headed inside, and took the booth where she had met Elisha. Fifties music echoed from a tinny speaker somewhere behind the grill. A couple of truckers at a table near the other end of the room stared at Jess before going back to their food.

A waitress walked over with a coffee pot in her hand. There was a mug, ready on the table. Jess turned it over, and the woman filled it with coffee. She left no room for cream, nor did she ask.

Jess ordered a salad and an omelet.

"Anything else?" said the waitress without looking up.

"Is the owner in today?"

The waitress looked at Jess. "Why?"

"Elisha Harvey is related to the owner of this place, right?"

"Marion Harvey. That's right," the waitress nodded.

"I'd like to meet her. Is she here?"

"You're the reporter?"

Jess nodded. "Why?"

"Nothing." She walked away.

Jess curled her fingers around the mug. The coffee was hot and strong. Steam curled up into the chill. Jess blew on it, twisting and turning its path in the air.

"You wanted to see me?" said a woman's voice.

Jess turned. The woman could be no one other than Elisha's sister. A little older perhaps, and a little heavier. "You're Marion?"

"Yeah." She sat in the booth, opposite Jess. "What do you need?"

"I was wondering, did you work at the Meisner estate when Crystal Mackie disappeared?"

"Didn't see that question coming." Marion pursed her lips and then nodded. "Yes."

"You gave a statement to the police at the time?"

"We all did."

"Did you know Crystal?"

"Everyone knew her. I mean, everyone at Meisner's. It's a big place, but the people who worked there, we kind of, like, bonded. We were a good team."

Jess leaned forward, both hands around the warm coffee mug. "What comes to mind when you think about her?"

"She was…happy-go-lucky. I mean, we all knew she was living with Spud, so…" Marion sighed. "You've got to have a wild streak to live with a guy like that. So, we all gave her some latitude."

"Latitude about what?"

Marion looked left and right, and back at Jess. "Like…her ups and downs, and if she was a little late or something. Life with Spud can do that to a girl."

"Is that experience talking?"

Marion grunted and shook her head.

"Was she often late?"

"Occasionally."

"I've read your police statement. You didn't mention any tardiness."

Marion shrugged. "I liked her. She'd gone missing. I wasn't going to say anything bad about her."

Jess shrugged. "I guess we're all late sometimes."

Marion shuffled to the open end of her bench seat and braced herself to stand.

"What other bad things were there that you didn't mention at the time?" Jess asked.

Marion stopped moving. Her hands on the table, taking her weight, ready to stand. She looked at Jess and looked away.

"Please. It could be important." Jess reached across and touched her hand.

Marion sank back into her seat. "I don't know…it…" She shook her head. "Senator Meisner. He told us not to spread rumors. To stick to the facts."

"Like what kind of rumors?"

"Well, you know, rumors… They're not facts. And it was a long time ago."

"It could still be important. Even now."

She nodded. "Well, he used to look at the girls. Always. Like you could tell he was staring. Every time he walked past." She shivered. "Most of us just thought he was a creep."

Jess kept her face impassive.

Marion looked at her hands. "I didn't want to mention it at the time. With him being recently married. You know?"

"It might still be important." Jess smiled reassuringly.

Marion sighed. "We had different shifts, right? Earlys, lates, on some days, off others. It was hard to know. To be sure, I mean. But…I, I don't think that was the first time Crystal had disappeared for a few days. And…"

Jess gazed steadily at Marion without flinching. "And, what?"

Marion shifted her weight. She looked up and down the length of the diner. She took a deep breath. "I didn't realize till later, and I might be wrong, but when Crystal wasn't around…Meisner wasn't either."

CHAPTER FIFTY-SIX

JESS LEFT THE DINER dialing Nelson. The moment the call connected, she said, "We need to talk to Yukon again."

"This is Jess Kimball, I presume?"

"Marion Harvey just told me that Crystal Mackie had disappeared before. She thinks Crystal disappeared at the same time Meisner was traveling." Jess paused, still standing in the parking lot. She glanced around to be sure no one was paying attention. "She didn't say so, but I could tell she thinks they might have been together."

Nelson sucked air in through his teeth. "There's no statement to that effect. No one has ever mentioned that before."

"Marion said she didn't want to speak badly about Crystal because she'd gone missing. Meisner prompted them not to spread rumors."

Nelson sighed. "She didn't say that in any formal statement, and she hasn't mentioned it in fourteen years."

"She was trying to keep her job. Meisner was fighting a

battle with the town over the right of way, Charlene's disappearance was stirring things up." Jess paused again. "Don't you see? Raising a suspicion like that would have been like bringing a burning match to a gas station."

"Is she willing to make a formal statement?"

Jess shook her head. "I didn't ask. But let's just talk to Yukon again. Maybe he'll open up or just remember something."

"Unfortunately he won't. One of the neighbors found him on his living room floor. Paramedics were too late. Looks like he overdosed."

CHAPTER FIFTY-SEVEN

BLACKSTAKE WATCHED JESS KIMBALL back her car out of the diner's parking lot and head toward the police station. He raised his window. The air was chill. Crisp. Refreshing. The ideal conditions for voices to travel. Something to do with compression ratios, or density, or other scientific terms he had little time for. To him, it only meant one thing. Kimball's phone call had been easy to overhear.

He dialed his phone and waited two rings. "She's still digging."

The boss swore.

"But they can't talk to Yukon any more. Apparently, he's OD'd."

"Apparently?"

"Absolutely definite."

"Now you just have to worry about Kimball and Nelson."

"Trust me. I'm not worried about them at all."

CHAPTER FIFTY-EIGHT

JESS PARKED IN THE Randolph police station lot and called
Mandy. By the fourth ring Jess expected voicemail, but Mandy's
voice came on the line.

"What's up?"

"I need you to dig up anything you can on Senator Meisner
from fourteen years ago. I'm interested in hotels he stayed in,
flights he took, cars he hired or rented. We need the same
information on Crystal Mackie as well. I'm looking for
commonality. Anything that overlapped."

"I've got the afternoon off." The pitch of Mandy's voice rose
an octave.

Jess stifled a sigh. "Okay. Then tomorrow will be fine. But
it's important, so first thing, okay?"

"First thing. No problem. I'm mostly done with Meisner
anyway."

Jess frowned. "Mostly done?"

"Carter had me dig out his background. He put me in touch

with the Berenstains. And not the bears. They're a political investigator unit in DC."

Jess pressed the phone closer to her ear. "And?"

"Well, I've got a ton of stuff on everything he voted for and against. Where his contributions come from. Ethics committee. All that sort of stuff."

"Any scandals? Staffers, males, females, constituents, donors, anything like that? Legal problems?"

"No sex scandals that we can find. He's married to big money. His wife keeps him on a short leash. He's had some long-running legal problem with the boundary of his estate, but the big thing is that he nearly went bankrupt."

"When?"

"Fourteen years ago, shortly after his first election. The Berenstains say his father died, left him the family fortune, and he spent it getting elected."

Jess checked her watch. "I don't suppose you…"

"I have a date."

Jess sagged back.

There was a long silence.

Mandy sighed. "All right. I'll find a way to remote-in to my secure email and send you what I can."

Jess smiled. "I owe you."

"Yes, you do." Mandy took a deep breath. "I haven't written it all up, so it'll just be a bunch of files. You'll have to figure it out."

"No problem."

The strains of an orchestra tuning up reverberated through the phone line. "This a good date?"

"A visiting conductor from Vienna."

"Interesting."

"He specializes in opera."

"Nice."

"I like opera."

"Since when?"

Mandy laughed. "Very recently. And he's starting, so I have to go."

The line went dead. Jess grinned as she tucked the phone in her pocket.

CHAPTER FIFTY-NINE

JESS WALKED INTO THE police station. Gardner was the only person visible. He stood up and met her at the counter.

"I need to talk to Nelson," Jess said.

Gardner stepped toward Jess, his arms outstretched, herding her back to the door. "We're flat out busy. I don't think he's going to want to talk to a reporter. Come back tomorrow."

"That's okay, Gardner," Nelson said.

Gardner turned. "Oh, I thought you were leaving."

"I wish."

"Where's Charlene?" Jess said.

Nelson checked his watch. "Shifts over. She's gone."

"What happened to Yukon?"

"The pathologist report will tell us, but I think it's safe to assume he OD'd on something. The paramedics noticed several syringes scattered around the living room."

"Good riddance," Gardner said.

Jess shook her head. "I can't say I'd ever have liked him, but it's a shame to see a life wasted."

Nelson nodded. "It's strange, though. He's been an addict for the best part of twenty years. He's been in and out of rehab and in and out of jail. Then right after we visit, he overdoses."

"You think there's a connection?"

He shrugged. "Hard to say at this point. I mean we took Laurie away, but I doubt that pushed him over the edge."

"Think he knew something?"

"Probably guilty as hell," Gardner said. "Finally got too much for him."

Jess frowned. "He didn't seem in the slightest concerned when we were there earlier."

Gardner laughed. "He was good at playing people. I mean, no offense, but look at him, he'd being doing it for years. He was an expert."

"Do you think Yukon was capable of killing someone?"

"You mean Crystal?" Gardner said. "Who knows? But he could have put the fear of God in her, and frightened her off. Either way, he's gone now, and that should put a lid on the Crystal Mackie case."

"We'll see," Nelson said. He beckoned Jess as he led the way back to his office, and closed the door.

"Gardner's not a fan of Yukon or Charlene. So, Crystal Mackie has always been a sore point with him. Far as he's concerned, they're trash and not worth the time of day."

"Do you think Yukon could be involved in her disappearance?"

He gestured to the boxes of evidence. "I've read everything that's been collected on the case, and I still have no strong feelings about what happened."

He leaned back in his chair. "So, Marion told you that Crystal and Meisner seemed to travel at the same time?"

"Yes."

"But she never thought to mention it in all this time?"

"She's not one to start rumors."

"In other words, she doesn't have proof."

Jess sighed. "Charlene showed me a picture of Crystal. Had it in her purse. She was wearing a black T-shirt with writing on it that I can't quite remember."

Nelson thumbed through the files in the box marked "C. Mackie #4." He found a faded green envelope and pulled out a photograph.

Jess took the picture. "This is the same one Charlene showed me."

Crystal's bright eyes stared back at her. Blond hair and high cheekbones. The tree she'd leaned against. Blue jeans and the black T-shirt with the heart-shaped American flag and "I love DC" stamped on it.

She turned the photo over. There was a date on the back. "This was taken the week before she disappeared."

"Apparently."

Crystal was carefree, smiling. She looked like a girl who thought she had a future. Confident. At peace in her world. "She knew she was leaving Yukon."

Nelson frowned. "You're a mind reader now?"

"She was pregnant, and Yukon wasn't the baby's father. Obviously, she had a plan. Her glowing face tells you that." Jess held up the picture for Nelson to see. "She thinks she's on the way to a better life."

Nelson frowned.

"This isn't the smile of a girl who's living in squalor with that scum. This is a girl who *knows* her life is getting better." Jess shook the picture. "Look at her eyes. She's absolutely one-hundred percent sure of it."

"If you say so."

"Exactly." Jess lowered the photograph. "Do you have a list of the things Crystal left behind?"

Nelson rummaged in the same box and found a twenty-three-page list and an envelope of photographs. He laid out the pictures on the desk and handed the list to Jess.

Jess skimmed the list. Most of it was unremarkable. Clothes, shoes, toiletries and the like. A shoe box containing old bank statements and other papers, and a smooth pink rock that must have held some sentimental value.

Everything on the list had been photographed and cross-referenced. She pored over the pictures.

Nelson shook his head. "I've looked at them for hours. Things a young woman would own. Nothing special about any of it."

Jess moved from picture to picture, resisting the temptation to skim to the end. Worn shoes. A broken watch. Sunglasses. The contents of the shoebox photographed on both sides of every page. Bills and receipts. Mundane. Tedious in life, irrelevant after.

Jess reached the end of the photographs. The last picture showed a dresser drawer. A comb, toiletries, and a few scraps of paper. One was a small square with a hole punched in it.

She handed the picture to Nelson. "She kept mementos. Things that meant something to her."

She pointed to the square. Printed on it was an American flag in the shape of a heart. The letter *D* was visible.

Nelson frowned. "She was so happy in the T-shirt, she kept the tag?"

"I love DC. Except it wasn't the T-shirt. She was really saying she loved what it represented."

Nelson shook his head. "You think she was planning to move to DC with Yukon?"

Jess shook her head. "She knew she was leaving Yukon. She was heading toward a better life. What do you need if you're going to start over?"

He frowned. "A dream? Hope? A lover?"

"Money. She'd already made plans to sell her baby. And maybe she planned to get more money from someone else, and," Jess pointed to Crystal's T-shirt.

"And what? Millions of people live in DC."

"But who did she know?"

Nelson shook his head. "You can't accuse a public figure with nothing to back up the charges but guesses."

"True." Jess nodded.

"Rumor has it he's starting a run for the presidency. That brings a whole machine down on you, me, and anyone else who dares say anything bad about him."

"I'm not writing fiction. I'll get confirmation."

"Confirmation? Confirmation isn't going to do squat. He'll chew you up and spit you out if you find anything less than Crystal Mackie's body."

CHAPTER SIXTY

JESS SAT IN THE police station parking lot and checked her phone. Another missed call from Agent Henry Morris, but he'd left no message, so whatever he wanted couldn't be all that urgent. The message from Mandy was better. She had found somewhere to connect to her email and forward the information she had collected on Meisner.

She flipped through the first few files. Lists of his voting records stacked against his declared investments. No obvious conflicts of interest, but if he was smart enough to manipulate legislation to his advantage, he was smart enough to cover up his activities.

One file was devoted to Meisner's legal battle over the right of way across his land. There were hundreds of pages of legal discussion. She skipped through, stopping at a series of diagrams of his estate.

Before the big fence was installed, the public pathway had curved much further into his estate than it did now. The diagrams included crosses, circles, and random capital letters. She searched the surrounding pages but found no explanations for them.

The file ended with the order establishing the new path. A compromise established by a judge after fourteen years of the trivial dispute. About the length of time Meisner had been a senator.

The final file covered Meisner's financial affairs. The Berenstains had acquired confidential information. Some of it must have been illegally obtained.

Politicians are not required to disclose tax returns, but Meisner's were included. His estate and holdings were sizeable, but his income wasn't. Around the time he was first elected to the senate, his tax bill approached the value of his entire holdings. Creditors threatened him with involuntary bankruptcy. Shortly afterward, somehow he'd paid all of his debts. Jess shook her head. How had he managed to employ such a big staff to maintain his house and grounds?

She found the answer in the next file. Fourteen years ago, Meisner had married Margot Palmer-Breton, daughter of one of America's few double-digit billionaires. George Palmer-Breton had started from nothing and in forty years built up a financial empire that was a watchword for integrity and independence.

Wedding pictures included a shot of Margot's father with his arm around Meisner. Both men smiling.

Two years later, Margot's father purchased Meisner's estate. Only Meisner still lived there. So it wasn't so much a purchase, as a way to transfer a large sum of money while avoiding any troublesome tax issues.

Jess whistled. Not only did Meisner no longer own his mansion or his estate, but he'd sold to his father-in-law three days after Crystal Mackie was reported missing.

CHAPTER SIXTY-ONE

SHE LOOKED AT THE map one last time and then closed it. Mandy's email reappeared with its long list of attachments running off the bottom of the phone's screen. Jess scrolled down. She had looked at most of the files, but she'd missed one at the very bottom. The last in the list was labeled *NEL gate*. She clicked to open it.

The images of a book appeared on the phone. They had been taken with a camera, not scanned in. The book was laid on a wood desk. The pages were open, the spine folded flat. Each page had a list of names. Each name was in different handwriting. Some were cursive, some were printed, and some were in capitals. There were dates and times in columns. The columns were marked *Entry* and *Exit*. The dates were for the past weekend.

Jess flipped on to the next image. It was the same book. The same folded flat pages and lists of names. The dates were older. She flipped back and forth. The dates were in pairs with gaps.

She counted from the current date. They were weekends. Saturday and Sunday with no more entries until the next Saturday.

She flipped on to the next page and traced her finger down the names. She stopped on the second to last name and frowned. The letters were heavily slanted. The sweep of a confident writer. A busy person dashing off a signature before rushing on to more important matters. She recognized the name. He was the Senate majority leader. His appointment had come with controversy. His face had been a staple of the evening news for a couple of weeks until the next big thing had moved him aside.

Jess ran back to the first image. There was no cover page or title. She skimmed a dozen pages and recognized the names of several senators. Twenty-five pages in, a gray cover appeared, with the words *North Entry Lower* covering the top half. Underneath were two dates, four years and seven months apart. She skimmed on.

Every fifty pages, a cover appeared with the same title and a new pair of dates. The book ran serially back in time. The dates kept up the weekend pattern. She recognized the names of more senators.

The document was long. The pictures changed. They were taken from a different angle. The lighting was different. Further on, the wood changed to marble and the gray covers to green.

She pressed on. Ignoring the names and concentrating on the dates. She stopped the week Peter Whiting was born fourteen years ago. The pictures were dim. A different camera. Older. Poorer resolution. The signatures had jagged edges. She went further back in time. A month. Two. Four.

She stopped at a name. Her skin tingled. She leaned closer to her phone. Closer to the image. Her eyes smoothed the handwriting's jagged lines, her mind envisaging the sweep of a pen. She zoomed in. Centering a name on the phone's small screen.

Alistaire Meisner.

The signature was unmistakable. Clear. Precise lines and confident curves.

Underneath was another name she recognized. Strong print. Individual letters. Same date, same time. No less clear. No less confident.

Crystal Mackie.

Jess punched the speed dial button for Mandy's cell phone. It seemed like ages before connecting. She took deep breaths as it rang and fell over to voicemail. Her assistant's jaunty voice invited her to leave a message and assured that she would reply as soon as possible.

"Mandy. It's Jess. The information you sent. From the Berenstains, or whatever their name was, I need to know where the North Entry Lower book came from. It's got a long list of signatures and dates. I need an answer as soon as possible."

She took a breath. "And thank you. I know you had to break up your date. I appreciate it, Mandy. I really do."

Jess hung up. She had a good idea she knew where the book came from, but why such a book existed and why it had so few names was a mystery.

Meisner denied knowing Crystal Mackie, and yet here were both names recorded in what was surely their individual handwriting. If Jess was right about the pages of the NEL book, the signatures had been made on the other side of the country.

Not a smoking gun, but definitely a new lead. Crystal Mackie might be leading a happy life somewhere. Or she might not be. Jess had a bad feeling about Crystal. She'd had that bad feeling from the beginning.

She heard Nelson's voice urging restraint, telling her she needed evidence.

CHAPTER SIXTY-TWO

LIGHT RAIN MISTED THE windshield of Jess's rental. She briefly considered her need to find a hotel for the night before studying the strange hand-drawn markings on the Meisner estate maps. The images in Mandy's files were copies that had been scanned or photographed from the originals with no indication of where the originals were located.

She switched off her phone and started her car. Maybe she could figure it out by comparing the map to the physical area. She rolled out toward the Meisner estate.

Within ten minutes, she found and parked at the place where Nelson had found her on her first day in town. The rain hadn't let up. She wished she still had her jacket. She turned up her collar and slid out of the car.

The ground was slippery. She kept to the side of the trail, making the most of the additional grip from the grassy edges.

She called out to Max, but he didn't reply, and she continued on to what she'd come to think of as Peter's tree. She stayed well into the woods, shadowed by the tree's canopy. She hoped Meisner's security team in the mansion couldn't see her.

She pulled out her phone and found Mandy's map. She visualized the computerized survey map, matching it to the physical presence it represented. As expected, the markings accurately referenced the location of the house and fence.

The handwritten marks on the plan were less obvious and less accurate. She walked further along the trail to a spot marked by a circle placed on the vicious looking fence. The circle lined up with the gate Meisner's security guards had used to escort her from the property. The gate was secured with a heavy-duty chain and padlock.

The map showed two more locations with circles. Probably two more gates. The persistent rain dissuaded her from investigating further.

The remaining hand-drawn mark on the fence was a cross. She'd passed that location already. She turned and walked back, bending down to peer through the woods as she approached the area.

She stood on the edge of the woods, beside the cover of another tree. The slope of the hill hid the lower two floors of the mansion. She looked along the roofline, searching for surveillance cameras. She saw none, but knew they must be there somewhere.

She stepped closer to the fence. The horizontal spars were thick wire placed at six-inch intervals. The vertical poles were single piece, heavy-duty metal moldings that ran straight into the ground. The horizontal wires ran through holes in the vertical poles. Three rows of barbed wire were secured to the tops of the poles.

She walked to the next vertical pole. The horizontal wires passed through holes here, too. She tossed a branch at the wires.

It bounced off. The wires vibrated but didn't arc or burn the branch. It looked like an electric fence, but either it wasn't electrified or the power was off.

The next vertical post was different. The horizontal wires didn't pass through the metal. They were attached to the post with bolts. The next set of wires ran from another set of bolts.

She stepped back. It was the dislodged post she had seen on her first visit to the tree. It sported a bright yellow label with black text identifying who to call for repairs. Nelson had said it was probably vandalism, but the more she looked, the less it looked like a random act.

The post was embedded in the ground, but the tension in the wires on either side contributed to holding it upright. She'd once read how counterbalanced loads kept suspension bridges from falling. She touched the wires. They were taut with little sign of sagging between the posts. The wires hadn't been sagging on her first visit, either. So the wires hadn't been cut.

She stepped back. A large area of ground had been dug up around the post. Much more than would have been required for a concrete base. Presumably, the foundations for the post also played a part in keeping it upright. And if the wires hadn't been cut, the foundations must have been undermined.

She looked at the old map. There was no question in her mind. Someone had marked the post on the old map. It had been something important. Something they wanted to remember.

And fourteen years later, someone had dug it up again.

She shook the wires that stretched from post to post. It was easy to see how the post could be pulled over if the force on either side wasn't balanced. Whoever had cut the wires knew that very well. It wasn't luck or spite or random vandalism that led him to this particular spot.

She held out her arms on each side of her body. Like most people, her outstretched arms from fingertip to fingertip were the same length as her height—five feet four. The churned up ground around the post was a good two feet longer than her extended arms.

She stared at the ground. Seven feet. Far more than was required to reinstall the fence post but, she took a deep breath, enough to bury Crystal Mackie's body.

Except that made no sense. Crystal Mackie disappeared fourteen years ago, but the fence post was repaired this week. Unless the body was someone other than Crystal. But that didn't make sense, either. Whoever buried the body had to know the fence post would be repaired. No one would bury a body expecting repairmen to dig it up again.

She turned off her flashlight. Blackness flooded in. The sun had given up for the day. The woods were silent. The activity of the daytime creatures handed over to the more cautious night dwellers.

In the distance, the mansion's lights illuminated brilliant white walls. The roof climbed into the misty black sky. Whatever secrets were hidden inside Meisner's mansion had waited for years. They'd wait another day.

CHAPTER SIXTY-THREE

JESS RETURNED TO HER rental, switched on the headlights, and drove back to town.

The Plum Inn was at the opposite end of town from The Montpelier. It wasn't just its location that was at the other end of the scale.

The property was a two-story motel with paint peeling from the siding. Wooden steps ran up the side of the property to the upper floor. The doors were navy blue upstairs, and green on the ground floor. They opened directly into the rooms. As Jess parked her car, she didn't hold out a lot of hope for room service.

The office was at one end of the building. It was a cramped space with a counter, a guest book, and an out-of-place old-fashioned cash register. Behind the counter was a door that, by the scent in the air, Jess guessed led to a laundry.

A woman followed her into the office. "Room?" she said, as she ducked under the counter.

Jess nodded. "Say a week." She had no idea how much

longer she would be in Randolph, but she wasn't going to risk being turned out of her last chance hotel.

The woman had a handwritten badge with Beth printed in large letters. Underneath it said *Enjoy your stay!* in faded blue marker.

Beth pushed the guest book toward Jess. "Name, address, and registration. I'll need ID."

Jess held out her driver's license and corporate credit card.

Beth examined the license and wrote down the number from the credit card.

Jess frowned.

The woman handed back the card. "We don't have a reader thing. I have to call the number in."

Jess smiled. "No problem."

The woman looked Jess up and down. "Forgive me, but you don't look short on money. There's a fancier place on down the road."

"The Montpellier?"

"Yeah. You know it?"

"I was there last night."

The woman raised her eyebrows. "Didn't like it?"

"They're full tonight. Apparently. Practically threw me out."

The woman tutted. "Old Meisner isn't known for his hospitality."

"The Montpellier is owned by Meisner?"

"Not Senator Meisner, Charlie Meisner. His brother. Though I should say Charles Meisner because he hates Charlie. One more stuck up than the other."

"You don't like them?"

The woman shrugged. "It's not a case of like or don't like. They don't spend their time with the likes of me."

Jess hummed. "Me neither, so it seems."

The woman held out an old key with a giant wooden key fob. "Well, you're welcome to stay here as long as you like."

Jess left the close confines of the office. The number twenty-seven was crudely chiseled into the wood. It was halfway between rustic charm and an amateur trying his hand at one of the million jobs that a small business has to perform to save every penny.

Room twenty-seven was on the upstairs deck. Jess carried her bag up the creaking steps. It was almost at the end of the row of blue doors.

The key slid into the lock with a well-worn ease. The door drifted open. The air inside was as chill as outside. Jess's breath condensed in front of her.

Two wall lights above the bed lit the room. One was brighter than the other, but neither was up to the task of illuminating the space.

The bed was close to the floor, and the springs squeaked as she dropped her bag on it. The sheets were clean, and there were several layers of blankets. The drapes didn't quite join in the center of the window.

The room had only three other items of furniture, a table and chair, and a chest of drawers beside the bed. A flyer on top of the dresser advertised a local pizza delivery place. She had no better option, so she ordered a small pepperoni and a salad.

There was an electric heater on the wall. She switched it on. Air wafted out. It took a minute until it was warm. Jess looked at the room. It was going to take a while to heat it all.

A narrow door led into a bathroom. The sink was a plastic molded one-piece unit. The large bathtub was old and did double duty as a shower. It rang as Jess tapped it. Cast iron.

She settled on the bed to catch up on her email.

Ten minutes later, her pizza arrived. She tipped the fresh-faced kid that delivered it and dug into the food as she pondered the Crystal Mackie case.

She'd demanded to talk to Meisner out of anger and frustration. She had so many puzzle pieces and still no idea of the picture. She sighed. Nelson might even be correct that all she was doing was stirring things up.

No.

She stood up. Someone wasn't taking revenge, and it wasn't random acts of vandalism. Someone was spooked. Someone was covering their tracks. The painful irony was that she might be the one connecting the dots for that very someone.

She sent a message to Mandy, asking if she was able to talk, and waited three minutes until her phone rang.

"Mandy," Jess said.

"The one and only."

"How's the date?"

"Good. I'm back home."

"Oh. Didn't work out?"

"No, no. This one's good, but he's a trainee, and practice didn't go well. So he's practicing some more."

"And you left?"

"It's opera."

Jess smiled. "I thought you liked opera?"

"I do. Kind of. It does go on."

"The novelty wears off."

"With the opera."

"And the trainee conductor?"

"We'll see. What do you want?"

"N.E.L. North Entrance Lower. The book of signatures you sent. Is that the North entrance of the Capitol?"

"The very one. The Capitol building in DC. I asked the Berenstains. There's several parking lots and entrances on the ground level, but that entrance is the least popular with senators."

"Least popular?"

"Yeah. Apparently, it smells and hasn't been renovated since the sixties."

"But the Berenstains have a copy of the register?"

"Yeah. Don't ask."

"Why not?"

"That's what the Berenstains said."

"But it's the least popular entrance."

"So it's only used by people who want to get in and out of their offices without attracting attention."

"Like a senator trying to impress his mistress."

Mandy groaned.

"What?" Jess said.

"You're going to make me hunt for Meisner's name, aren't you?"

"I've already found his name. And Crystal Mackie's. Right next to each other. Same date, same time."

Mandy's voice lightened. "Good. Because I don't mind searching it, but not tonight. Tomorrow. At the office where I can use optical character recognition."

"Do that, and send me the list."

Jess said goodbye and hung up.

The least popular entrance? She shook her head. It was a good link, but could he still use the plausible deniability argument?

The bed creaked as she sat on it.

She was seeing half the picture. When Peter Whiting's name

had been pushed into the news, it had set off a series of events. The destruction of the Whitings' home, the murder of Norah Fender, maybe even Johnny Yukon's overdose, they were all linked through Peter.

Yet the only thing that felt as if it could be significant was the question over Peter's father. And why would being Peter's father be a reason for murder? Why would anyone want to cover it up so badly?

She had no answer.

CHAPTER SIXTY-FOUR

JESS'S LAPTOP SAT ON the end of the bed. It called to her. She should be making notes. Documenting her day. Recording the seemingly insignificant. It was the way she found her best leads, in the tiny details.

She sat on the bed, her back against the headboard. She needed to think. There was too much going on. Nothing seemed connected, yet she knew, positively, that somewhere there was a connection.

She closed her eyes. The room was warming up. Her limbs felt weighted. She let them sink down. The sounds of passing cars faded.

Images drifted in front of her. Dreams of boats and piers and sails meshed into a mad reality. She was floating away. She reached to hold on and hit something. Something hard.

Her eyes snapped open. She couldn't see anything in the inky room. She felt something on her face, across her mouth. She struggled to breathe. Her hands flew to her face. Duct tape.

The silhouette of a man loomed over her, a ski mask over his face. He lunged with his right hand. Jess grabbed his forearm. Something glinted in his hand. He swung his other arm, smashing Jess across the face. She kicked up at his side and twisted the man's arm.

In the faint glow from the street lights that crept between the curtains, the glinting object became a glass and steel tube. A syringe.

The man shifted more weight to his right. She dug her nails into the man's arm. The needle hovered inches from her neck.

She brought a knee up between her and the attacker. She snorted air through her nose.

He angled the needle toward her face, the tip was so close she could barely focus on it.

She pressed the air down into her lungs, tensing her muscles, and rammed his hand sideways. The needle scraped across her shoulder and smashed into the chest of drawers, snapping off the syringe.

The man snarled, and threw his weight back and forth, ripping his arm from Jess's grasp, and bringing his knee down on her chest.

Her lungs burned. She felt two hands around her neck. Tight. She squirmed and bucked. Shifting her weight. Using her legs to angle her sideways across the bed.

The man tightened his grip. Closing around her throat.

She gagged hard. The skin around her mouth strained against the strong tape. She ran her hands up the man's arms, searching for his face. She couldn't reach.

She kicked up her legs. Bringing her knees up. Hard and high. Her attacker grunted.

Blood pounded in her ears. Her face throbbed. She pulled on

the man's elbows. A hard jerk. Widening the distance between his arms. Bringing his face closer to hers.

She whipped her hand upward. Fist clenched. Shoving hard. Reaching soft flesh and bone. Under his chin. His neck. Ramming her knuckles into his windpipe. He gagged and twisted his torso, deflecting her blow.

She couldn't escape his chokehold. She punched again. Barely reaching. He'd pulled back. His face out of her reach. Her head pounded. Vibrating as hard as a jackhammer. Her lungs strained to suck the gallons of oxygen her body was demanding through her nostrils.

She threw her legs to one side. Away from the door. Away from the man. Leverage to escape the confines of her bed and his grip. Her movements were slow. Her arms wavered, fell back down, laid across her chest.

No. She mustn't stop. She forced her hand upward. Slow. Like moving lead through treacle. Her head rolled forward, desperate to ease the crushing force on her windpipe. She felt the man's jacket. She pulled. Too weak. She slid her fingers along its edge and felt leather and cold metal. She fumbled and gripped. Her fingers searching. The metal moved. She felt a click.

Light flashed. Intense and white. A roar filled her ears, half percussion and half the hissing of a thousand snakes. A hot blast ripped her grip away. The white faded to black. Not pitch black. Not everywhere. A silhouette. Broad shoulders. Thick arms. A ski mask.

The man jerked sideways. She felt his hands slide from her neck. His body tumbled onto her side. Away from the door. Her arms wouldn't move. Her legs were numb. She rolled to push him off. Just a small tilt of her body.

His tumble continued. Onto the floor. His head smashed hard

into the thin carpet. His arms clattered over the metal edge of the bed. His boots thumped, toes first.

She rolled her head forward, curling her neck around the screaming pain in her windpipe.

She brought her fingers up to her mouth. They grabbed at her chin. She forced them up to her mouth, but they scraped through her hair. She willed them back down, over her eyelids and her nose. Down to the rough tape across her mouth.

Her vision was no more than spots. Her head throbbed, and her heartbeat swooshed in her ears.

She scraped with her nails, catching an edge of the tape. Picking at it with the tips of her fingers. She rolled up a corner. Gripping the sticky backing, she gave it a hard yank.

Pain erupted across her face. Air rushed into her lungs. She choked and coughed. She rolled forward, curling slightly. She drank air in giant lungfuls, gasping and choking and fighting to keep herself from swallowing her tongue.

She pried one eye open, squinting at the painful bright light. She felt something wet on her hands, and an acrid burning smell drifted into her nose.

There was noise. Voices. Or one voice. The buzzing and pounding in her head stopped the voice from getting through. She was rolled onto her side. Her legs were moved, curled up halfway. Her arms were pulled from under her.

A scream rang out. High pitched. Short. The physical impact of shock. There were more noises. Definitely more voices. The ringing in her ears was fading. She panted. People meant protection. Safety in numbers.

A siren wailed in the distance.

The voices grew louder. Beth's face appeared above Jess. Her lips moved. Jess heard nothing but the ringing and the siren.

Beth lay a cold towel on Jess's forehead. A couple came into the room and stared. The woman had her hands over her mouth. Beth pushed them out.

The whistling faded as the siren came louder.

Beth looked at the man on the floor.

"He attacked me," Jess said, though her words were incoherent.

Beth patted Jess's arm.

"He attacked me," she said again, her words more intelligible this time.

Beth nodded. Slow. Deliberate. "Well, you killed him. That's for sure."

The siren was close. It stopped. Two paramedics hustled into the room. Jess didn't move. She wanted to tell them what had happened, but her jaw stayed still and locked.

They knelt on either side of her and moved her arms. They shined a bright light in her eyes. She stared at it. She blinked once, which made it better and went back to staring. They took the light away. A black spot drifted in front of her. They attached an oxygen mask to her face and stuck a needle in her arm. She saw a transparent bag hanging on a hook above her.

"I wum-um wag-ah when," she said. The mask was muffling her voice. She reached for it. One of the medics pulled her hand away, and shook his head.

They slid her onto a stretcher and carried her out of the room. The body lay on the floor, its arms and legs at awkward angles, an irregular pool of blood around its chest.

At the bottom of the stairs, Nelson appeared in her field of view.

"E attaracked me," she said, "Did a kill 'im?"

Nelson nodded. "Looks like you did."

CHAPTER SIXTY-FIVE

JESS GROANED. SHE ROLLED sideways. Soft, crisp cotton brushed against her face. Her throat was dry and sore. A machine bleeped in the distance.

She opened her eyes. She was in a hospital bed. Wires and tubes dangled beside her pillow. She followed them down. They were attached to her. She reached for her neck. Taut plastic and tape pulled at her skin. An IV.

Elisha Harvey's face appeared at the door. "Take it easy."

Jess grunted.

Elisha checked a machine by the bed. "You're going to have a headache."

Jess grunted again. "I already have a headache." Her voice rasped. "What happened?"

"I wasn't there. Captain Nelson will have to fill you in."

Jess lay back. "And no doubt give me a lecture."

"Damn right," Nelson said from the door.

Elisha made her excuses and left the room.

They stared at each other in silence. Nelson whistled. "Your lawyer is outside."

"Do I need him?" Jess rasped.

"You might. A CSI team from Seattle has been camped in your motel room all night, and I now have more help than I can use."

She frowned.

"State police. Two people murdered in two states. One person at both scenes. Bound to get their interest."

Nelson opened the door.

Miller walked in. He smiled. "You've been busy. How you feeling?"

Jess lifted her arm with its IV. "Been better." She pointed at Nelson. "You let him talk to me without you."

"We've had plenty of time to catch up. The short summary is that the crime scene shows you shot the man with his own gun."

Jess frowned.

"It was still in his holster. An open thing. Quick release. Just a couple of straps. You must have caught the trigger."

"He was trying to strangle me."

Miller rubbed his hand over his neck. "As your bruises show."

"He nearly succeeded."

Miller took a deep breath and let it out slowly.

"Why strangle me if he had a gun?"

Miller smiled. "You apparently left a note at the front desk informing them you were checking out first thing."

"I—"

"We know. You didn't write it. You didn't write the text

you sent Carter saying you were taking a week off, either."

She shook her head.

"Car rental company got a call to extend your contract a week, and that you'd be dropping it off in LA."

Jess lifted her head and opened her mouth.

Miller held up his hand. "Yes. Someone was setting you up. That appears obvious."

Jess lay her head down. "He had a syringe as well."

"Like Norah Fender. It's being analyzed," Nelson said.

"I broke it."

Nelson nodded. "Blood tests show you have traces of scopolamine in your blood."

"A date rape drug."

"And worse. Looks like it was only scratched across your skin, but the syringe had enough to quell an ox."

She rolled her eyes. "Oh, thank you."

"Figure of speech."

"More importantly, he was apparently trying to abduct you, and you killed him in self-defense," Miller said.

"A working theory," said Nelson.

"Oh, come on—"

Nelson held up his hand. "We are still gathering evidence."

"Which will only support—"

"I am not jumping to a premature conclusion."

"There's—"

"No! There appears enough evidence to not detain Miss Kimball, but I will not judge the investigation until we have completed our inquiries."

Jess sighed. "More importantly, who attacked me and why?"

"We don't have answers to either yet."

"Fingerprints?"

"Haven't turned up anything yet."

"A mystery man comes to little old Randolph just to kill me?"

"Abduct you," Nelson said.

"A fine distinction."

He shrugged. His phone rang. He checked the display and muted the ringer. "The doctor will probably let you out this afternoon, but you're not to leave Randolph. Under any circumstances. Understand?"

She nodded.

He looked at Miller. "And I'm expecting you to ensure she doesn't forget."

Miller nodded. "Nothing less than life threatening."

"If it's life threatening, you come to me."

"If that is practical."

Nelson harrumphed. "Don't push your luck." He left the room, dialing on his phone.

Miller drew a chair to the side of the bed. "What's going on, Jess?"

She closed her eyes. "According to the signatures on the hospital records, Peter Whiting could be Crystal Mackie's son. Crystal Mackie disappeared right after the birth. A nurse was involved in selling the baby. Fourteen years after the boy is sold, the nurse gets killed. Right as we go to interview her."

"We?"

"Crystal's mother, Charlene Mackie and I."

"And she didn't do it?"

"I was with her all the time."

"Right."

"Nelson and I started looking for the father. Crystal's boyfriend is sterile."

"Nelson said you think it might be Meisner?"

"Crystal was last seen headed in the direction of his estate."

"Nelson told me."

She sighed. "He's denied any connection with Crystal, but I found his name in an entry log at the Capitol building."

"North Entry Lower. Mandy told me."

"We need to talk to Meisner."

Miller shook his head. "Nelson has. He said she was just visiting. Said he wasn't going to turn away one of his employees who came to visit."

"Even on the weekend?"

"Yes. And it's funny she turned up on a weekend when he happened to be working, don't you think?"

"It's as suspicious as hell."

"Even so, plausible deniability is the hardest thing to fight."

"The owner of The Montpellier is Meisner's brother. He practically threw me out. That's why I ended up in The Plum. A much easier place to attack a sleeping guest."

Miller nodded. "I wondered why you were in that place."

"Apparently, The Montpellier was full."

"I passed by this morning. Didn't seem busy."

"I had the feeling it was an excuse."

"I'll check. Might be something we could use."

Jess lifted her head. Her balance swam. She closed one eye and stared at Miller. "When can I get out of here?"

He laughed. "When you don't need to close one eye to stop the world spinning."

She lay back. The warmth and the cotton and the softness rose up to meet her.

"Touché," she murmured.

CHAPTER SIXTY-SIX

THREE HOURS LATER, JESS sat on the edge of her bed. The doctor had checked her reflexes and declared her free of the drug. Elisha removed the IV and the heart monitor's sticky electrodes. The latter activity was enough to ensure she was truly free from the drug's sedative effects.

Miller was waiting in the lobby. He gestured to his car, and they walked in silence. She buckled her seatbelt.

"The man you shot was Karl Blackstake," he said.

"Never heard of him."

"No surprise. He's spent a long time keeping his name under the radar. They found him on a twenty-year-old driver's license in West Virginia. And he has a record. One conviction for auto theft at age nineteen. The car he used when he attacked you was stolen, too."

"So presumably he was someone's hired hand."

Miller hummed. "Indeed. And I just heard that one of Meisner's security detail identified him."

She raised her eyebrows.

"Appears he did occasional work for the senator."

Jess twisted around in her seat to look directly at Miller. "They said that?"

"It took a while, but yes."

"Well? What does Meisner say?"

"Nelson is interviewing him."

"At the station?"

Miller laughed. "At his mansion."

Jess sat forward. "But if he worked for him. That's a heck of a link."

"Doesn't mean Meisner knew what he was doing."

"Whoa—"

"No. It's a link between them, but it doesn't mean he was acting under Meisner's orders."

She exhaled. "You mean he just decided to hold a grudge against me?"

"It's what they'd say in court." He shrugged. "It's what I'd say."

"This is insane."

"No. It's called a lack of evidence."

"He set up the attack on me. And if Meisner was having a relationship with Crystal Mackie—"

"But think about it. Even if he was having a relationship with Crystal Mackie, it doesn't mean he had anything to do with her disappearance."

"It gives a motive."

"But Crystal Mackie might still be alive."

"Since I started linking Peter Whiting to Crystal Mackie and a possible father, people have died. I was almost killed. Someone is trying to stop us from finding something."

"Exactly. Someone. You don't have anything other than conjecture."

"The spouse or lover is always the most likely—"

"'Most likely' isn't evidence Jess."

Jess sat in silence while Miller drove twenty miles toward Seattle. They stopped at a mall where Jess bought toiletries and new clothes. Three miles farther on, he pulled into the parking lot of a fifteen-story Marriott.

"We have rooms on the top floor," he said.

"I thought you were in charge of keeping me in Randolph."

"I told Nelson. He eventually agreed you might be safer out here."

"You know, Meisner's achieved what he wanted. He's driven us off."

"You don't have evidence it was Meisner, and you're lucky to be alive. Leave it to the police. From what I've seen of Nelson, he won't do anything without strong evidence. That's the definition of good police work."

She sighed. "Sometimes you have to take a leap of faith."

"Take a shortcut, you mean."

"Meisner is laughing at us."

"He might be doing all sorts of things, but if he's guilty, he'll play the plausible deniability card like a grand master. If we don't have him tied up tight, we don't have him tied up at all."

"Even though his man tried to kill me."

Miller gave a sympathetic smile. "At least he didn't succeed."

"If Blackstake was working for Meisner, and he's gone, I wonder what Meisner's going to do?"

Miller shrugged. "Surely nothing now the spotlight's on him."

"So, it'd be a good time to spook him. Make him do something he wouldn't normally do. Now. While he's under pressure."

Miller shook his head. "Don't do anything, Jess. Scaring Meisner might make you feel good, but it won't make Nelson's job any easier."

She got out of the car. "I don't want easy. I want justice."

CHAPTER SIXTY-SEVEN

MILLER HAD BOOKED THEM rooms. They were checked in quickly. Jess dropped her things on the bed and sat in an armchair beside a picture window that looked out over an expanse of small industrial units. The light was fading. Street lamps were coming on.

Miller was right. The police would be best suited to investigate Meisner. They had the resources. Norah Fender's murder and her own attempted murder weren't things that could be trivialized and ignored.

She opened her email and skimmed the plethora of messages looking for Mandy's name. She found three emails, two checking on her condition, and one with a spreadsheet of names from the NEL register.

The spreadsheet made it easy to find Crystal Mackie's name. Her shoulders sagged as she searched the document. Crystal's name appeared only once. She'd hoped for more to prove a stronger connection.

She sorted the spreadsheet to show Meisner's name. Apparently, he wasn't a workaholic. In fifteen years in office, he had only worked the weekends on eleven occasions. All of the dates were in the two years after Crystal Mackie's visit.

She expanded the spreadsheet to show people who had signed in on the same day as Meisner. On four occasions a female name was listed at the same time as his signature. One of the four was Crystal, but the other names were unfamiliar.

She searched the internet for the first name: Louisa Smith. A long list of social media and dating sites came up. Several sites offered to do background checks. She flipped to the second and third pages of search results. On the fourth page, she found an article in *The Alpharetta Chronicle* reporting that the twenty-three-year-old Louisa Smith had gone missing.

Jess clicked on the link. The newspaper's sympathetic article reported the parent's torment. There was a picture. Louisa Smith was a tall blonde with bright blue eyes and a brilliant white smile. The article ended with her sister's request for people to pray for her safe return.

Jess searched for the second name, Susan Parker, and found requests from the Phoenix Police Department for information on the girl's whereabouts. The photo on the missing person's page showed a bright-eyed blonde with a captivating smile. The police article was eleven years old, and the page still listed her as missing.

Jess leaned back in the armchair. Goosebumps prickled on her arms. Missing women. Just like Crystal. Young women who arrived at the Capitol building with Alistaire Meisner. Same date, same time.

Same outcome.

Missing. For years.

She gritted her teeth and searched for the last name: Georgia McCarthy. Newspaper articles and police reports appeared. She'd been twenty-five when she disappeared. Pretty. Blonde. Her car had been found three hundred miles away. The gas had run out. There was a book in the glove box. *A Thousand Things to do in LA*. The parents had set up a website for people to report tips. It had pictures. There was a simple box to fill in details. There was a checkbox for an anonymous submission. They offered a reward. Jess looked at the plain black text. The words begged for help.

Jess's hand trembled. Four blondes. Spread across the country. One common thread. Not coincidence. Orchestrated, organized, planned. Alistaire Meisner had been killing off his girlfriends, and when Peter Whiting was born, he'd killed Crystal Mackie, too.

That didn't seem quite right.

She put her hand to her forehead. It wasn't Peter's birth that had pushed Meisner over the edge with Crystal. Two months before Peter was born, Alistaire Meisner had married Margot Palmer-Breton.

She stood up.

Damn. Palmer-Breton ran a squeaky clean family business. Meisner's father-in-law was the face of Palmer-Breton. His money had rescued Meisner from a messy bankruptcy. It was likely that Palmer-Breton's financial benevolence carried conditions.

She clenched her fists. Meisner married for money. Stood to reason that he'd made damn sure the skeletons in his past would stay buried.

She paced the length of her room. He must have thought he was clever. Different women in different cities. All far from home. No chance any of them would intersect. No chance the glare of the public spotlight would uncover his infidelity.

She sank onto the bed. Four lives. For what? Killed to protect his marriage? Or more accurately, protect the money his marriage gave him?

She shivered at the memory of shaking his slimy hand. His obsequious voice came back to her. She rolled her shoulders. She wanted to deal with him before he could do more harm.

She called up the Georgia McCarthy police report on her phone. The last victim she had that was connected to him. The last piece of information that placed him and the missing women in the same location at the same time.

Except…Georgia McCarthy might not be the last.

Blackstake had attempted to abduct Jess. He sent messages to indicate she had moved on from Randolph. He didn't shoot her because he wanted everyone to think she had left Randolph of her own free will. The same as Crystal and the other girls. Jess lowered her head.

Meisner was a serial killer who had used Blackstake to work his evil. She wrapped her arms around herself. He would use plausible deniability to get out of any link she could find. She had no choice.

If she was going to tie Meisner up tight, she needed to find a body.

CHAPTER SIXTY-EIGHT

JESS PACED HER ROOM. Four girls? Just to hide his infidelity and save his miserable skin from bankruptcy? She furrowed her brow. If the girls had been killed to make sure his marriage into money wasn't disturbed, what had happened when Peter came onto the scene?

She'd arrived in Randolph the same day Peter fell, and the following day the Whitings' house had been burned down. Jess hadn't known the link to Crystal when she arrived, nor had the police. So Meisner must have been spooked by Peter from the moment he fell from the tree.

Jess slapped her hand to her forehead. How dumb could she be? Peter Whiting had left them photographic evidence.

She grabbed her laptop and watched Peter Whiting's drone video more intently this time. The camera soared its way across the field around the Meisner mansion. It hovered and drifted slowly along the rows of windows. She scanned back and forward, peering into the glass, unable to make out any details.

The drone pulled away from the house and raced for the woods. The sun reflected off the dew. Jess couldn't see Peter, but she could see the ill-fated tree. The drone tilted, using its helicopter blades to slow its headlong rush. Slowly it entered the woods before it lurched upward and crashed into the tree.

Jess reversed the video. The video panned across the fence. A small patch caught her eye. She stabbed the pause button. The shutter speed and the rate of motion had combined to blur the image, but the shapes were there.

She scrubbed back and forward. A shape moved between the camera's frames. Someone was working along the inside of the fence.

She couldn't tell if the figure was male or female. The camera had captured only a few frames, but whoever it was, was a hundred feet away and had what looked like a wheelbarrow.

She reversed the video. The drone flew backward from the woods, up the incline to the house. She stopped the video halfway. The figure was small in the camera's field of view.

A dark line ran across the dew glistening in the early morning sun. She zoomed in, tracing the line with her finger. It ran from the figure, close to the fence, all the way to the larger woods, far behind the mansion. She zoomed in, but the woods were a mottled blur.

She played the video in full. There were no more sightings of the figure along the fence, but the video told her two things.

The first was that she needed to get back to Meisner's estate as soon as she could, and the second was that there had been someone close by when Peter had climbed the tree. He was so close to Peter he must have been there when he fell.

He must have heard his cries.

He must have investigated.

He must have looked at him on the ground.

He must have seen the blood.

He left him to die.

He was a monster.

She balled her hands into fists.

Peter had survived his fall. She was going to make damn sure this monster's fall was fatal.

CHAPTER SIXTY-NINE

JESS LOOKED OUT THE window and watched street lights click on. Things were coming together. She had an idea. It was almost a plan. She couldn't do it on her own, but neither Miller nor Nelson would approve. She had only one option left.

She dialed Charlene Mackie. The call rolled over to voicemail. Charlene's recorded voice mumbled and then was cut off. "Hello," Charlene said.

"This is Jess." She paused. "Look, I need some help. I need to get into the woods along the side of Meisner's estate without being seen on his cameras. Can you help?"

"I've been in the woods plenty of times. Practically lived there. But I don't know about the cameras."

"Did you knock down the fence?"

"Trust me, I would bulldoze the entire fence flat if I thought I could get away with it." Charlene's voice delivered the mundane truth. "But I didn't knock down his precious fence. And I don't know how to avoid the cameras."

Jess ran her fingers through her curls. "I need to get out there without being seen."

Charlene thought for a moment. "There's a homeless guy who lives out there. Max. I'll bet he knows."

"Yes. I met him. Do you think he'd show me?"

"We can ask him. He's at Grace's Church. North end of Randolph. He goes there sometimes to dry out. Meaning to both get off the booze and stay out of the rain."

"Is he capable of making sense during all of that?"

"Well, he's trying to postpone having a bath for as long as he can, but other than that he's fine." Charlene cleared her throat. "There's one problem, though. He's scared Meisner will have him evicted from his land."

"I could pay him."

"Not a good plan. He'd spend the money on booze." Charlene sighed. "But I'll talk to him. After you've told me why you want to get into those woods without being seen."

"I have a hunch." Jess pursed her lips. She didn't want to say more to Charlene just yet. "I need a ride."

Charlene took a deep breath. "Where are you?"

CHAPTER SEVENTY

JESS GAVE THE HOTEL name to Charlene. Then she called Miller and told him she was turning in for the night. Twenty minutes later she took the stairs down fifteen floors to the lobby.

Charlene's Crown Vic pulled into the parking lot. Jess waved. Charlene popped open the passenger door, and a few moments later they were heading back to the main road, headlights holding back the rapidly settling night.

Charlene accelerated. "So. What have you got?"

"Peter Whiting was flying a drone around Meisner's estate."

"Nelson told me."

"I think he captured something on the video that Meisner didn't want to be spread around."

Charlene drove on. "You know Nelson won't be happy if he finds out we're going back there. Meisner's been complaining about you. This won't help."

"That's more of a problem for you than me." Jess shrugged. "I don't answer to Nelson. You do."

"And I need my job." Charlene nodded.

Jess didn't reply because she didn't know what to say. Not yet, anyway.

Charlene adjusted her grip on the wheel. Jess watched the speedometer needle climb past eighty.

Grace Church turned out to be the end unit of a strip mall. Colorful murals were painted on the windows depicting scenes of a baby in a manger and Jesus on the cross. Light slipped from an unpainted section at the top of the windows.

"Wait here," Charlene said.

She knocked on the main entrance. The door opened. A red-haired man in jeans and a precisely trimmed beard opened the door. Charlene went inside. Several minutes later she emerged, a steadying hand on Max's shoulder.

She ushered Max into the back seat. Jess smiled at him. He grunted.

"Where exactly do you want to look?" Charlene said.

Jess brought up Peter's video and selected a frame that showed the moving smudge that was a person, and the track across the dew. She held the phone in front of Max and pointed. "Here and here."

He leaned forward staring at the screen. Jess held the phone steady, inhaled and held the air in her lungs to avoid his rancid breath.

He pointed. "Can't walk there without being seen." He shook his head almost violently as if he'd had bad experiences that proved his point. "Have to walk out of the woods."

"We can do that."

He leaned back. "Have yer eaten?"

Charlene looked at him in the rearview mirror. "Aren't they feeding you at Grace's?"

He shook his head. "Salad."

Jess pointed at a fast food burger place across the road. "My treat."

Max smiled.

Charlene pulled over. She left the air-conditioning running to freshen the air. They ate in silence. Despite Max's unwashed and disheveled presence, he couldn't have been starving. He didn't wolf his food, but ate his fries one at a time. Jess ordered a refill for his sugary soda. She figured he needed every calorie he could get.

When he finished, he wiped his fingers on a napkin and stepped out of the car to deposit his waste in the trash.

Charlene pulled out of the parking lot.

"North," Max said, pointing in that direction.

They looped around Randolph and drove from the north down the side of Meisner's estate.

"Slow," he said.

He leaned over Jess and pointed to the side of the road. "Stop."

Charlene pulled off the road. Max got out and led the way. Jess and Charlene followed him into the forest.

Inside the thick woods, all light was eliminated. Zero visibility. Jess followed Max's unwashed scent. He said, "Wait. Let your eyes adjust."

They stood in a line and waited. After a full minute, Jess noticed that Max had his eyes closed. She closed hers. When she opened them again, her vision had adjusted to the blackness.

Jess glanced around. There was little to see and only creaking branches and rustling leaves to hear. Lush decay and damp aromas permeated the air. She breathed quietly and watched Max as he rotated his head.

"Listening," he said, scowling, presumably picking up sound and its direction. His scowl faded, and he opened his eyes. "No one nearby."

He walked on, ducking and holding back branches as Charlene and Jess passed, then stepping past them to regain the lead. He veered around thick clumps of undergrowth and changed direction seemingly at random. They followed.

The thick trees looked the same in every direction. She felt like she was walking in circles. Without Max, Jess would have been completely lost.

Max came to a stop and held up his hand. He crouched and gestured. Jess crouched, too. She saw the fence, silhouetted by the light spilling from Meisner's mansion.

She angled her head. Meisner's mansion didn't provide enough ambient light to be able to make out the nature of the ground's surface around the fence posts.

Max extended his right arm like a referee. He moved parallel to the fence, bent double and taking exaggerated steps, lifting his feet high.

Jess followed suit, lifting her feet, and wondering if they were trying to avoid tripwires. She glanced back at Charlene executing the same deliberate high-lift gait. Charlene shrugged.

Max crouched down and pointed. "There."

Jess squinted. The fence posts were easy to make out, but the ground was a blanket of blackness. "Can I go out there?"

Max nodded, then pointed left and right. "Cameras. Pointing away from here."

"What about cameras at the house?"

He frowned. "Those you be seen."

She took a deep breath and accepted the risk. She moved out of the trees, crossed twenty feet in the open, and knelt by the fence post. The post towered above her, but she stared at her feet. The ground had the uneven look of dug soil. The damp and rain had smoothed over mounds of earth giving them the sheen of age. She lowered her head to within a couple of inches off the ground. The mounds weren't that large, but it was easy to believe they were shovel sized. She exhaled. Nothing short of excavating the area would yield further clues.

The muddy soil was an area three feet wide and seven feet long. It had a ragged edge, well-worn by work boots that had blurred the line between the soil and the field grass.

She moved around the edge on her side of the fence. She ran her hands through the grass and felt nothing but mud and stones.

She sighed, and sat on her haunches. Was there something buried here? Or was her imagination out of control?

CHAPTER SEVENTY-ONE

JESS RETURNED TO THE cover of the trees.

Charlene said, "What? What is it?"

"I want to see some more."

"Oh come on! We're sneaking about, with you doing who-knows-what, and we're supposed to just follow along?"

"I—"

"We're not out here to enjoy the night air." Charlene's eyes glistened in the light from the house.

Jess wondered if it was tears. She nodded. "This is crazy. I might…" She took a deep breath. "I found Meisner's name in a register. An entry record into the Capitol building." A gap appeared between Charlene's lips. "Crystal's name was in the same book. Same date. Same time."

Jess paused to let her words sink in. "It was a Saturday morning. It seems a little hard to believe that he coincidently arrived at that particular entrance at the same time as Crystal."

"He was having an affair with her." Charlene breathed deep,

her lungs laboring in the cold, damp air. "I always suspected. I never knew."

She took Jess's arm and moved her sideways. She nodded to the fence post. She tried to speak. Grunts and labored breathing were all she could call up.

Jess shook her head. "I don't think that's where your daughter is buried."

Charlene's lips trembled. She rocked back and forth. Her breathing was hard. Short breaths, panted into the night.

Jess put her hand on Charlene's arm. "I'm sorry. But we need to find out."

Tears glistened on Charlene's cheeks. She wiped her nose on the back of her hand. She jerked her head in Jess's direction. "Where is she?"

Jess squeezed Charlene's shoulder. "I might be wrong."

Charlene gripped Jess's arm. She nodded. "She could have left from DC. Gone somewhere." She stared into Jess's eyes. "Couldn't she?"

Jess nodded. "She really could." She squeezed Charlene's arm. "But I found other names."

Charlene's mouth hung open.

"Three more women. From different states. Their signatures with Meisner's. In the same book. Always on weekends." Jess swallowed. Her stomach churned. She breathed in, holding the air in her lungs to calm her emotions, before she said, "They're all missing."

Charlene squared her shoulders. Her nostrils flared, and her eyes widened. "You're telling me that Alistaire Meisner murdered all four of those girls?"

"Maybe."

"Are they buried here?"

"I don't know."

"Is Crystal?"

Jess squeezed Charlene's arm. "We need to find out."

"Damn right we do. If you're right, I'll kill that bastard myself." Charlene's chin jutted forward. "Let's get to it. What's your plan?"

Jess pulled out her phone and brought up the image from the video, the dew and the fence and the blur of a moving figure. She pointed to the far end of the trail through the dew.

Max gave a single nod and put his hand over the phone's screen. "They can see the light."

Charlene said, "Why did you look at the fence?"

"I think Crystal may have been buried under that post at one time."

Charlene stared at the fence post. "Why buried there?"

"Because fourteen years ago, that post was being installed, along with all the other posts for this fence. There was a big hole in the ground."

Her eyes widened again. "And Meisner threw her in it."

"Or Blackstake. And after the court order, they had to move her because this fence is going to be relocated. I saw someone working by that post on Peter's video."

"So where is she buried now?"

"The video shows a track in the dew. It looks like an animal track, but I think it was the path he followed after exhuming the body."

Charlene stood up. "Then let's go."

"It's on the other side of the woods. Max said we have to go back to the road to avoid the cameras."

"The hell with that. Let the bastard come out here and face

me. If he dares." Charlene pushed Jess back a step and marched off, traveling parallel to the fence.

Jess hurried to catch up. Max matched his step to Jess.

Walking alongside the fence was easier going than trudging through the woods. Max pointed up to a camera on a pole. The camera tracked them as they passed. Jess sped up, grabbed Charlene by the arm, and veered her into the woods. Charlene fought back.

Jess tightened her grip. "They may have seen us on the cameras already. They'll send men. We need time to search before they get here."

Jess took her flashlight from her pocket, turned it on and waved it around. "We want them to think we're right here. Maybe they'll waste their time searching the wrong part of the woods and buy us a little time."

Max nodded. He set off deeper into the trees, beckoning. Charlene followed.

Jess switched off the light and trotted ahead to join the others. Max picked up his pace, walking fast under tree limbs and jumping ditches. In minutes they were panting, but they were making good time. Meisner's mansion was hidden by the slope of the ground, but its lights glowed on the clouds above.

CHAPTER SEVENTY-TWO

"DON'T ANSWER THAT PHONE, Alistaire. We're right in the middle of dinner," Margot Meisner said, a crystal wine glass in her hand.

"I'll only be a moment, dear," he replied. He pushed his chair from the table and took the call in the next room where he could see the monitor.

The activity in the guard house was short lived. The automatic cameras had spotted movement. Infrared showed three bodies. There had been a flash of light, but apart from that, they were walking in the darkness. The unusual activity would have normally triggered a call to Karl Blackstake, but that was no longer an option.

Meisner watched the camera's feed. After a few moments, he made his decision. "The security team can stand down. No action required."

He ended the call and returned to the dining room prepared to cajole his wife from her pouting.

CHAPTER SEVENTY-THREE

MAX KEPT UP HIS fast pace. Despite his disheveled appearance and poor diet, he had plenty of stamina. Jess had to keep moving her head from side to side to make the most of the pale glimmers of moonlight in her peripheral vision.

They emerged onto a rutted track. Jess stretched her back. Charlene paused ahead of her.

"Lot of trails around here," Max said. He came to a stop, his arm out, pointing. "There."

"The trail I showed you led there?" Jess asked.

He nodded. "Yeah. The dew trail. There. What I said."

Jess squeezed past Charlene and crept in the direction Max had pointed, to the edge of the woods.

Max strolled over and stood by her side. "No cameras over here."

She nodded and stepped out of the trees. The forest was a wall of blackness stretching far in either direction. The fields behind her rose to a horizon defined by the glow beyond, the stray light from Meisner's mansion.

She frowned at Max. "You sure?"

He stepped out of the woods and pointed to a tree leaning at a forty-five-degree angle. "Lightning strike. A couple of years ago. Can't miss that." He nodded at the woods. "Definitely. It's here."

Jess fished out her flashlight.

Max waved his hand. "Not here. They'll see."

Jess nodded.

"I have to go." Max shook his head. "Security catch me, they never let me back. I live here."

Jess nodded. "I understand. Thanks for the help."

He gave a toothless smile, and walked off, across the fields.

Jess moved into the cover of the trees, placed her hand over the lens on her flashlight, and switched it on. The light made a small irregular shape on the ground. Satisfied it would be harder to detect, she walked back along the trail, staring at the ground. Charlene followed.

"Is this still Meisner's property?" Jess said.

"Yes," Charlene said.

Swinging the dimmed flashlight beam across the width of the track, Jess worked her way along the trail. Undergrowth curled over the ground, working its way toward cutting off the path. A spindly branch scraped across the top of her head. She brushed it away. It shuffled from the tree above and fell to the ground.

Charlene turned on the phone's light. It was more of a glow than a beam. She held the phone close to the ground. "You think someone came this way?"

"Maybe."

A second trail curved off the first. Jess shined her light along the path. Ten yards down, the undergrowth had reclaimed the space. She stayed on the same trail.

"Over there," Charlene said, pointing to the left.

Jess scanned the area with the flashlight. "What did you see?"

Charlene stared. "Nothing."

Jess moved on. She placed her feet with care, checking the ground before putting her weight down. She had to rock her foot to free it from the path's muddy surface. Finally, she stopped.

"What?" Charlene said.

"The ground is soft, but no footprints. Branches and undergrowth are everywhere, but I haven't seen as much as a suspicious broken twig."

"This end of the woods covers a large area. We aren't likely to find what we're looking for in the dark."

"I know." Jess sighed. "They saw us on cameras back there. It's not long until Meisner's security goons figure out where we are."

"Maybe we organize a full-out search as soon as the sun comes up. In the daylight, we should be able to find…" Charlene swallowed. "A new grave. If one exists."

"It makes sense, but it won't happen. You know it won't. Meisner will have a court order on us in a hot second. And we don't have any evidence."

"You have some. The names."

Jess shook her head. "Deniable."

"Then what the hell isn't deniable?"

Jess weighed her options. None of them were good, but Charlene deserved the truth more than she needed sympathy. "A body."

Charlene took the flashlight from Jess's hand, restoring its full beam. "Well, we're here now. Let's do the best with what we have."

Charlene started down the trail, waving the light from side to side, stopping to kneel by occasional branches or clumps of vegetation. Jess kept close behind to make the most of the light.

They reached a side path. Jess put her hand over Charlene's to steer the light. The overgrowth was thick. Charlene pushed into the pathway.

Jess tugged at her arm. "Slowly. We want to see evidence of someone passing this way."

"Meisner or his goons." She scowled and patted her gun. "I hope they're still here."

Charlene reached the end of the path. She waved the light up and down the diminishing end of the narrow trail.

Jess held her phone's weak light close to the leaves and thorn-covered creepers. Among the green was a trace of white. Perhaps not pure white, but glaring bright in the dark. Charlene pointed the flashlight. The white was a tear, a rip in the green outer covering of a thick bramble stem.

Jess leaned in.

Charlene eased the light down toward the ground.

Jess grabbed another broken stem. And another.

Charlene jerked the light over the vegetation in a wild dance. Searching and stopping. Telltale patches of brightness shone in the night.

Charlene flipped up the hood to her thick jacket. She faced away from the thorny undergrowth and plunged backward.

Jess stepped away.

Charlene pushed into the bushes, branches cracking and

creepers snapping. She rolled from side to side, shaking off the thorns that ripped into her clothes. She grunted.

Jess cringed. The vegetation wasn't giving in easily. Charlene had her hands on her face, and Jess could see blood.

With a cry, Charlene fell backward and disappeared through the wall of undergrowth. There was a thump followed by a crunch when Charlene landed.

"You okay?" Jess said.

"Yeah. Not great, but fine." She flashed the light. "The path goes on from here."

Jess could see the flashlight beam flickering through the leaves. "Wait for me."

"Hurry," Charlene said, her voice already heading away.

Jess had no covering for her head. Pushing through the thorns would be seriously painful. She raced back along the path. The overgrowth thinned. She peered left and right, wishing Max hadn't left.

She took a promising gap between the trees and pushed through hip-deep weeds. Creepers dangled from trees. She ducked and twisted, throwing them off before they snared her.

The light from her phone barely illuminated the ground at her feet. She kept looking around, trying to keep her sense of direction and heading toward where she guessed Charlene would be.

The bushes rustled and shook. Jess swung her phone in the direction of the noise. The line of bushes trembled. A deer heading away from her. She breathed her relief.

The undergrowth thinned. Charlene's flashlight flickered. They were no more than fifty feet apart.

Jess stopped. In the dim light of her phone, a line cut through the undergrowth. A path. The line was clear. The undergrowth had been crushed. It was recovering, but not fully. One end of the thick weeds headed toward the path Charlene was on. The other end extended beyond the light of her phone.

Jess moved parallel to the line of undergrowth. It curved around into a wall of weeds and vines and brambles. Jess knelt down to a gap below the green canopy of wild vegetation.

Close by, she sensed something moving. Branches and leaves were being pushed aside. Not Charlene. She was still a good distance away.

Jess turned off her phone. Blackness closed in. Rustling and creaking and the sound of a million bugs filled her ears, but one thing sounded clear above all else.

Footsteps.

Jess crouched down. The steps were slow. Deliberate. Irregular. She couldn't tell if she heard two feet or four.

She twisted her head around, searching behind her as much as in front. The footsteps definitely sounded in the direction of Charlene and the flashlight.

She frowned. Perhaps it was a trick of the cold. Perhaps the sound of Charlene's footsteps carried on the damp air. Jess listened a few more moments. The footsteps had stopped.

She pushed her way into the gap in the wall of undergrowth. She emerged into an open space large enough to park a car. The wall of vegetation ringed the space. She caught glimpses of Charlene's flickering flashlight through the leaves.

Jess crouched inside the space. A layer of weeds covered the ground. They crunched as she walked. She kicked at them with her boot. They moved but didn't spring back into place.

She knelt. The weeds covered the ground, but they had been torn from their roots. She kicked them away and cleared a rough five-foot circle.

She sat on her haunches. The ground had been freshly dug. It had the same lumpy appearance as the area by the fence post. Someone had buried something using a shovel. Something five or six feet in size.

She fished her knife from her pocket and dug into the ground as best she could with the thin blade. The earth was soft. She scraped with her blade. The mud rolled back into the hole as she dug. She scooped it back with her hands. The soil was separated into clumps. Cut lines and air gaps were everywhere. It had been dug, and recently.

Jess stared at the ragged hole she'd dug. It would take a shovel and some effort to confirm what seemed obvious, but it was obvious enough. She was in the middle of nowhere with a man-made ring of vegetation to hide the location. She couldn't put off the inevitable. She closed her switchblade.

Jess found Charlene's number on her phone.

A man's voice came from behind her. "Drop it."

Jess held her phone out and turned slowly.

A shadowy figure stood in the gap she had used to enter the circle. He held a gun out. His arm was low, his elbow bent. Not a good posture for using a handgun.

He shook the gun at her. "I said drop it."

The voice was filled with the tremble of adrenaline, but she knew its owner.

"Gardner?"

He stepped forward, straightening his arm until the gun was just a foot from her face. "Drop. It."

"It's me. Jess."

"And it's me. The man who locked you up." His tone was smug. "Surprise."

Her mouth went dry. "You're working for Meisner."

"How clever you are. Pity you're not going to be able to tell anyone."

Jess held up her phone. "Okay, okay. I'm putting it down." She sank down on her haunches, lowering the phone to the ground with her right hand. His eyes followed the phone. She tossed it the last few inches and threw herself in the opposite direction.

He twisted, retracting his arm to wield his gun in the confined space.

She mashed her left thumb on her switchblade's latch, and threw her arm around his leg, whipping the blade back across his Achilles' tendon.

He screamed. His gun boomed. A wave of heat from the exhaust gases washed over Jess's head. He'd missed. She lunged with her right hand for his gun, using her legs to ram her shoulder into his ribs. He stumbled back. She clung to his gun. He wrenched his hand back, flicking the gun from his grip.

He wrapped his arm around Jess's head. Squeezing.

She stabbed at his chest. The knife bounced back. He was wearing a bulletproof vest.

He grabbed her knife hand, crushing her knuckles and shaking her arm. Her knife flicked from her fingers.

She shoved herself backward. His rigid grip on her head pulled him with her. He screamed as he limped along.

She had to make the most of his damaged leg. She kicked, wrapping her foot around to hit his wound.

He growled and pushed her away from him. She spun around from the force of his movement, swinging her right foot. A toe punt. Plenty of follow through. Her shoe against the bloodied flesh of his severed Achilles. He screamed, collapsing on one knee. She brought her foot up, and back down, centered on the back of his skull. He sagged forward, face down in the undergrowth.

With his Achilles destroyed, he wasn't going anywhere.

Jess stood and breathed, calming her nerves. Meisner must have seen them on one of their cameras and sent Gardner in place of Blackstake. He must have had him on his payroll all along.

She cussed. Her adrenaline still pumped her blood hard. Meisner had used people to do his dirty work, but he was going to suffer in court. She was going to make damn sure.

CHAPTER SEVENTY-FOUR

JESS DIALED CHARLENE'S PHONE. In the distance, she heard the ringer.

Charlene answered. "What was that?"

"Gardner just attacked me."

Charlene's voice went up an octave. "What?"

"Really. Held a gun on me. I stabbed him, and he's down."

Charlene remained silent for a good ten seconds. "I've always hated that man."

"With good reason, it seems."

"Where are you?"

"There's something else." Jess kept her voice low, but there was no easy way to break the news. "I think I've found a grave."

No response.

"Charlene?"

Charlene gasped. "Where?"

Jess pushed out of the space. "Hold the flashlight in front of you and turn around. Slowly."

In the distance, the light bounced through gaps and reflected off the greenery. When Jess guessed the flashlight was pointed in her direction, she said, "Stop. Walk in that direction."

The flashlight bobbed up and down.

"What have you found?" Charlene asked.

"Freshly dug earth inside a wall of undergrowth. The ground seems to have been sprinkled with weeds that haven't taken over yet."

The light bounced. Charlene was running.

A second light flashed. Blinding and brief. A loud noise traveled through the air. Deep and percussive. Gunfire.

Charlene screamed. A second gunshot.

The flashlight's broken beams twisted around, slicing across the tree canopy.

Jess moved toward the light. It fell still. Staring upward, illuminating a tree trunk.

She stopped. "Charlene?" she whispered into her phone. No reply. She hung up.

Charlene's flashlight went out.

Jess crouched down. She held her mouth open and breathed hard, oxygenating her blood with minimum noise. Meisner's security detail? As well as Gardner? How many of them were there?

She had no gun, and Gardner's had been lost in their fight. She had only a vague idea of which direction led to the main roadway, and she couldn't leave Charlene here alone. She kept still.

The footsteps she had heard earlier resumed. Louder and quicker this time. Each footstep clear. Twigs and leaves crunched loudly under heavy boots.

She cocked her head, trying to get a bearing on the noise.

She couldn't tell if he moved left or right. The noise grew louder as he pushed through the undergrowth.

A sharp burst of adrenaline shot through Jess's body. Whoever it was, they were heading straight for her.

She knelt, keeping close to the ground. She turned ninety degrees and moved away from the shooter's path. She lifted her feet high as Max had done, hoping to quiet her movement through the vegetation.

A light went on. A sharp and focused beam. It speared into the wall of undergrowth. Dancing left and right.

She crouched down again. Bright light reflected off the wet leaves, spraying out, blinding to her night-adjusted eyes, silhouetting everything behind the beam.

The shooter held a large gun, made even larger by a giant silencer. The gun pointed forward, into the wall of undergrowth and the sheltered area beyond. Black clothes, head to toe. Face hidden behind a ski mask. The light swung around the gun following its arc.

Jess abandoned all attempts at stealth. She kept down and ran. The weeds dragged on her legs. The light jerked toward her. She changed direction. The light slewed around, covering the space and angles as it searched for her.

She dove for a tree, absorbing the impact as her back thumped into the unyielding trunk. She ducked her head into the undergrowth as the light flitted across the branches above.

The shooter was on the move, plowing through the undergrowth behind her.

Jess eased her head up. The light caught her. She ducked and rolled. Three shots hammered into the tree where she'd been crouching a moment before. Chunks of wood spun through the air.

She kept rolling. Her shoulder hit a broken tree limb, fifteen inches in diameter and a straight four-feet long, tapering at one end. She hugged it and threw herself over.

Two shots hissed through the air above her. The flashlight was close.

She jumped up and ran. She dove for a thick tree, keeping it between her and the shooter.

The flashlight beam danced over the undergrowth. She panted through her open mouth, fighting the adrenaline that begged her to flee.

She picked up the fallen tree limb and held it like a baseball bat. The light shook and danced. She steadied her breathing.

Behind the big tree trunk, she was protected. She couldn't see her stalker, but she heard jogging footfalls through the prolific vegetation.

The light bounced over the undergrowth to her right.

The shooter had abandoned all caution. Desperate and confident and under matched. Holding a flashlight, a clear target. Yet Jess hadn't fired a shot. Which proved that she wasn't armed.

Her only chance was to strike first.

The flashlight beam narrowed. The shooter was getting close.

She judged he would pass ten to fifteen feet from her, an ocean of distance for her improvised club against that gun.

She re-doubled her grip.

The light was close now. The crunch of leaves came closer.

She breathed hard.

She would leap out, swinging her club.

The shooter would bring the gun around.

She leaned back, ready to throw her weight forward.

She dipped down. Her hand flailed around in the undergrowth and found a large rock. She rose up with the makeshift weapon in her grip.

The shooter stopped. Jess had made a noise. The shooter knew where she was.

She stretched her arm around the tree and threw the rock.

It arced through the air. Silent.

It landed behind the shooter. Out of the dazzling light.

The big rock thumped into a tree trunk and crashed noisily into the undergrowth.

The shooter moved. Rustling the leaves. Sweeping the flashlight behind and firing off two rounds.

The sound told Jess exactly where he stood.

She threw herself forward. Her arms bent. Her club high over her shoulder.

The shooter turned halfway.

The gun and the flashlight pointed away from Jess.

The shooter steered the beam, searching for the source of the noise.

Jess made two long strides, and pulled the club forward and left.

The shooter turned, facing the club.

Jess swept the club in a slicing arc. A baseball player's swing. Hard. Fast. Flat.

The shooter twisted the gun and the light, bringing him around.

The club hit the shooter's head. Ten-pound mass. Perhaps thirty miles an hour. A whipping motion. A solid impact. Wood meets flesh. Momentum against bone.

The shooter's head twisted. The body leaned. The gun and the light angled down.

Jess drove on. The club's rough surface tearing across the shooter's face before whipping behind her.

The shooter's head came up. The light and the gun followed. Whether recoiling from the blow or using the momentum to advantage. The gun waved past her kneecaps.

Jess threw the club back. Reversing the blow. Sweeping left. Catching him under the nose. Tearing the lip. Smashing the teeth. Tossing the head back.

The shooter's arms flailed. The gun spun into the air. Up. Overhead. On and on. Spiraling through the trees. Curling out of light and sight.

The shooter toppled backward, groaning. Hands raised to the face. Blood ran between the fingers.

The flashlight disappeared beneath the canopy of weeds.

Jess stepped in the direction of the gun.

The shooter groaned.

The ground was a mass of mottled shapes and darkness. Without the light, she would never find the gun, and with the light she would be a perfect target if he found the gun first.

Jess ran, fighting through the creepers and vines, batting branches away from her face with her forearms. She angled left, toward Charlene and, she hoped, the road beyond the forest.

She held the club in front of her face as branches whipped at her. She fell in a pothole, waving her arms to stay upright, and kept moving forward. Away from the shooter and the gun.

The light between the trees flickered. It bounced and shook. The shooter was on his feet.

She plied on, searching the ground, her pace halfway between desperate and careful.

The light grew brighter, phasing in and out between the trees. Moving fast, straight toward Jess.

She reached a narrow trail. The flickering light revealed glimpses in either direction. If this was the correct path, Charlene would be to the right.

She swallowed. The light was also to her right. He was trying to head her off. Stop her from reaching the road. Which meant she was headed in the right direction.

She sprinted into the darkness, the club in front of her face to fend off the branches. Head up to keep a clear airway for oxygen into her lungs.

Her peripheral vision monitored the flickering light. She slowed and stopped. Charlene's body was splayed on the ground.

The light emerged between Jess and Charlene.

The shooter stepped in and filled the narrow path. A knife glinted in his hand. He panted hard. The ski mask was ragged and torn. He reached up and peeled it off his head, and threw it aside.

Face wet and glistening. Blood covered cheeks and neck. The mouth was a ragged bloody shape.

Jess's skin tingled. She stared, her jaw locked open.

The shooter's head shook back and forth. Long hair tumbled down to her shoulders.

Jess redoubled her grip on her club. "Margot."

Margot Meisner's jaw jutted forward. "That's Mrs. Meisner, to you." She turned the knife over, making sure Jess saw it.

"So the big, important senator has his wife doing his dirty work."

"He's never had what it takes to make it and stay on top." Margot snorted. "You think he's a real man? He's a sniveling mess without me. Can't find his ass with both hands."

Jess cocked her head. "You killed those girls."

"Of course I did. You would have, too." Margot nodded.

"They were trash. They thought they'd found a meal ticket. All of them. Crystal Mackie was the worst. Trying to blackmail my husband with her bastard. She deserved everything she got. They all did." She shook her head and wiped blood from her mouth with the back of her hand. "Just like you. You think you can bring him down, don't you? Ruin his career? Not a chance."

"How did you kill Crystal?" Jess hefted the club, inching her hands to a thicker section. The branch didn't carry the fear of cold steel, but she would neither run nor beg.

"She came around, asking for money. We fought. I didn't have the chance to finish her off. She fell right under my horse. Frightened him, the stupid bitch. He trampled her to death. Served her right." Margot nodded, her voice rough with anger and exertion.

"And Blackstake cleaned up after you."

Margot shrugged. "I paid him well for the work he did."

Jess moved her feet to keep her muscles limber. "Nelson is on his way."

"No, he isn't." Margot's hand gripped the knife expertly. "If Nelson was on the way, you wouldn't have been crawling around out here. You'd have waited for better lights and reinforcements."

Jess raised the club to shoulder height and said nothing.

Margot leaped forward, the knife blade backward in her hand, slashing through the air.

Jess sidestepped, and the blade swept past her. She raised the club and swung it down on Margot's arm. It made hard contact.

Margot grunted and whipped the knife back, retracing its arc through the air.

Jess swung the club around, keeping up its momentum, but Margot lunged forward, the knife reaching for Jess's ribs. Jess sucked in her stomach, bending to keep air between her and the tip of the knife, the club frozen above her head.

Margot stepped forward, swinging the knife. Jess stepped back, holding both ends of the club to thwart the blade.

Margot grabbed Jess's shirt with her free hand. Jess brought the club around and down on the side of Margot's head, slamming hard and tearing across her ear.

Margot jerked away, screaming.

Jess brought the club up. Arcing through the air.

Margot bent backward, lashing out.

The end of the club caught Margot's chin. A glancing blow. A tiny flick. She stumbled into the undergrowth.

Jess kicked. The toe of her boot caught Margot's kneecap. She doubled over, screaming and growling.

The club was high. Jess tensed her muscles, resting her weight solidly on her feet, and heaved the club down.

Despite her pain, Margot lurched sideways, swinging the knife.

Jess was committed, her body locked in place. The club swung past Margot's side, harmless in the air.

Margot's knife slashed through Jess's jacket. Tearing the lining. Ripping a foot-long scar across the front. A burning pain erupted in her abdomen. An electric spasm that built and built. She grunted hard.

The pain screamed for attention, but she held onto the club and swung for Margot. Low speed. A small run up.

Margot raised her arm, absorbing the momentum of the blow, and wrapped her hand around the shaft of the club. She tugged on the club, dragging Jess toward her with one hand as she stabbed the knife forward with the other.

Jess slid her hands back and then shoved on the club with all of her strength. Her momentum was in sync with Margot's force, and the blow pushed the woman backward, into a tree, and sideways onto her knees.

Jess ran past Margot, toward Charlene's body, and the open road. She had mere moments of advantage. The undergrowth clawed at her legs, and branches slashed her face.

Jess dove for Charlene's arms. The chance of carrying her and escaping Margot's blade were impossibly slim, but she wouldn't leave Charlene.

Margot was climbing from the undergrowth.

Jess wrenched Charlene into a sitting position.

Charlene screamed.

Margot stumbled forward. Closing the gap.

Jess threw Charlene's arm over her shoulder.

Charlene grunted and moaned.

Jess braced for the weight. "We have to run." She stood. Dragging Charlene along.

Charlene screamed. Hard and long. Deafening in Jess's ear.

Jess gritted her teeth as Charlene's belt tore across her abdomen.

Margot crouched ten feet away.

Charlene twisted to free herself from Jess.

Jess's stomach wound burned.

Charlene bent, levering herself from Jess and collapsing onto her knees.

Margot growled, her knife ready, twisted backward in her hand. The ideal position for ripping and tearing. The grip that provided maximum force and damage. If it connected, Jess would die.

Margot leaped forward, sweeping the blade through the air. Backhand. Tip first.

Charlene drew her gun from its holster and swung it around. One arc. Smooth. Fast.

Margot was only feet away. Directly in front of them. Barely any need to aim. Charlene's left hand rested on top of her right wrist. Bracing for the inevitable shock waves.

The gun boomed. A nine millimeter round. An unstoppable force. The explosion cracked the air. Jess's eardrums bottomed out. Silencing the real world.

Charlene didn't flinch.

The flash illuminated Margot's face. A single strobe that showed anger and venom and hate.

The bullet rammed Margot backward.

A gaping hole appeared in her sternum, bloody and ragged. Fragments and red mist burst into the air behind her.

Her legs gave way. Her knees buckled, her torso collapsed slowly.

Her arms stayed at her sides.

Her face hit the ground, and the knife tumbled away.

Charlene kept her gun trained, her finger on the trigger.

Margot didn't move.

Jess breathed deep and emptied her lungs with a gasp.

Charlene lowered the gun.

Jess knelt beside her and lowered her backward onto the ground. "It'll be all right."

Charlene moaned in pain.

Jess switched on her phone's light. Charlene was pale. Her eyes were closed.

She dialed 911 and gave her uncertain location. At the operator's urging, she kept the line open and put her phone on speaker.

Charlene's pulse was weak.

"Hang in there. Help is on the way," Jess urged.

Charlene opened her eyes a fraction and nodded.

CHAPTER SEVENTY-FIVE

Randolph, Washington
Two weeks later

THE TAXI THREADED ITS way down the lane. The line of cars perched half on and half off the grassy shoulder slowed its progress.

Jess recognized some of the vehicles. Their owners had already left. She checked her watch. She was later than she had hoped, but she would be on time.

The taxi stopped at an arch, the words "Memorial Park" formed in wrought iron above.

Jess stepped out and tightened her coat around her. The damp Washington air was colder than she remembered. Fall had turned to winter. She opened her umbrella and wished she'd worn an extra layer.

The taxi left, waiting until it had reached the end of the road to pick up speed and head for its next fare.

Memorial Park wasn't large. Country paths made a zig-zag patchwork of the graves, but the group assembled under a temporary canopy in the far right corner couldn't be missed. She worked her way along the grass tracks.

Nelson broke away from the assembly and headed toward her. She shook his hand.

"Never been to a funeral when it isn't raining," he said.

She nodded. "Maybe that tells us something."

"You'll want to know." Nelson cleared his throat. "The medical examiner said Crystal's body was consistent with having been trampled by a horse. But she was already dead when it happened."

"So Margot lied about Crystal's death."

"She might not have realized the horse didn't kill Crystal. Either way, Margot was responsible." Nelson paused. "They haven't found the other girls."

Jess took a deep breath and released it slowly. "I'd hoped for more progress."

"It's a federal investigation now, Jess. They've got the resources. But with both Margot Meisner and Blackstake dead, they might never find the bodies. We need to accept that."

"What about Alistaire Meisner?"

Nelson grunted. "The ex-senator? He still has his highly paid lawyers covering for him. Claims he knows nothing, of course."

"You're not going to let him get away with that, are you?"

"He won't get away with anything. Trust me." Nelson shook his head. "But it's the feds' deal now."

"Let's hope they turn something up."

"They will. Gardner will talk. They figure at least one of the bodies is probably buried somewhere on Meisner's property. All they need is to tie him to one of the victims." Nelson grinned. "His father-in-law has evicted him from the mansion. He's living in a rental place and struggling to pay his legal bills. He'll crack eventually."

"Let's hope."

He pointed his chin toward the group under the canopy. "At least we got some measure of justice here."

Jess looked at the black-clad figures.

He nodded again. "Charlene's okay. Coping."

"At least she knows for sure what happened to her daughter now." Jess wondered whether that knowledge was welcome or whether Charlene would have preferred uncertainty. It was a question Jess wrestled with all the time. "And Peter Whiting is her grandson. At least she has him now, too."

"The DNA checked out. The Whitings said they never met the birth mother, but Charlene is definitely in Peter's maternal line and that could only mean Crystal was his mother." He looked at Jess. "You knew that, I presume?"

She nodded and spoke the words she'd rehearsed. "The blood on the rock didn't compare to mine at all."

Jess rubbed the soreness on her chest. She'd had two weeks to get past the ache, and it was still there. When she'd held the report in her hand, she'd felt an actual stabbing pain to her heart that lingered and stole her breath away.

She'd investigated false leads before. But this time had *felt* different, from Stephenson's first phone call right up until she saw the solid black on white words from the DNA lab.

She'd always believed her mother's intuition would lead her to her son. She'd welcomed those early feelings when she first heard about Peter Whiting. She simply *knew*, in her bones, that Peter was her son.

She'd been wrong. Completely wrong.

The knowledge still took her breath away. Because if her

mother's intuition was faulty, if she couldn't count on it to lead her to her only child, how would she ever find him?

Nelson shifted his weight. "I won't say I understand what you've gone through. But if it is any consolation, a lot of suffering has been eased by what you did." He glanced back to the group. "Charlene's for sure."

They stood in silence a moment longer, then Nelson turned to go. Jess caught him by the arm. "Did you ever learn why Peter Whiting went to Meisner's estate that morning?"

"John Whiting was scared they were going to be conned. So he followed Norah Fender. She led him to Crystal, and Crystal led him to Meisner. He kept notes of his activities. Peter found the notes."

"And the rest is history."

"Unfortunately."

"Why the secrecy about the adoption in the first place, though?"

"John was convicted of armed robbery. Sentenced to fifteen years. He got let out in seven, but he wouldn't have been a good candidate for adopting a child. He and Barbara weren't willing to wait that long, anyway."

"You knew all about that, didn't you? That's why you didn't want me to interview them."

Nelson nodded. "I watched him. Under pressure."

"At the hospital."

"He's a good father," Nelson said. "No one wants Peter taken from his parents. Not even Charlene."

Jess joined the group. She spoke to the people she recognized. Beth from the Plum Inn. Elisha and her sister, Marion.

John and Barbara Whiting smiled while holding onto their

boy. Jess had met them briefly at the hospital. They seemed to genuinely love the child. Peter wore a large coat that was buttoned up to the collar. A thick white bandage was wrapped around the right side of his head, covering his ear and eye. He waved to Jess, and she waved back. He would be okay, but she'd keep track of him like she did all the others.

Charlene separated herself from an elderly lady's tight grip on her arm and limped to Jess. "You came."

"Of course."

Charlene squeezed her lips into a thin line. She gripped Jess's hand and nodded.

Jess squeezed back. They said nothing. No words were needed.

The red-haired pastor from Grace's Church gave the service. Nelson and a fresh-faced police officer lowered the coffin.

Charlene wiped tears from her cheek. Jess steadied her as she sprinkled earth on the grave.

The pastor finished the service. The mourners filed past Charlene; hugging, shaking hands, and expressing their sympathies.

The Whitings came by with sheepish smiles. Barbara held Peter's hand.

"So much anguish," John said.

"It wasn't your fault, but you could have helped," Jess said. "Charlene is a good person. Peter needs a grandmother."

John looked down. "Yeah. We just..." He put his arm around Peter's shoulder.

There was a long silence.

"Life goes on," Charlene said.

"Yes," said John.

"Thank you," Barbara said.

Peter hugged his newfound grandmother, and the Whitings left.

In the end, only Charlene and Jess stood by the grave.

"She's at peace," Jess said.

Charlene nodded. "I wish she was still here."

"I know."

"I still have her picture on my desk."

Jess nodded.

"Do you keep your son's picture with you?"

Jess swallowed. "Yes."

They left the shelter of the canopy as two men shoveled earth into the grave.

Charlene huddled under Jess's umbrella. "Your Peter is out there. You'll find him."

"I hope so."

"You found mine, you'll find yours." She squeezed Jess's arm. "You just have to keep looking."

"I am." Jess took a deep breath. "Always."

She gave Charlene one last hug and headed toward the car. Her work was done here. It was time for Jess to move on, professionally and personally.

She pulled out her phone, quickly found the number, and pressed the button to dial. Henry Morris picked up on the second ring. "Jess?"

"I'm on my way back to Denver. How's your schedule?"

"Wide open."

"Any chance your dinner offer still stands?"

He laughed. "I think I can squeeze you into my tight schedule. Eight o'clock?"

"Sounds good."

"I'll pick you up."

"Even better."

He waited a beat. "It'll be good to see you again."

"You, too. I'm looking forward to it."

She slipped the phone in her pocket, and headed back to Denver.

Smiling.

THE END

ABOUT THE AUTHOR

DIANE CAPRI is the *New York Times*, *USA Today*, and worldwide bestselling author. She's a recovering lawyer and snowbird who divides her time between Florida and Michigan. An active member of Mystery Writers of America, Authors Guild, International Thriller Writers, Alliance of Independent Authors, and Sisters in Crime, she loves to hear from readers and is hard at work on her next novel.

Please connect with Diane online:
http://www.DianeCapri.com
Twitter: http://twitter.com/@DianeCapri
Facebook: http://www.facebook.com/Diane.Capri1
http://www.facebook.com/DianeCapriBooks